My Little Pony
Friends Forever

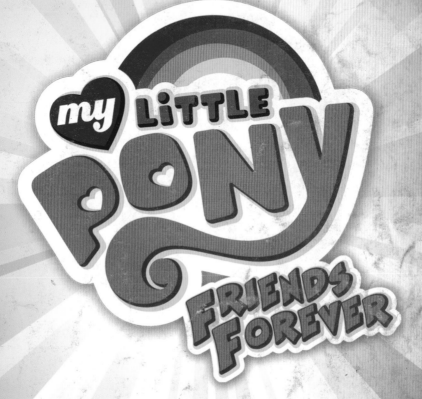

My Little Pony: Friends Forever

Pinkie Pie & Applejack

Written and Lettered by
Alex De Campi

Art by
Carla Speed McNeil

Colored by
Jenn Manley Lee
and **Bill Mudron**

Cutie Mark Crusaders & Discord

Written by
Jeremy Whitley

Art by
Tony Fleecs

Color Flats by
Lauren Perry

Lettered by
Neil Uyetake

Special thanks to Erin Comella, Robert Fewkes, Joe Furfaro, Heather Hopkins, Pat Jarret, Ed Lane, Brian Lenard, Marissa Mansolillo, Donna Tobin, Michael Vogel, and Michael Kelly for their invaluable assistance.

ISBN: 978-1-61377-981-1

17 16 15 14   1 2 3 4

 Licensed By: [Hasbro]

www.IDWPUBLISHING.com
IDW founded by Ted Adams, Alex Garner, Kris Oprisko, and Robbie Robbins

Ted Adams, CEO & Publisher
Greg Goldstein, President & COO
Robbie Robbins, EVP/Sr. Graphic Artist
Chris Ryall, Chief Creative Officer/Editor-in-Chief
Matthew Ruzicka, CPA, Chief Financial Officer
Alan Payne, VP of Sales
Dirk Wood, VP of Marketing
Lorelei Bunjes, VP of Digital Services
Jeff Webber, VP of Digital Publishing & Business Development

Facebook: facebook.com/idwpublishing
Twitter: @idwpublishing
YouTube: youtube.com/idwpublishing
Instagram: instagram.com/idwpublishing
deviantART: idwpublishing.deviantart.com
Pinterest: pinterest.com/idwpublishing/idw-staff-faves

PRINCESS CELESTIA & SPIKE

Written by
Ted Anderson

Art by
Agnes Garbowska

Lettered by
Neil Uyetake

TWILIGHT SPARKLE & SHINING ARMOR

Written by
Rob Anderson

Art by
Amy Mebberson

Colored by
Heather Breckel

Lettered by
Neil Uyetake

Cover by
Andy Price

Series Edits by
Bobby Curnow

Collection Edits by
Justin Eisinger & Alonzo Simon

Collection Design by
Neil Uyetake

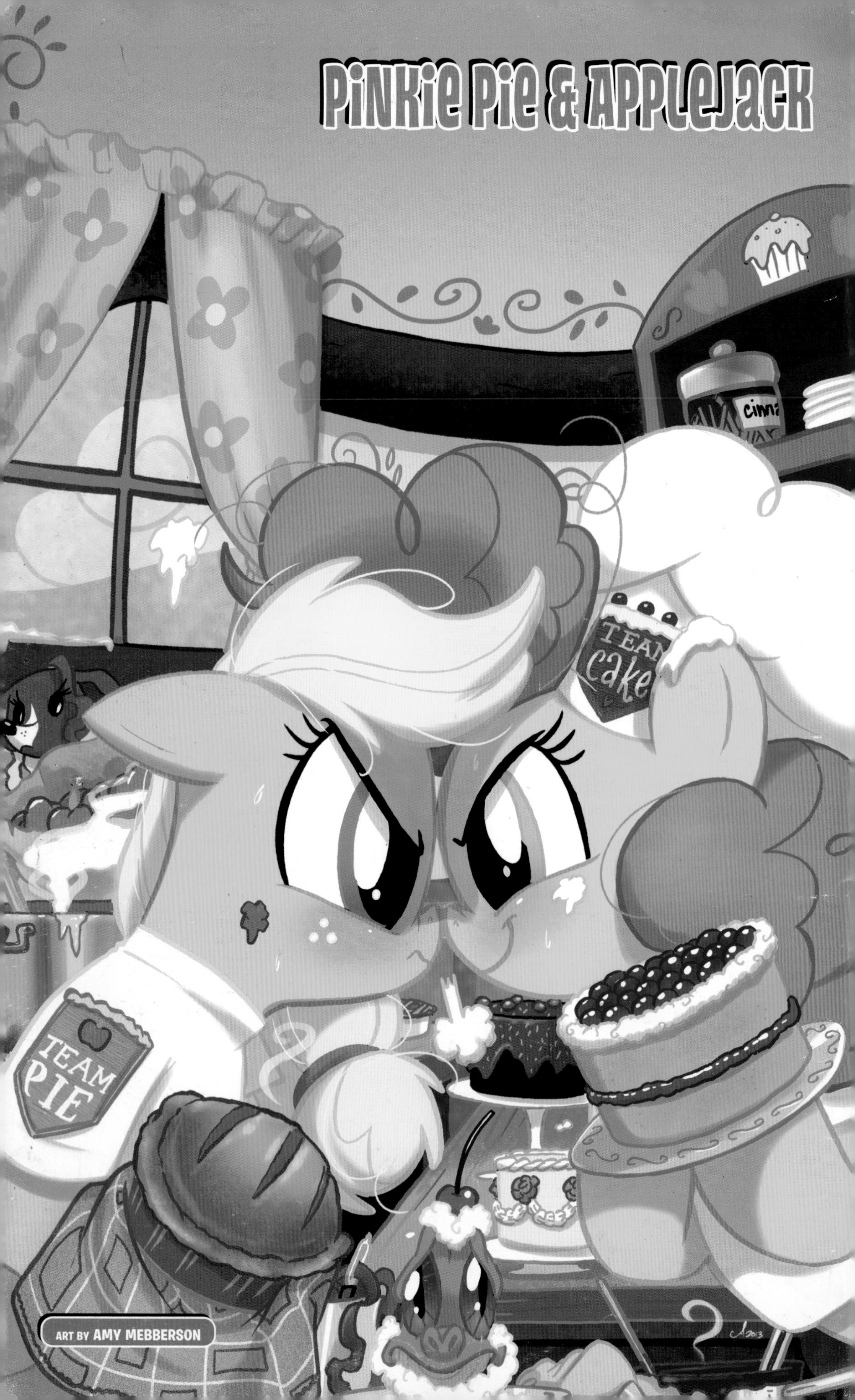
Pinkie Pie & Applejack
cinna
TEAM
cake
TEAM
PIE
ART BY AMY MEBBERSON

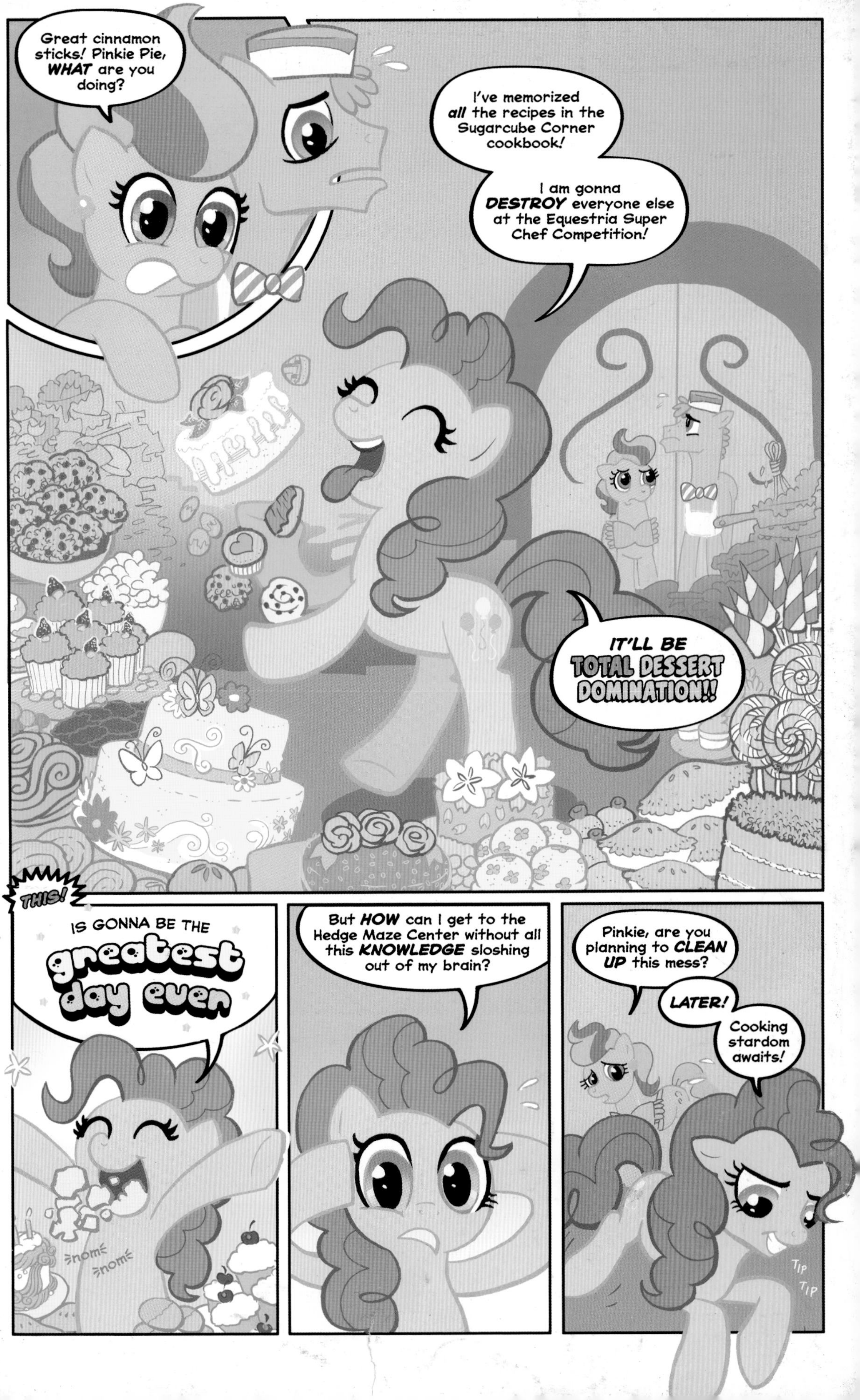
Great cinnamon sticks! Pinkie Pie, WHAT are you doing?
I've memorized all the recipes in the Sugarcube Corner cookbook!
I am gonna DESTROY everyone else at the Equestria Super Chef Competition!
IT'LL BE TOTAL DESSERT DOMINATION!!
THIS!
IS GONNA BE THE greatest day ever
nom nom
But HOW can I get to the Hedge Maze Center without all this KNOWLEDGE sloshing out of my brain?
Pinkie, are you planning to CLEAN UP this mess?
LATER!
Cooking stardom awaits!
TIP TIP

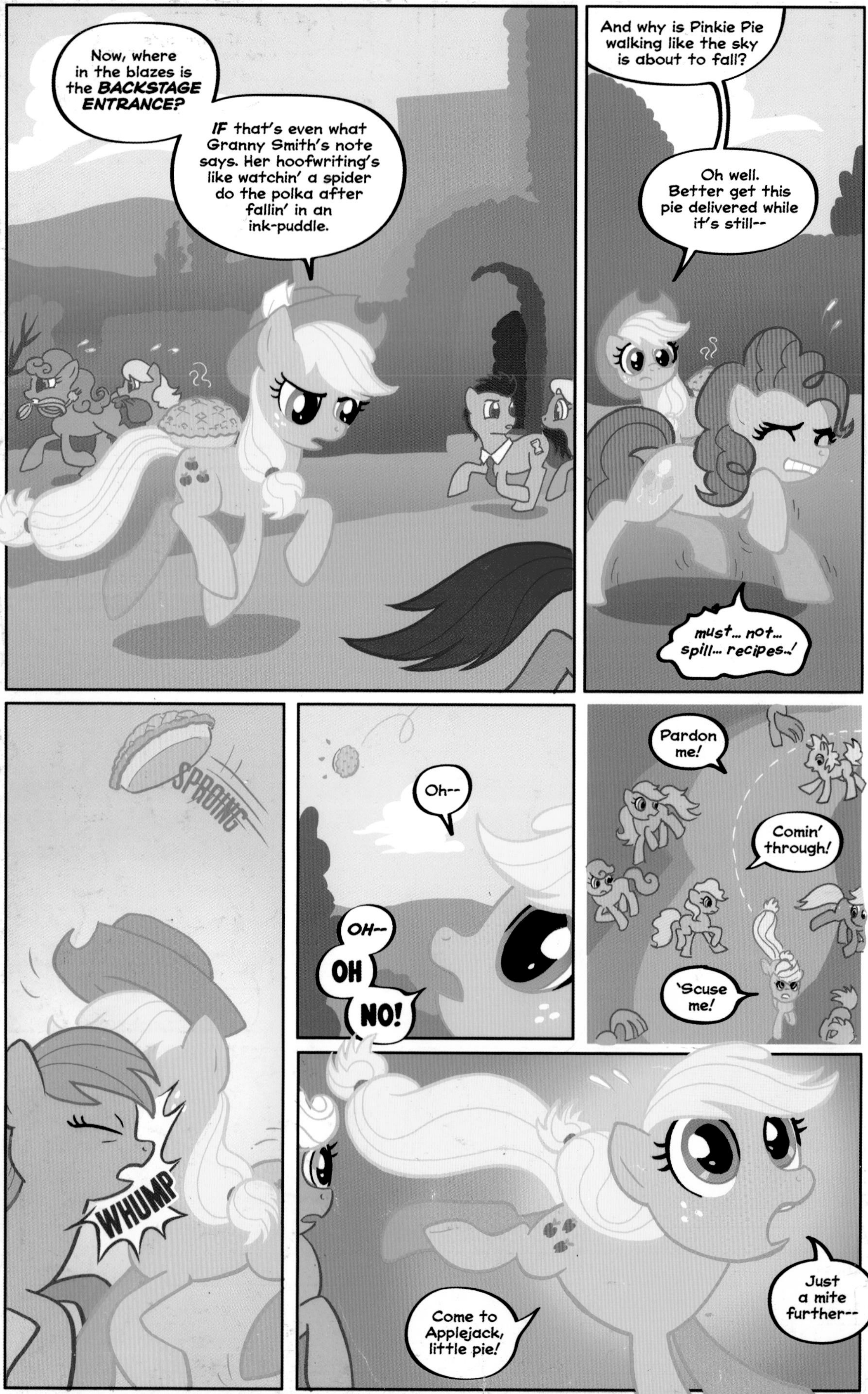
Now, where in the blazes is the BACKSTAGE ENTRANCE?
IF that's even what Granny Smith's note says. Her hoofwriting's like watchin' a spider do the polka after fallin' in an ink-puddle.
And why is Pinkie Pie walking like the sky is about to fall?
Oh well. Better get this pie delivered while it's still--
must... not... spill... recipes...!
SPROING
WHUMP
Oh--
OH--
OH
NO!
Pardon me!
Comin' through!
'Scuse me!
Come to Applejack, little pie!
Just a mite further--

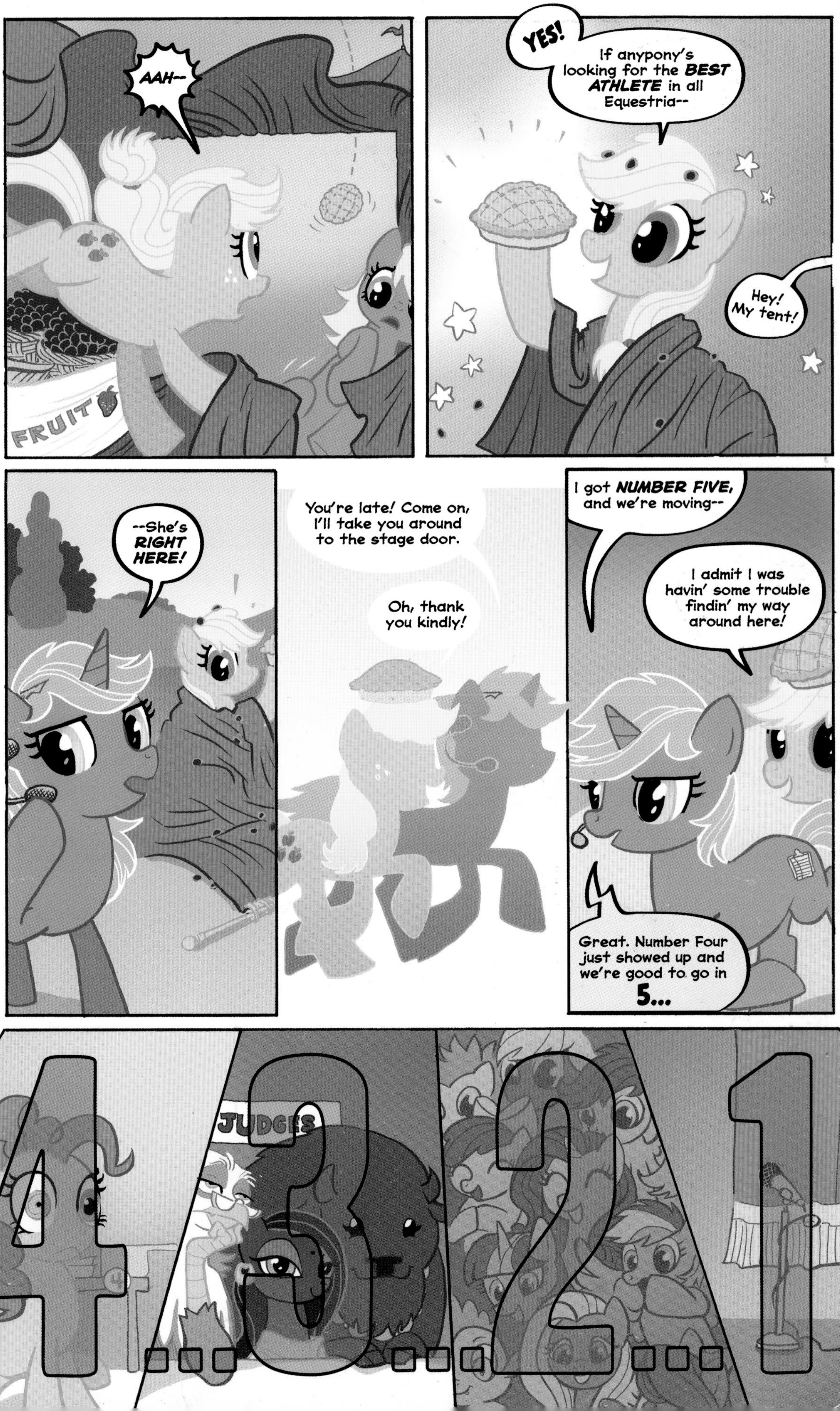
AAH--
YES!
If anypony's looking for the BEST ATHLETE in all Equestria--
Hey! My tent!
--She's RIGHT HERE!
You're late! Come on, I'll take you around to the stage door.
Oh, thank you kindly!
I got NUMBER FIVE, and we're moving--
I admit I was havin' some trouble findin' my way around here!
Great. Number Four just showed up and we're good to go in
5...
4...
JUDGES
3...
2...
1
FRUIT

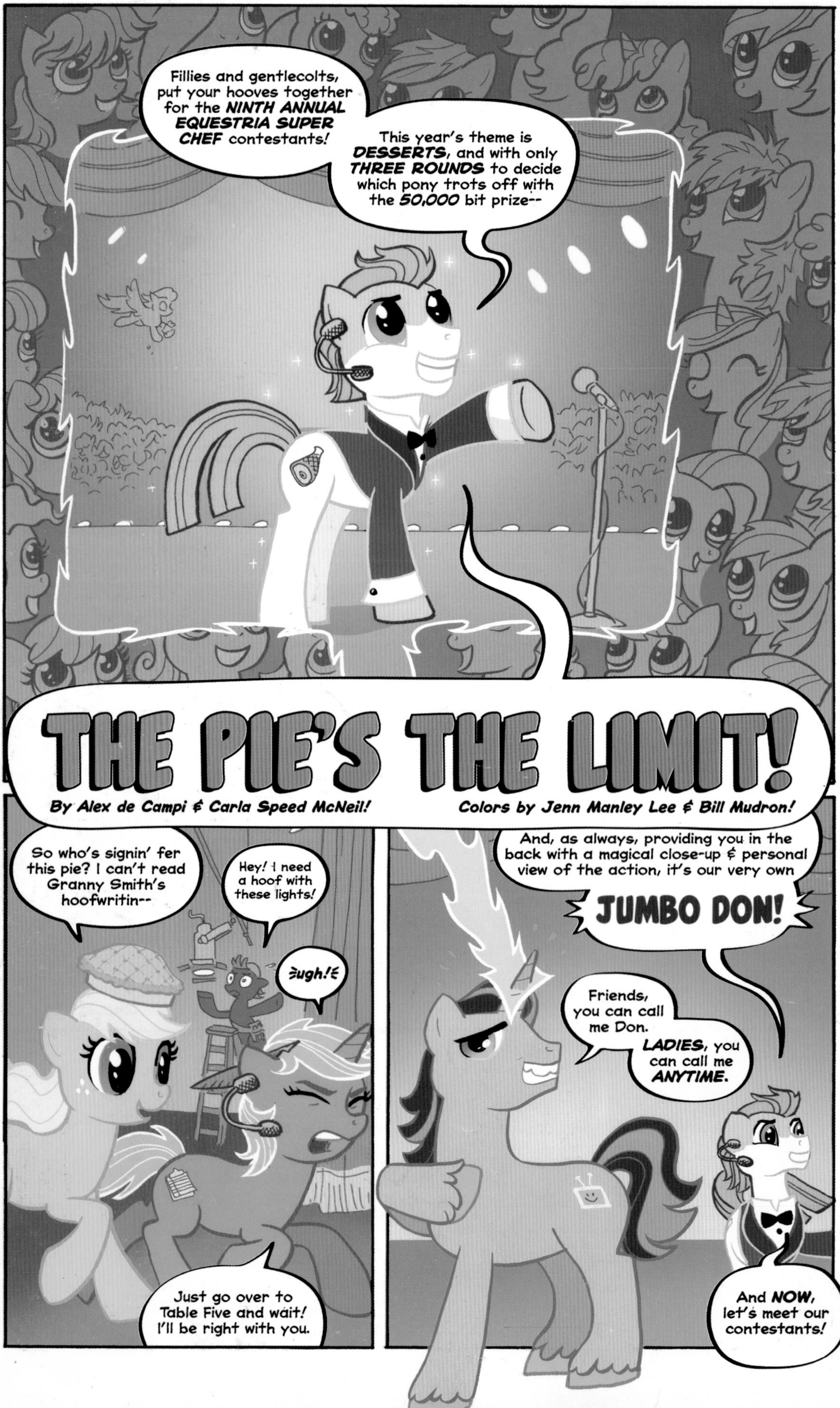
Fillies and gentlecolts, put your hooves together for the NINTH ANNUAL EQUESTRIA SUPER CHEF contestants!
This year's theme is DESSERTS, and with only THREE ROUNDS to decide which pony trots off with the 50,000 bit prize--
THE PIE'S THE LIMIT!
By Alex de Campi & Carla Speed McNeil!
Colors by Jenn Manley Lee & Bill Mudron!
So who's signin' fer this pie? I can't read Granny Smith's hoofwritin--
Hey! I need a hoof with these lights!
ugh!
Just go over to Table Five and wait! I'll be right with you.
And, as always, providing you in the back with a magical close-up & personal view of the action, it's our very own
JUMBO DON!
Friends, you can call me Don.
LADIES, you can call me ANYTIME.
And NOW, let's meet our contestants!

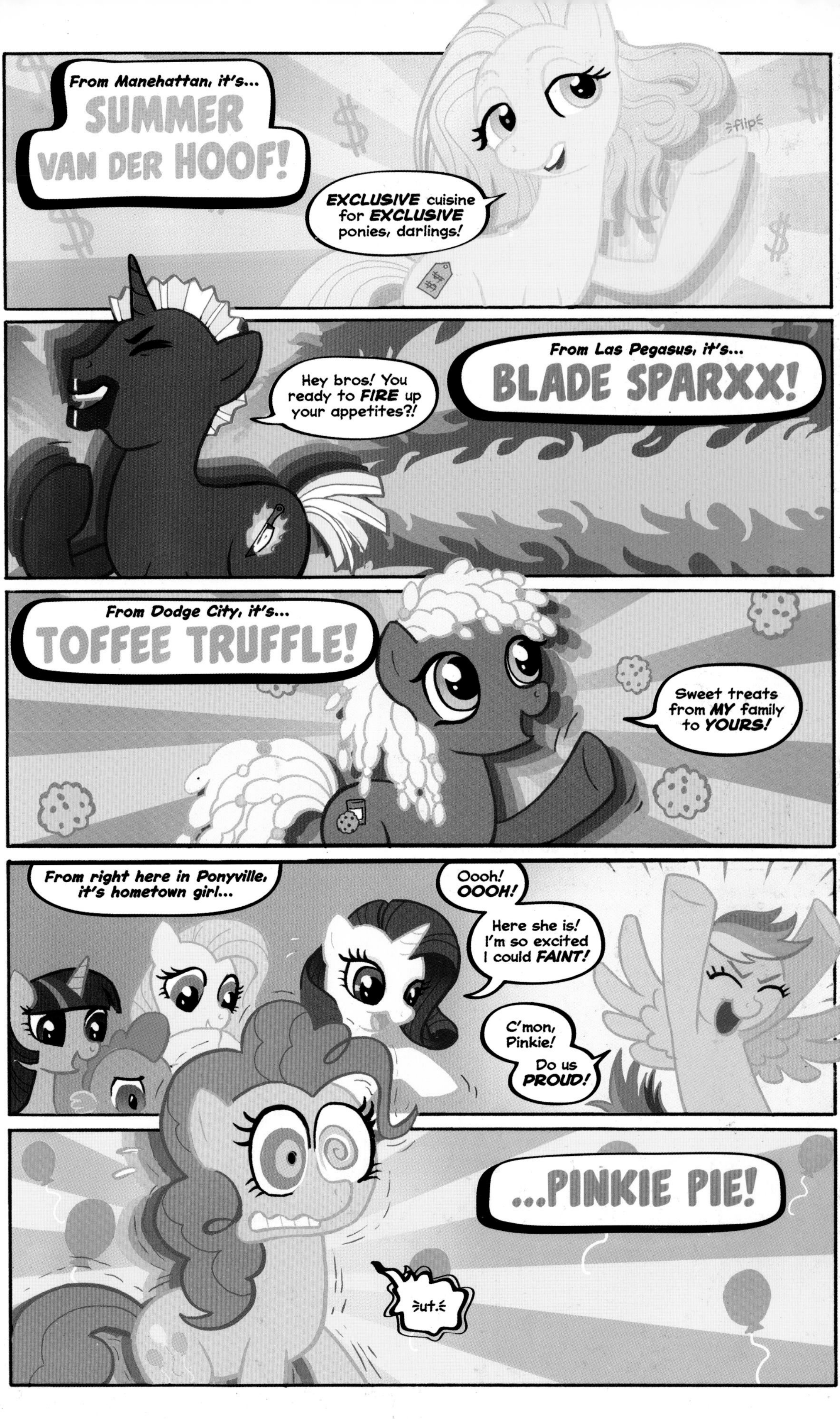
From Manehattan, it's...
SUMMER VAN DER HOOF!
flip
EXCLUSIVE cuisine for EXCLUSIVE ponies, darlings!
From Las Pegasus, it's...
BLADE SPARXX!
Hey bros! You ready to FIRE up your appetites?!
From Dodge City, it's...
TOFFEE TRUFFLE!
Sweet treats from MY family to YOURS!
From right here in Ponyville, it's hometown girl...
Oooh! OOOH!
Here she is! I'm so excited I could FAINT!
C'mon, Pinkie!
Do us PROUD!
...PINKIE PIE!
ut.

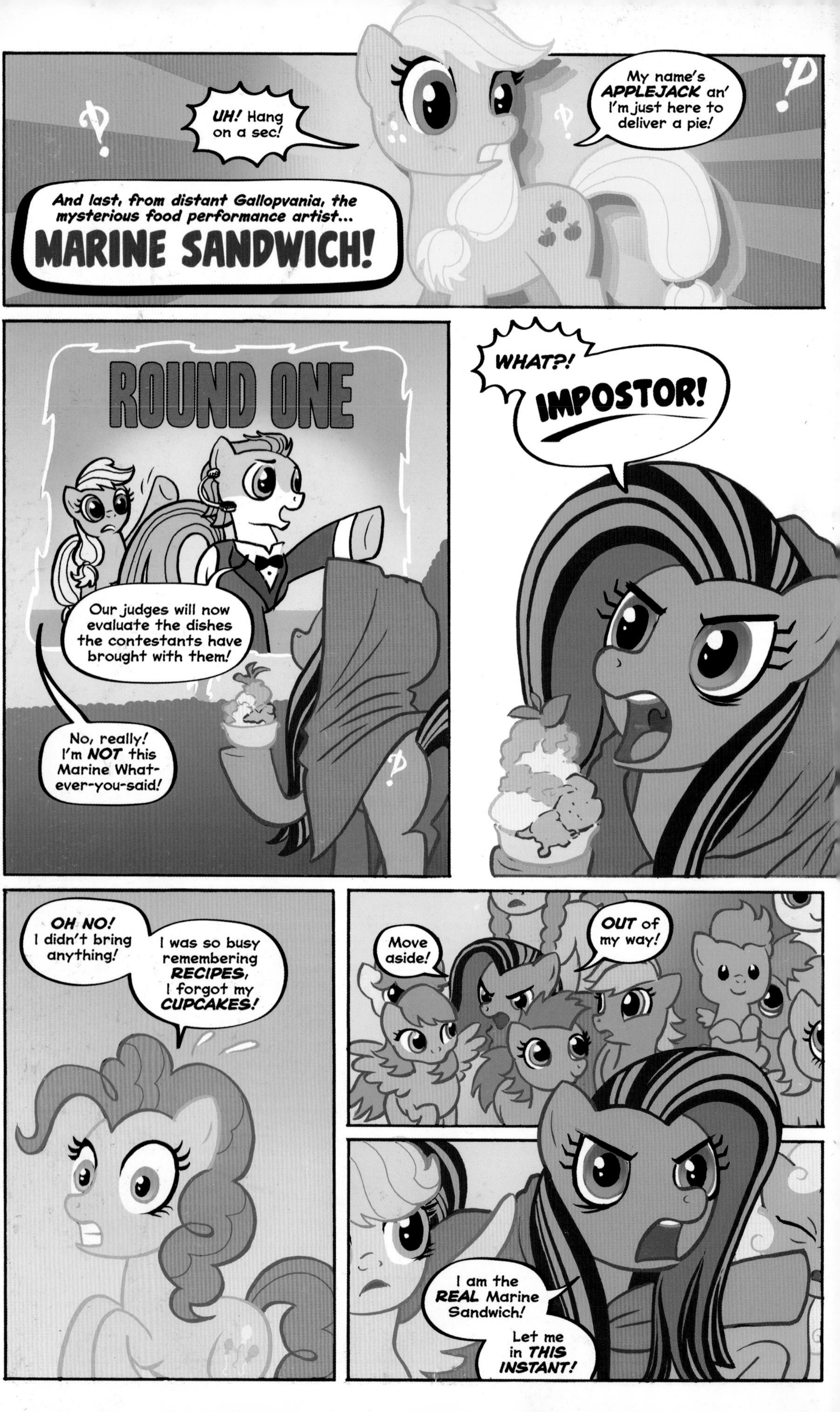

UH! Hang on a sec!
My name's APPLEJACK an' I'm just here to deliver a pie!
And last, from distant Gallopvania, the mysterious food performance artist...
MARINE SANDWICH!
ROUND ONE
Our judges will now evaluate the dishes the contestants have brought with them!
No, really! I'm NOT this Marine Whatever-you-said!
WHAT?!
IMPOSTOR!
OH NO! I didn't bring anything!
I was so busy remembering RECIPES, I forgot my CUPCAKES!
Move aside!
OUT of my way!
I am the REAL Marine Sandwich!
Let me in THIS INSTANT!

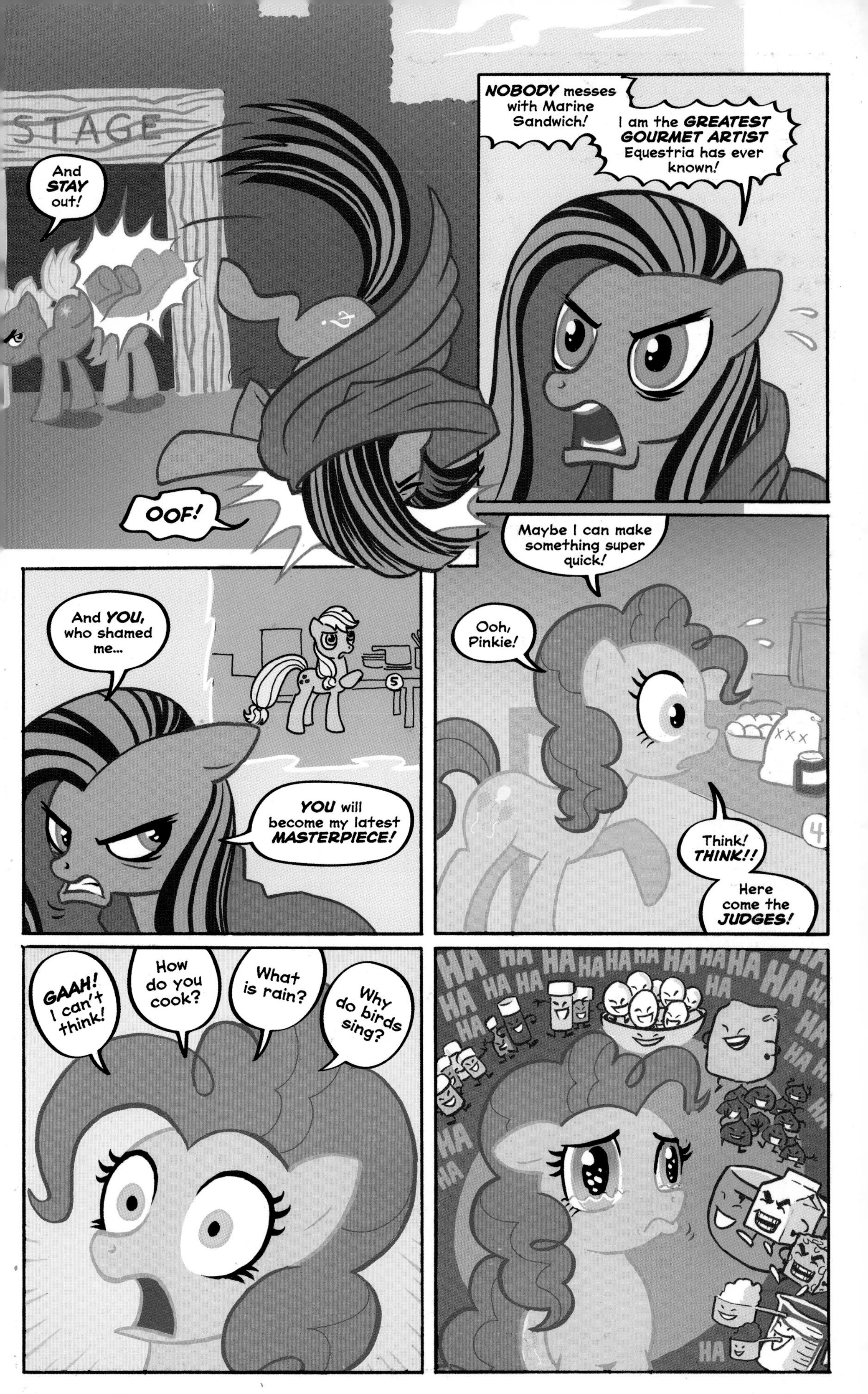
STAGE
And STAY out!
OOF!
NOBODY messes with Marine Sandwich!
I am the GREATEST GOURMET ARTIST Equestria has ever known!
And YOU, who shamed me...
YOU will become my latest MASTERPIECE!
Maybe I can make something super quick!
Ooh, Pinkie!
Think! THINK!!
Here come the JUDGES!
GAAH! I can't think!
How do you cook?
What is rain?
Why do birds sing?
HA HA HA HA HA HA HA HA HA HA HA HA HA HA HA HA HA HA HA HA HA HA HA HA HA

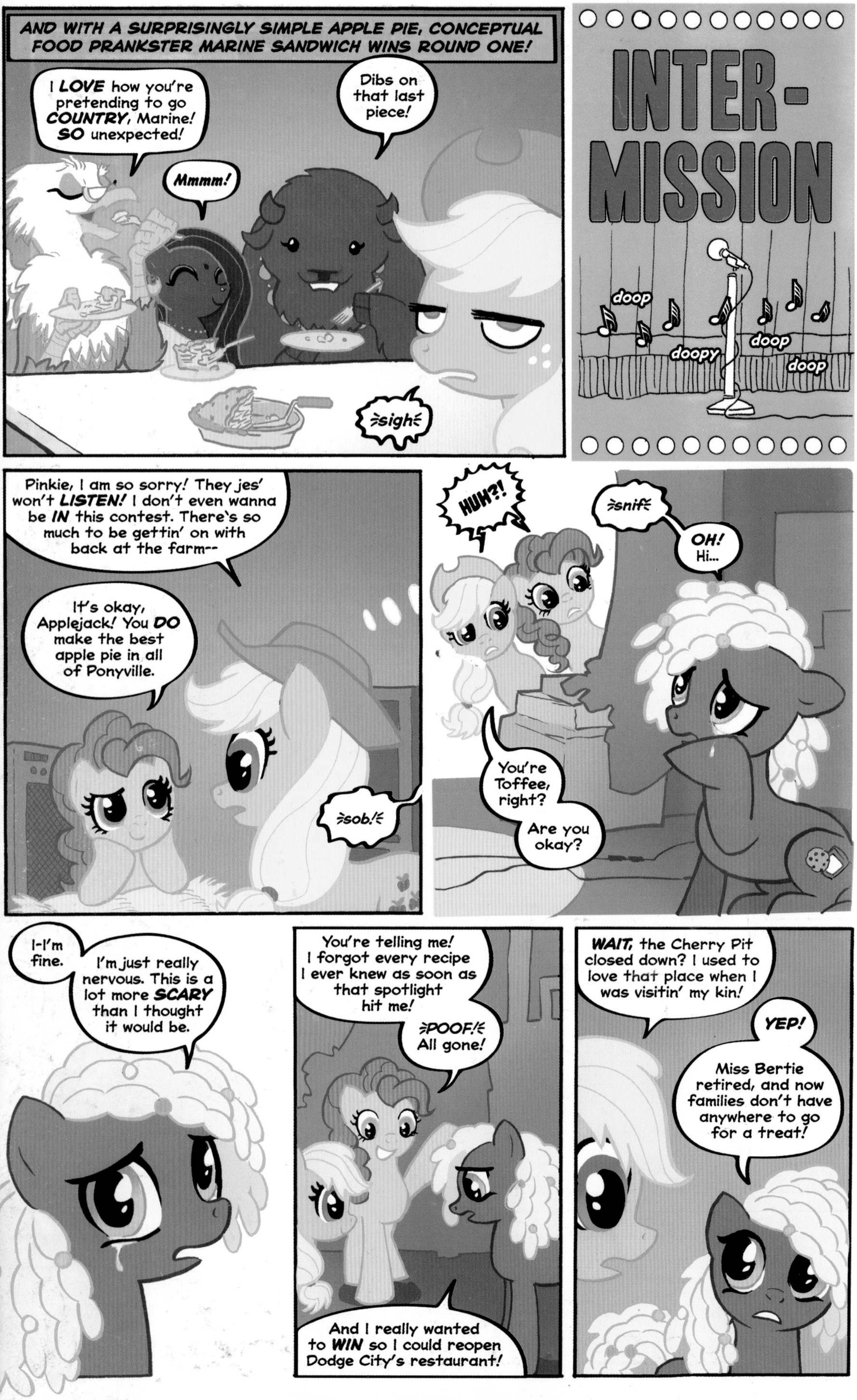

AND WITH A SURPRISINGLY SIMPLE APPLE PIE, CONCEPTUAL FOOD PRANKSTER MARINE SANDWICH WINS ROUND ONE!
I LOVE how you're pretending to go COUNTRY, Marine! SO unexpected!
Mmmm!
Dibs on that last piece!
sigh
INTER-MISSION
doop
doopy
doop
doop
Pinkie, I am so sorry! They jes' won't LISTEN! I don't even wanna be IN this contest. There's so much to be gettin' on with back at the farm--
It's okay, Applejack! You DO make the best apple pie in all of Ponyville.
sob!
HUH?!
snif
OH! Hi...
You're Toffee, right?
Are you okay?
I-I'm fine.
I'm just really nervous. This is a lot more SCARY than I thought it would be.
You're telling me! I forgot every recipe I ever knew as soon as that spotlight hit me!
POOF! All gone!
And I really wanted to WIN so I could reopen Dodge City's restaurant!
WAIT, the Cherry Pit closed down? I used to love that place when I was visitin' my kin!
YEP!
Miss Bertie retired, and now families don't have anywhere to go for a treat!

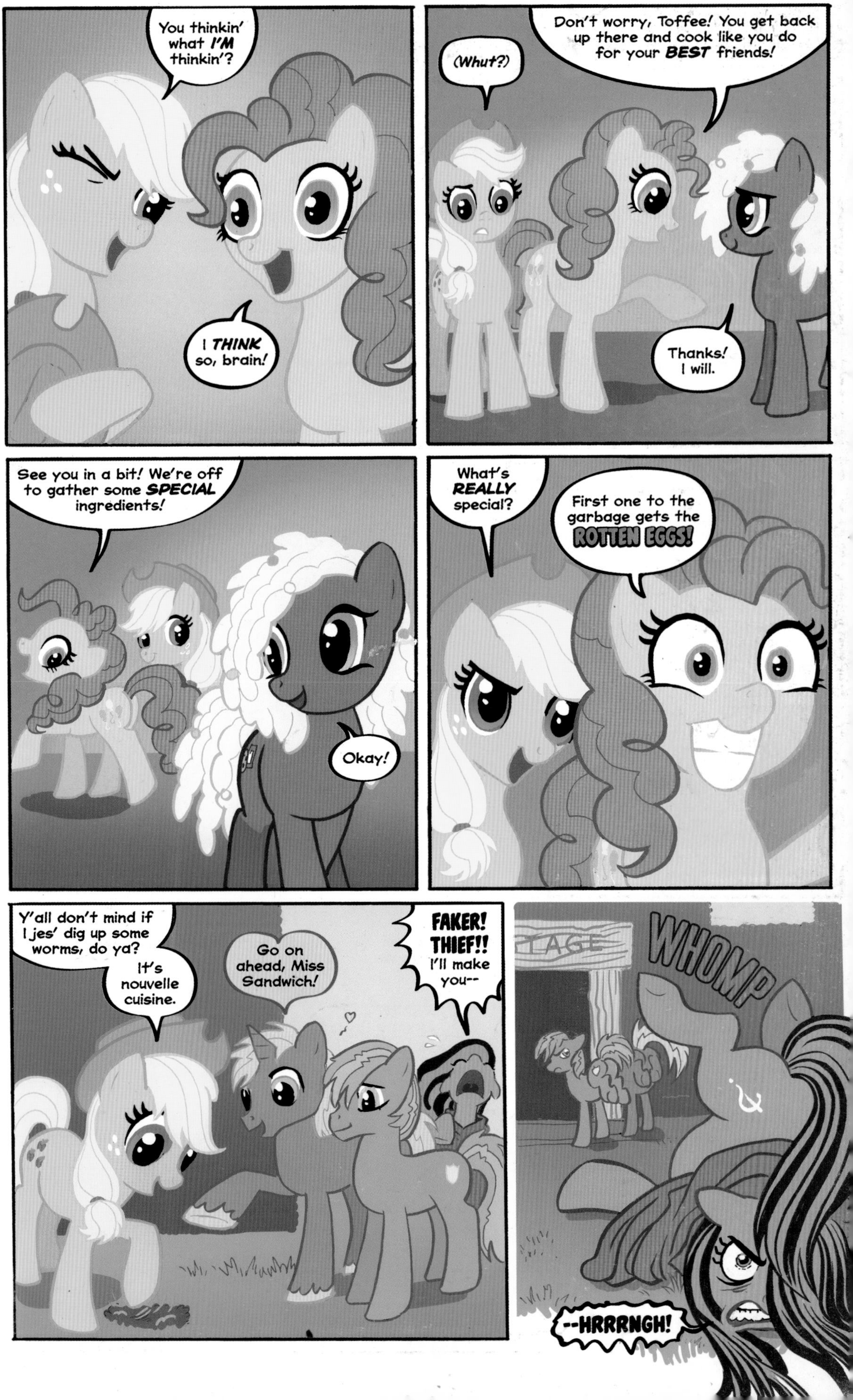
You thinkin' what I'M thinkin'?
I THINK so, brain!
(Whut?)
Don't worry, Toffee! You get back up there and cook like you do for your BEST friends!
Thanks! I will.
See you in a bit! We're off to gather some SPECIAL ingredients!
Okay!
What's REALLY special?
First one to the garbage gets the ROTTEN EGGS!
Y'all don't mind if I jes' dig up some worms, do ya? It's nouvelle cuisine.
Go on ahead, Miss Sandwich!
FAKER! THIEF!! I'll make you--
WHOMP
--HRRRNGH!

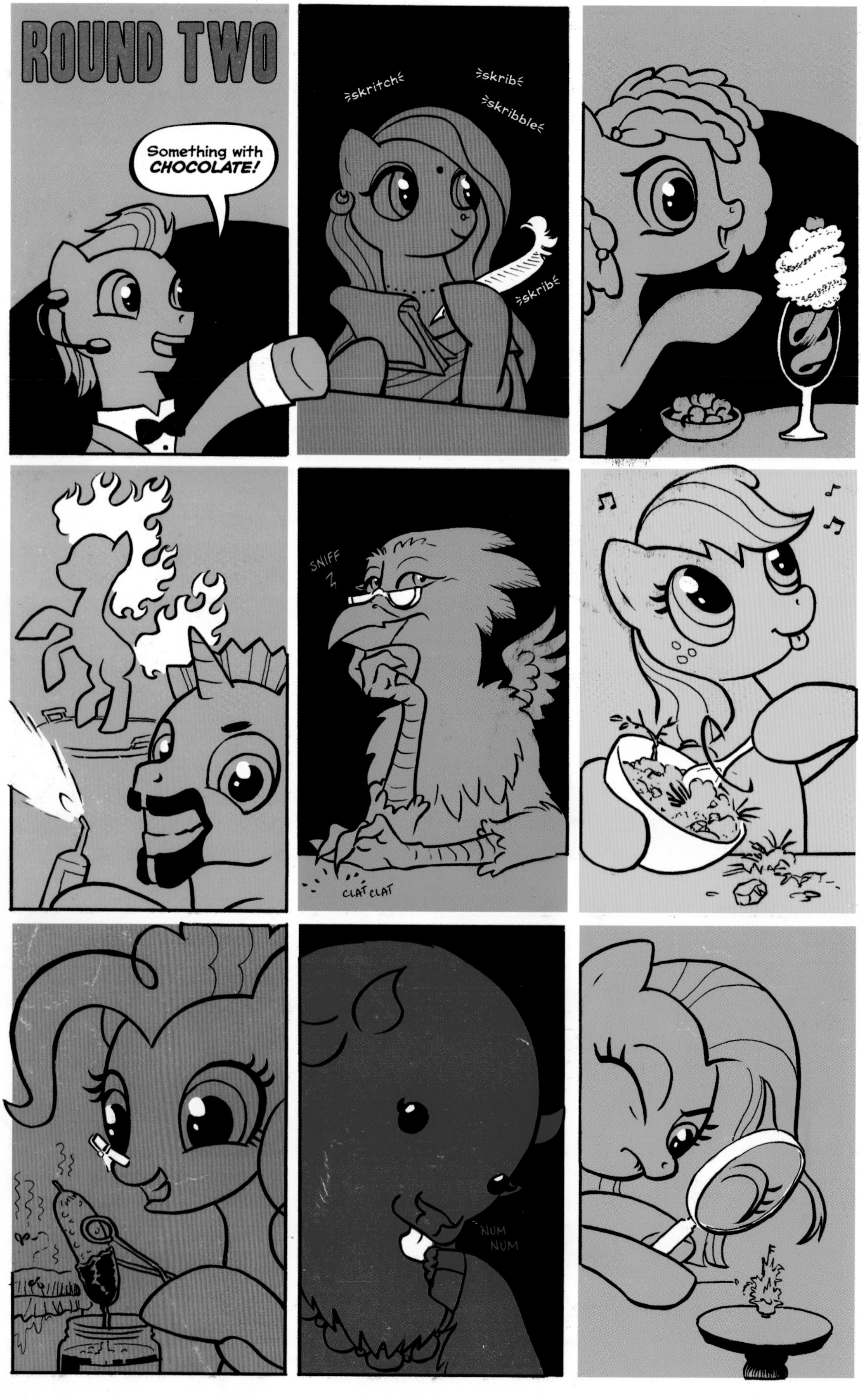
ROUND TWO
Something with CHOCOLATE!
skritch
skrib
skribble
skrib
SNIFF
CLAT CLAT
NUM NUM

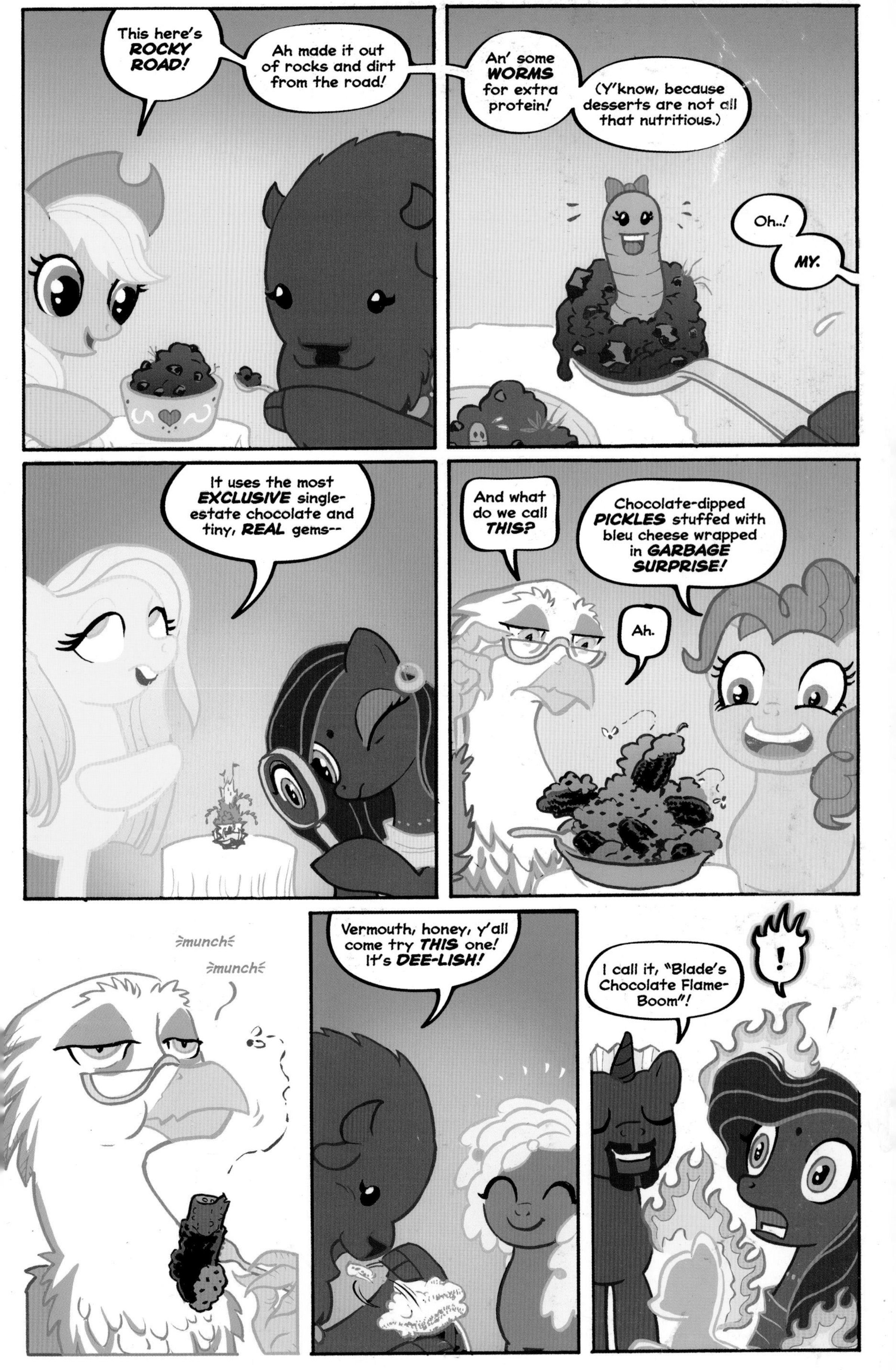
This here's ROCKY ROAD!
Ah made it out of rocks and dirt from the road!
An' some WORMS for extra protein!
(Y'know, because desserts are not all that nutritious.)
Oh..!
MY.
It uses the most EXCLUSIVE single-estate chocolate and tiny, REAL gems--
And what do we call THIS?
Chocolate-dipped PICKLES stuffed with bleu cheese wrapped in GARBAGE SURPRISE!
Ah.
munch
munch
Vermouth, honey, y'all come try THIS one! It's DEE-LISH!
I call it, "Blade's Chocolate Flame-Boom"!
!

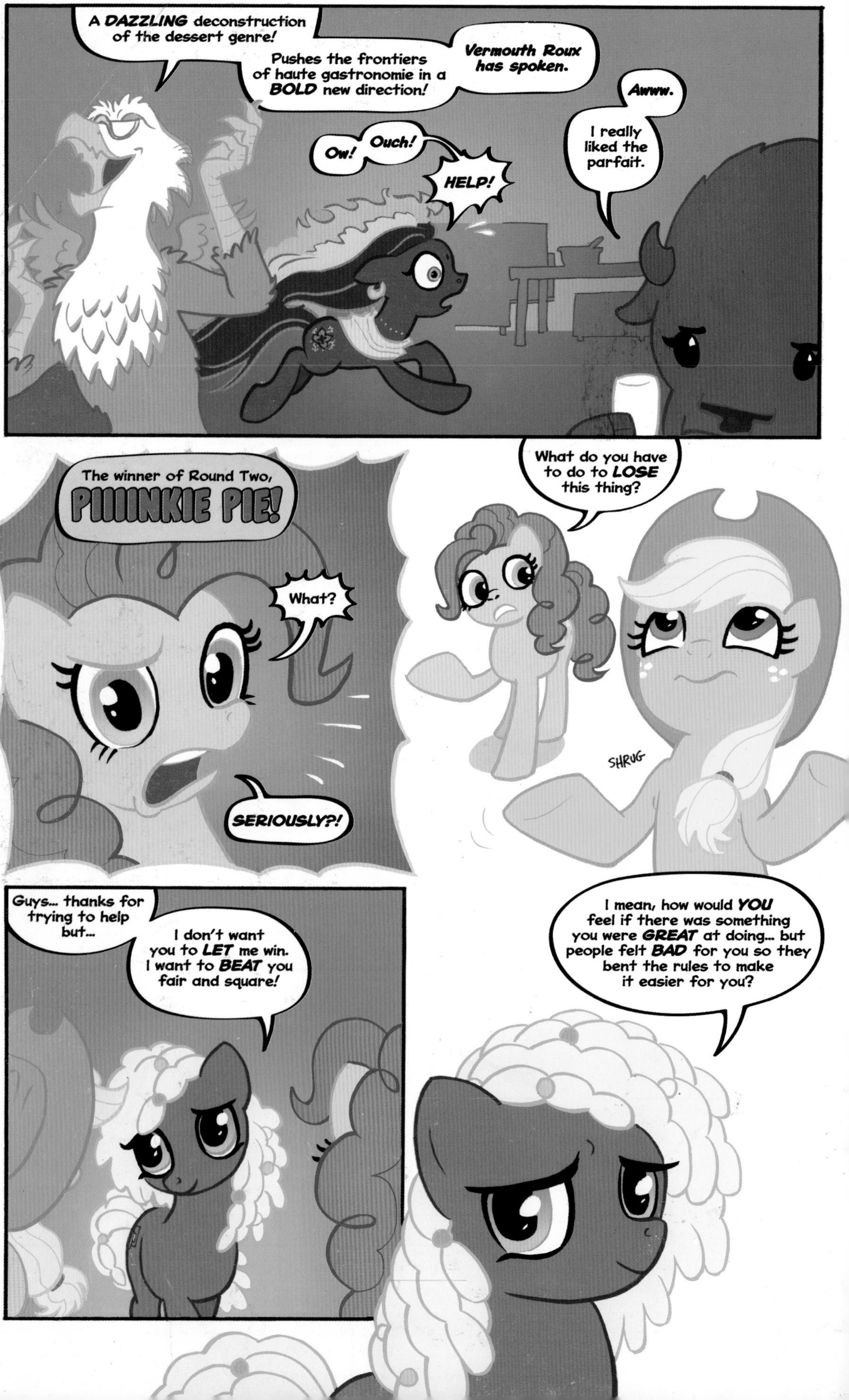

A DAZZLING deconstruction of the dessert genre!
Pushes the frontiers of haute gastronomie in a BOLD new direction!
Vermouth Roux has spoken.
Awww.
I really liked the parfait.
Ow!
Ouch!
HELP!
The winner of Round Two, PIIIINKIE PIE!
What?
SERIOUSLY?!
What do you have to do to LOSE this thing?
SHRUG
Guys... thanks for trying to help but...
I don't want you to LET me win. I want to BEAT you fair and square!
I mean, how would YOU feel if there was something you were GREAT at doing... but people felt BAD for you so they bent the rules to make it easier for you?

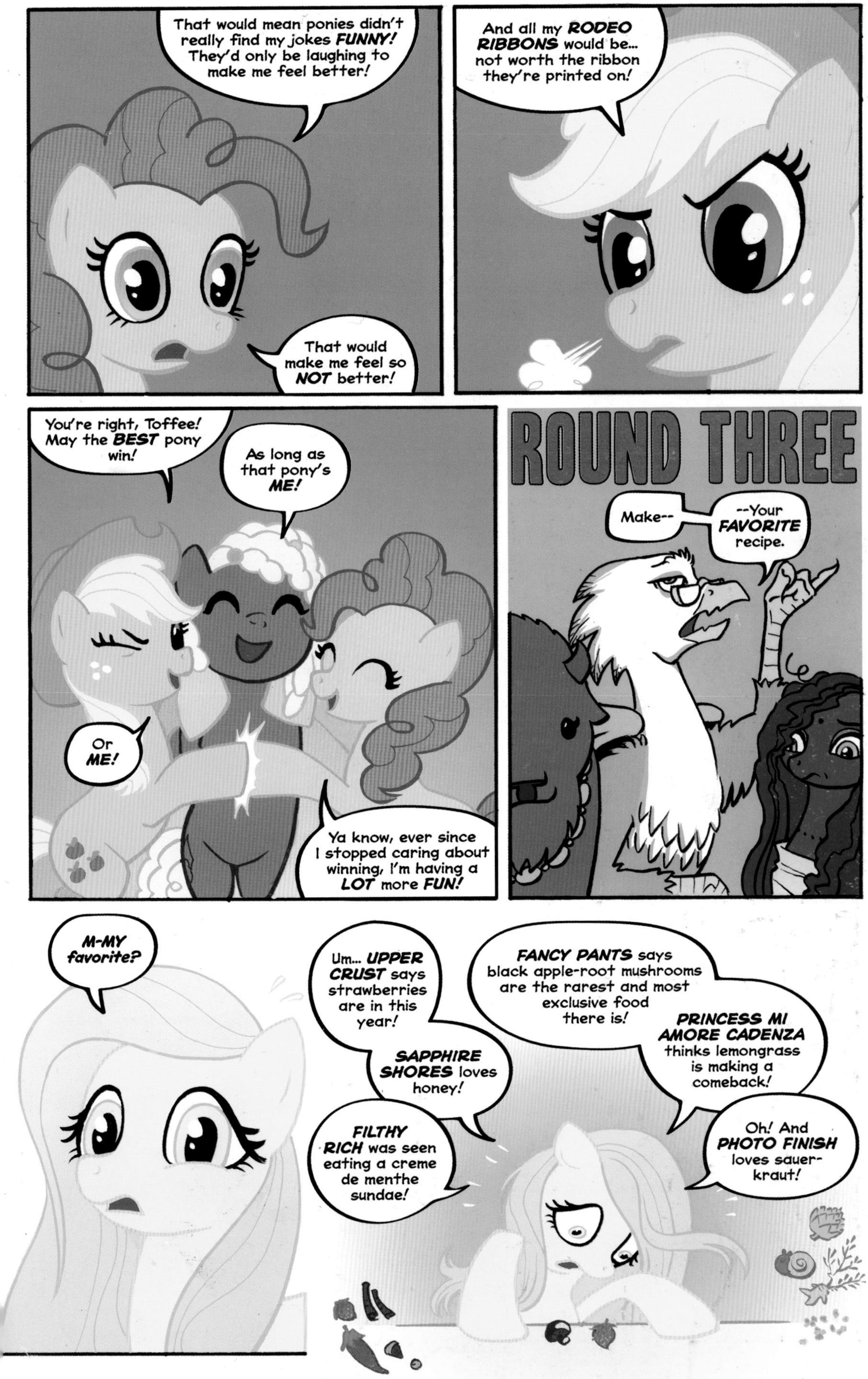

That would mean ponies didn't really find my jokes FUNNY! They'd only be laughing to make me feel better!
That would make me feel so NOT better!
And all my RODEO RIBBONS would be... not worth the ribbon they're printed on!
You're right, Toffee! May the BEST pony win!
As long as that pony's ME!
Or ME!
Ya know, ever since I stopped caring about winning, I'm having a LOT more FUN!
ROUND THREE
Make--
--Your FAVORITE recipe.
M-MY favorite?
Um... UPPER CRUST says strawberries are in this year!
SAPPHIRE SHORES loves honey!
FILTHY RICH was seen eating a creme de menthe sundae!
FANCY PANTS says black apple-root mushrooms are the rarest and most exclusive food there is!
PRINCESS MI AMORE CADENZA thinks lemongrass is making a comeback!
Oh! And PHOTO FINISH loves sauer-kraut!

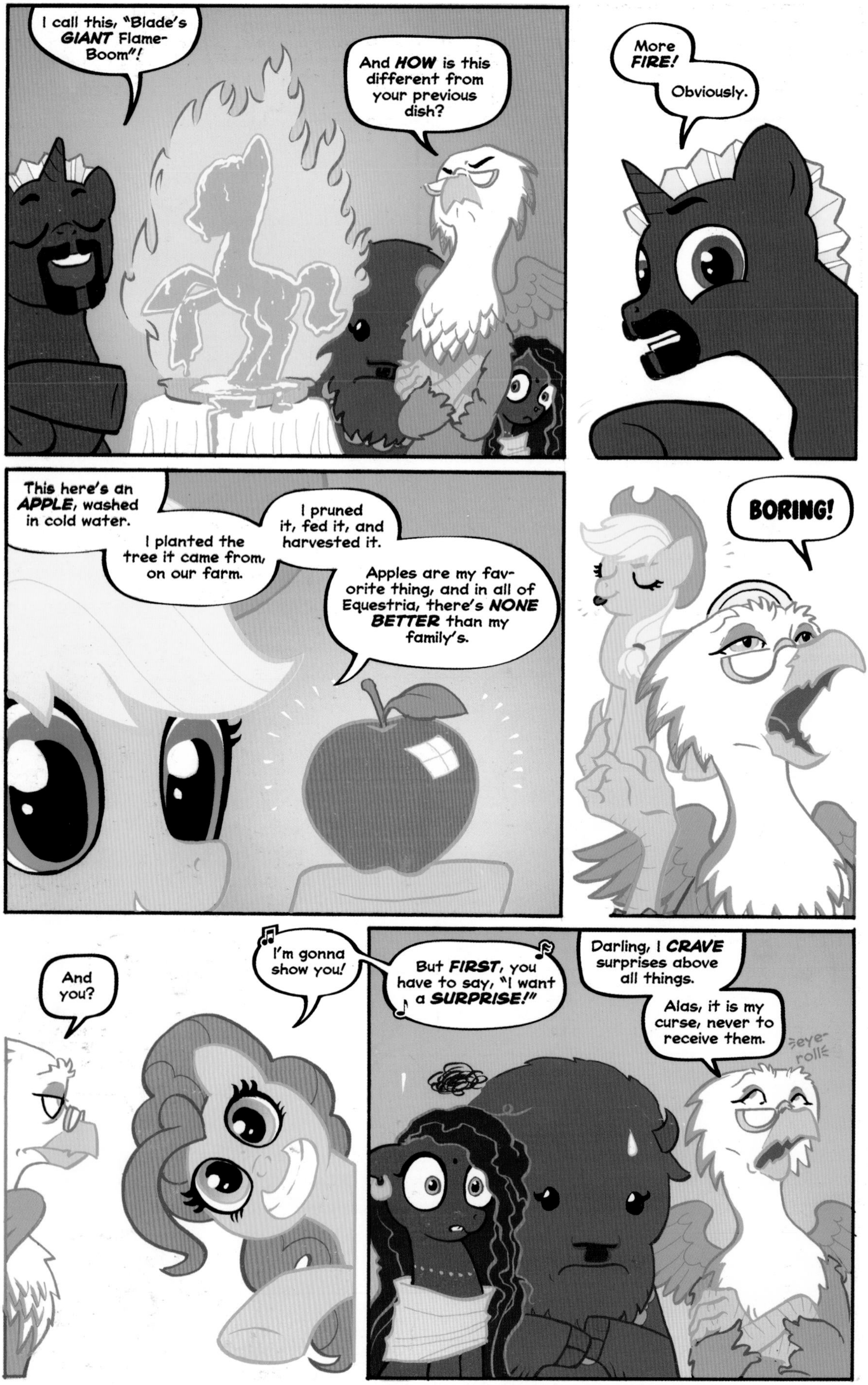
I call this, "Blade's GIANT Flame-Boom"!
And HOW is this different from your previous dish?
More FIRE!
Obviously.
This here's an APPLE, washed in cold water.
I planted the tree it came from, on our farm.
I pruned it, fed it, and harvested it.
Apples are my favorite thing, and in all of Equestria, there's NONE BETTER than my family's.
BORING!
And you?
I'm gonna show you!
But FIRST, you have to say, "I want a SURPRISE!"
Darling, I CRAVE surprises above all things.
Alas, it is my curse, never to receive them.
eye-roll

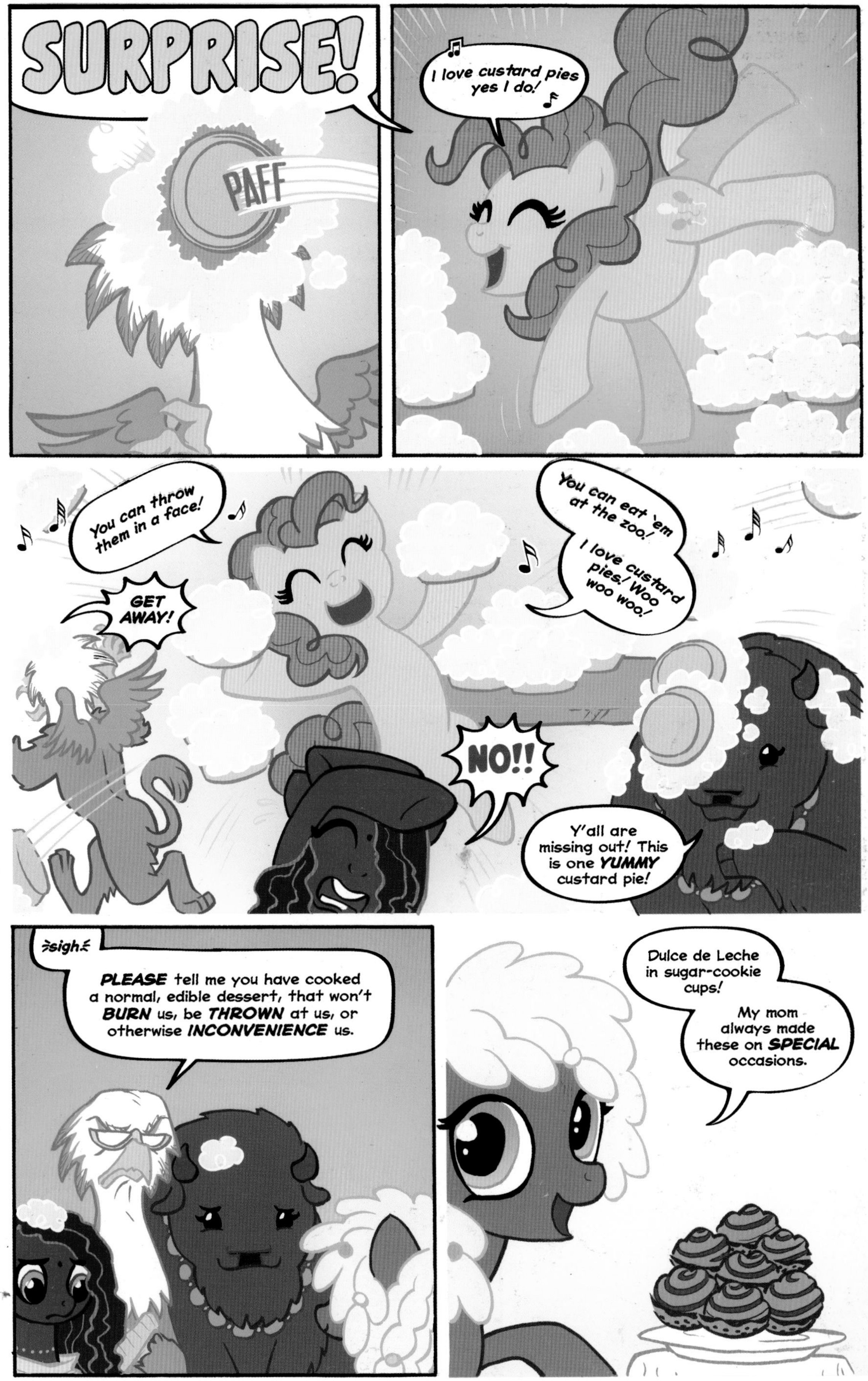
SURPRISE!
PAFF
I love custard pies yes I do!
You can throw them in a face!
GET AWAY!
You can eat 'em at the zoo!
I love custard pies! Woo woo woo!
NO!!
Y'all are missing out! This is one YUMMY custard pie!
sigh
PLEASE tell me you have cooked a normal, edible dessert, that won't BURN us, be THROWN at us, or otherwise INCONVENIENCE us.
Dulce de Leche in sugar-cookie cups!
My mom always made these on SPECIAL occasions.

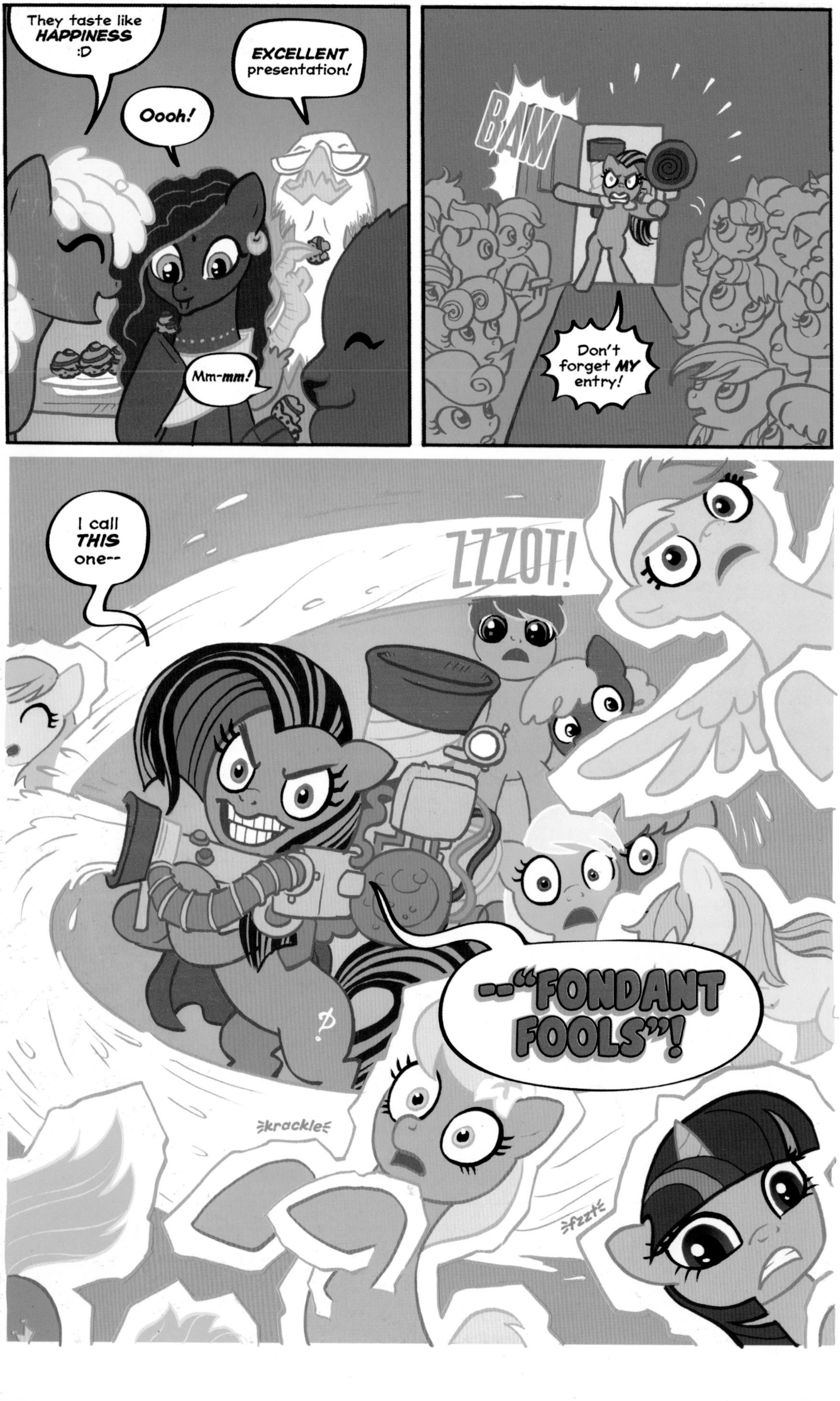
They taste like HAPPINESS :D
Oooh!
EXCELLENT presentation!
Mm-mm!
BAM
Don't forget MY entry!
I call THIS one--
ZZZOT!
--"FONDANT FOOLS"!
krackle
fzzt

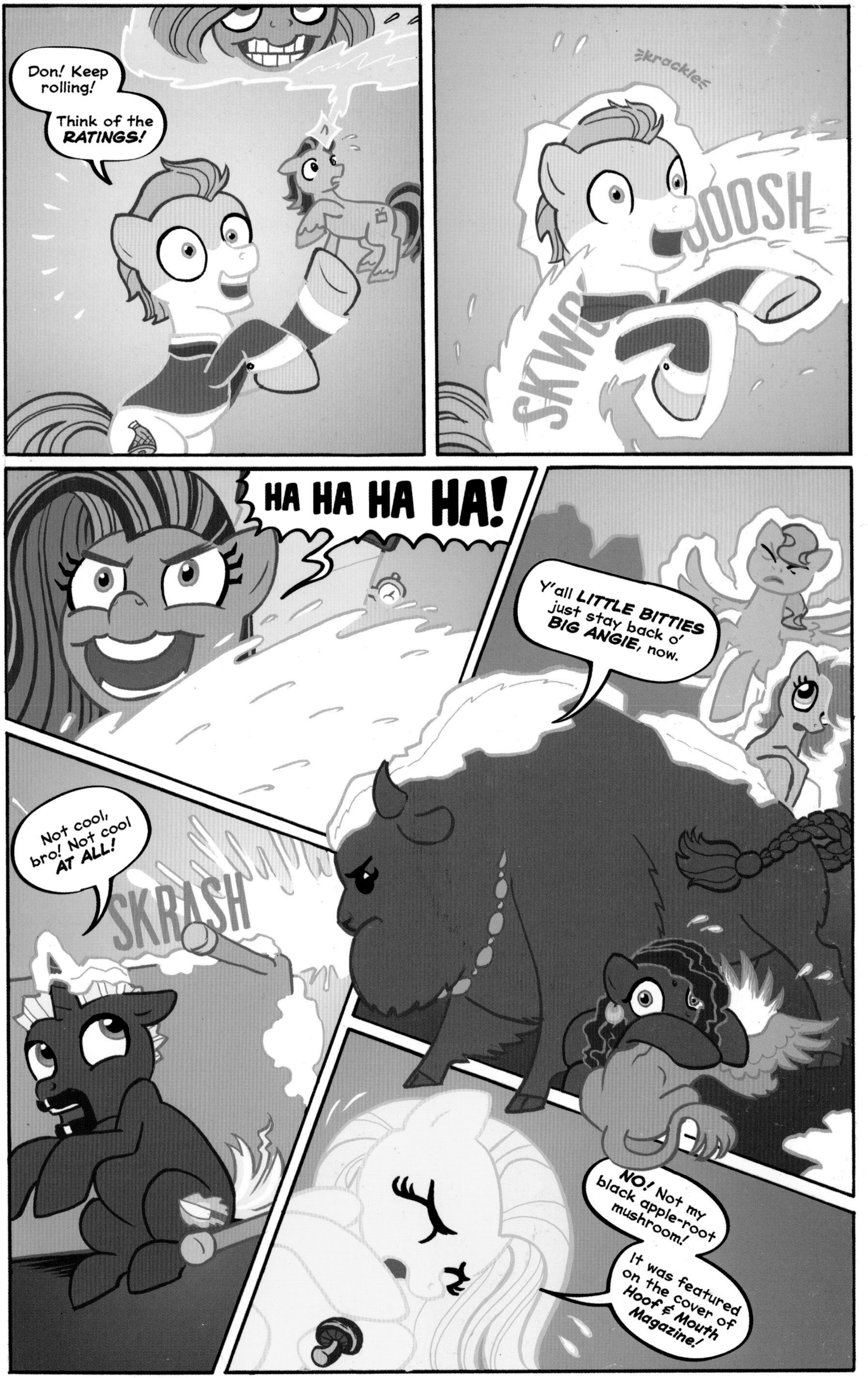
Don! Keep rolling!
Think of the RATINGS!
krackle
SKWOOSH
HA HA HA HA!
Y'all LITTLE BITTIES just stay back o' BIG ANGIE, now.
Not cool, bro! Not cool AT ALL!
SKRASH
NO! Not my black apple-root mushroom!
It was featured on the cover of Hoof & Mouth Magazine!

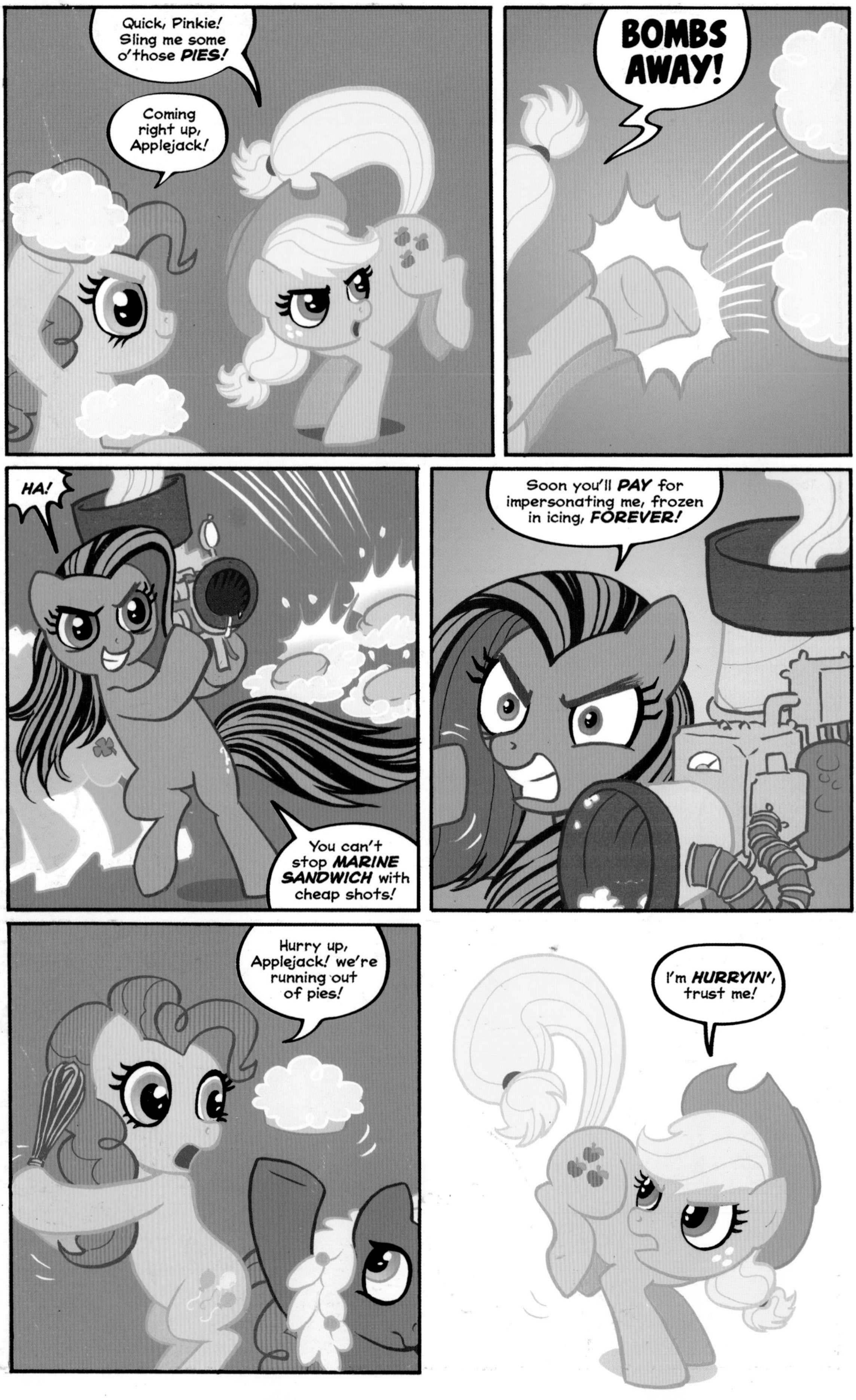
Quick, Pinkie! Sling me some o' those PIES!
Coming right up, Applejack!
BOMBS AWAY!
HA!
You can't stop MARINE SANDWICH with cheap shots!
Soon you'll PAY for impersonating me, frozen in icing, FOREVER!
Hurry up, Applejack! we're running out of pies!
I'm HURRYIN', trust me!

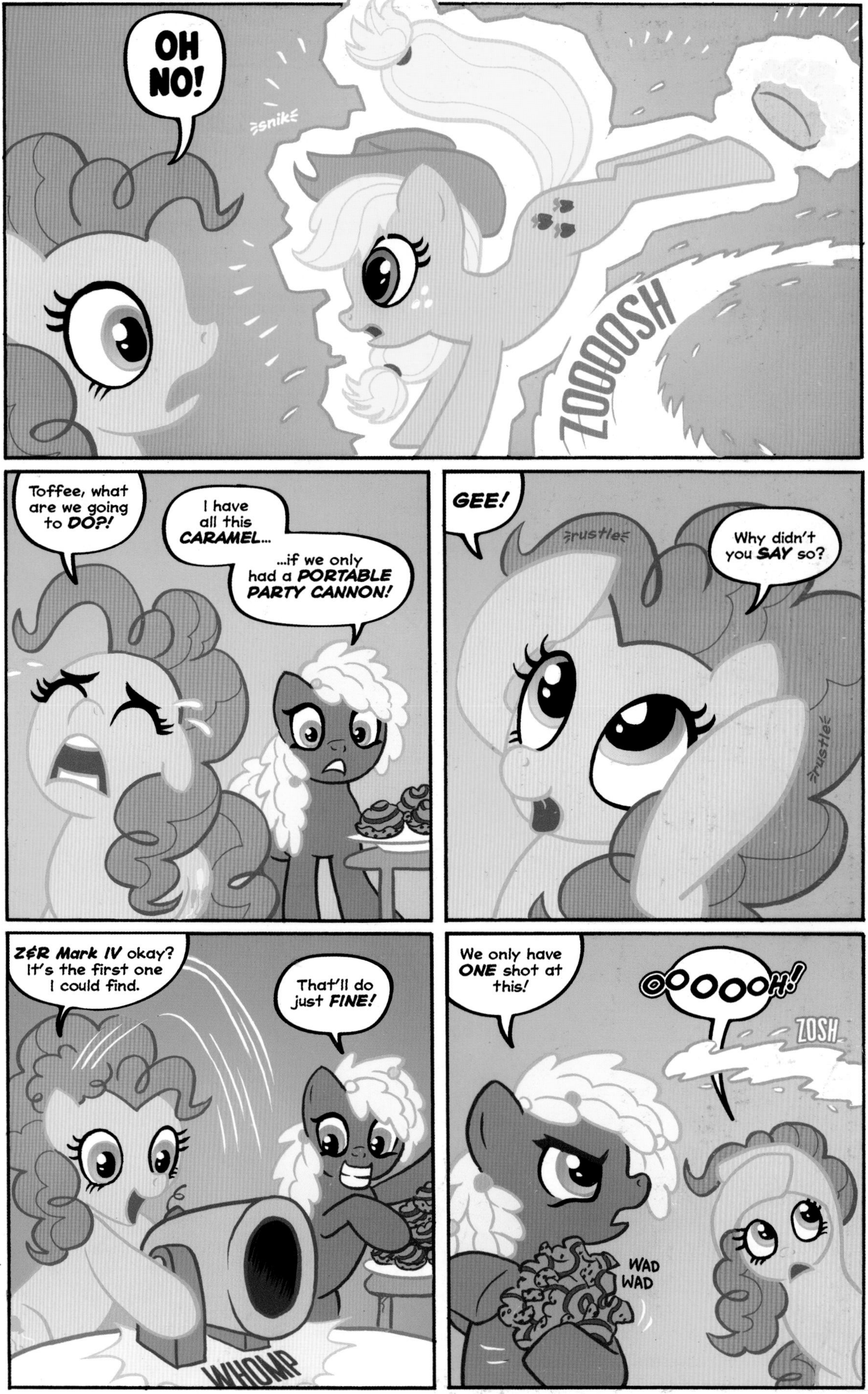
OH NO!
snik
ZOOOOSH
Toffee, what are we going to DO?!
I have all this CARAMEL...
...if we only had a PORTABLE PARTY CANNON!
GEE!
rustle
Why didn't you SAY so?
rustle
Z&R Mark IV okay? It's the first one I could find.
That'll do just FINE!
WHOMP
We only have ONE shot at this!
OOOOOH!
ZOSH
WAD WAD

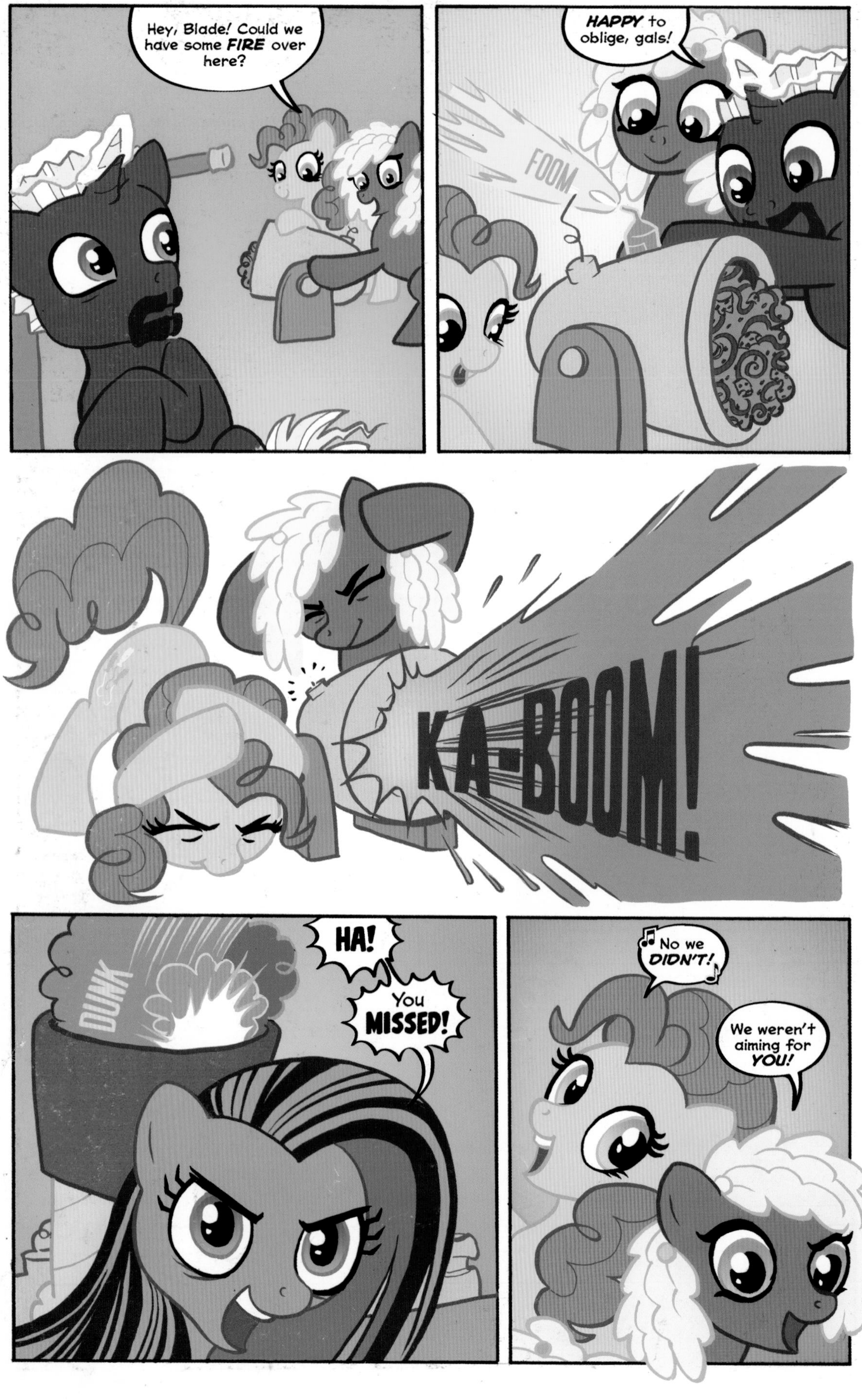
Hey, Blade! Could we have some **FIRE** over here?
HAPPY to oblige, gals!
FOOM
KA-BOOM!
HA!
You **MISSED!**
DUNK
No we **DIDN'T!**
We weren't aiming for **YOU!**

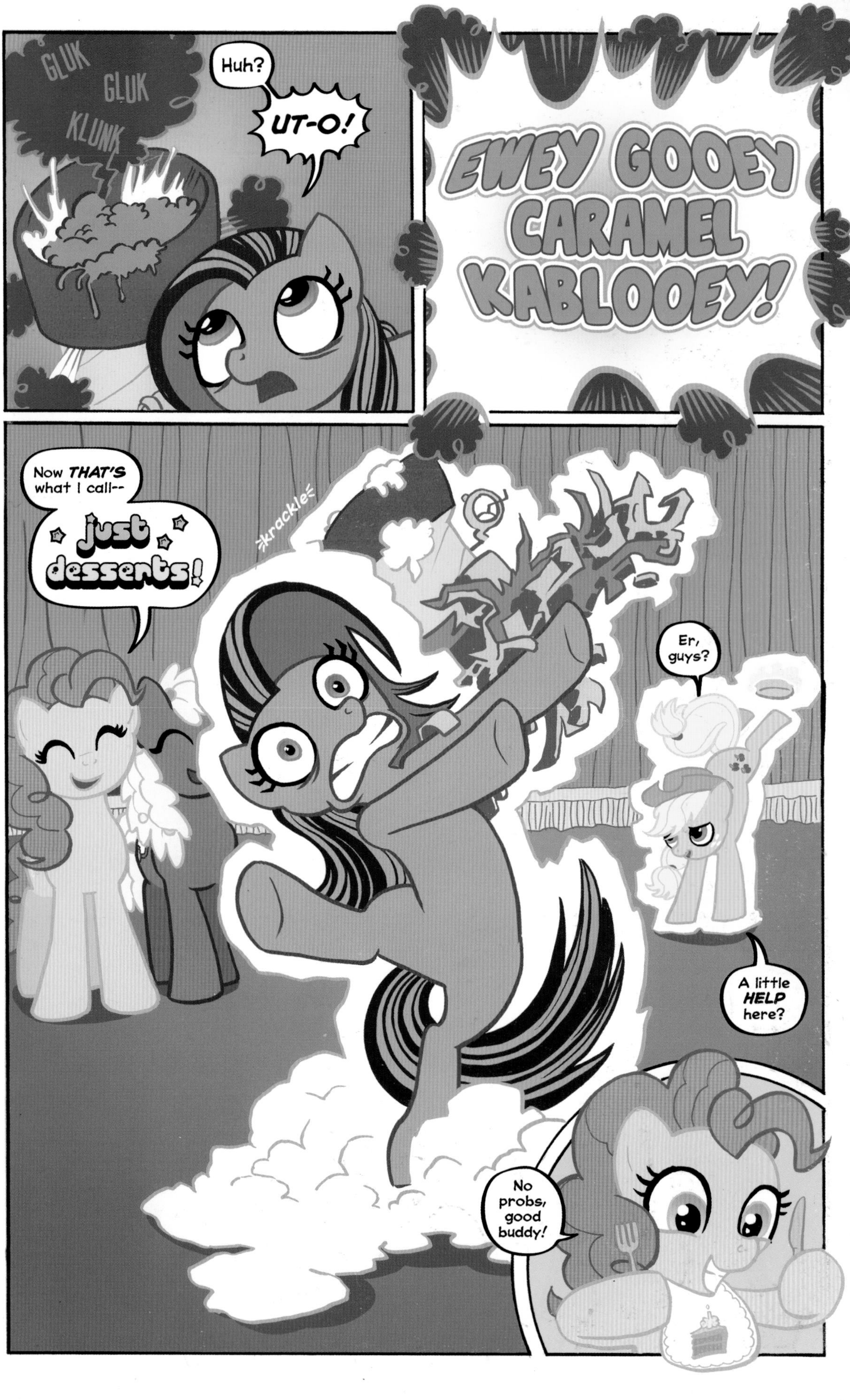
GLUK
GLUK
KLUNK
Huh?
UT-O!
EWEY GOOEY CARAMEL KABLOOEY!
Now THAT'S what I call--
just dessents!
krackle
Er, guys?
A little HELP here?
No probs, good buddy!

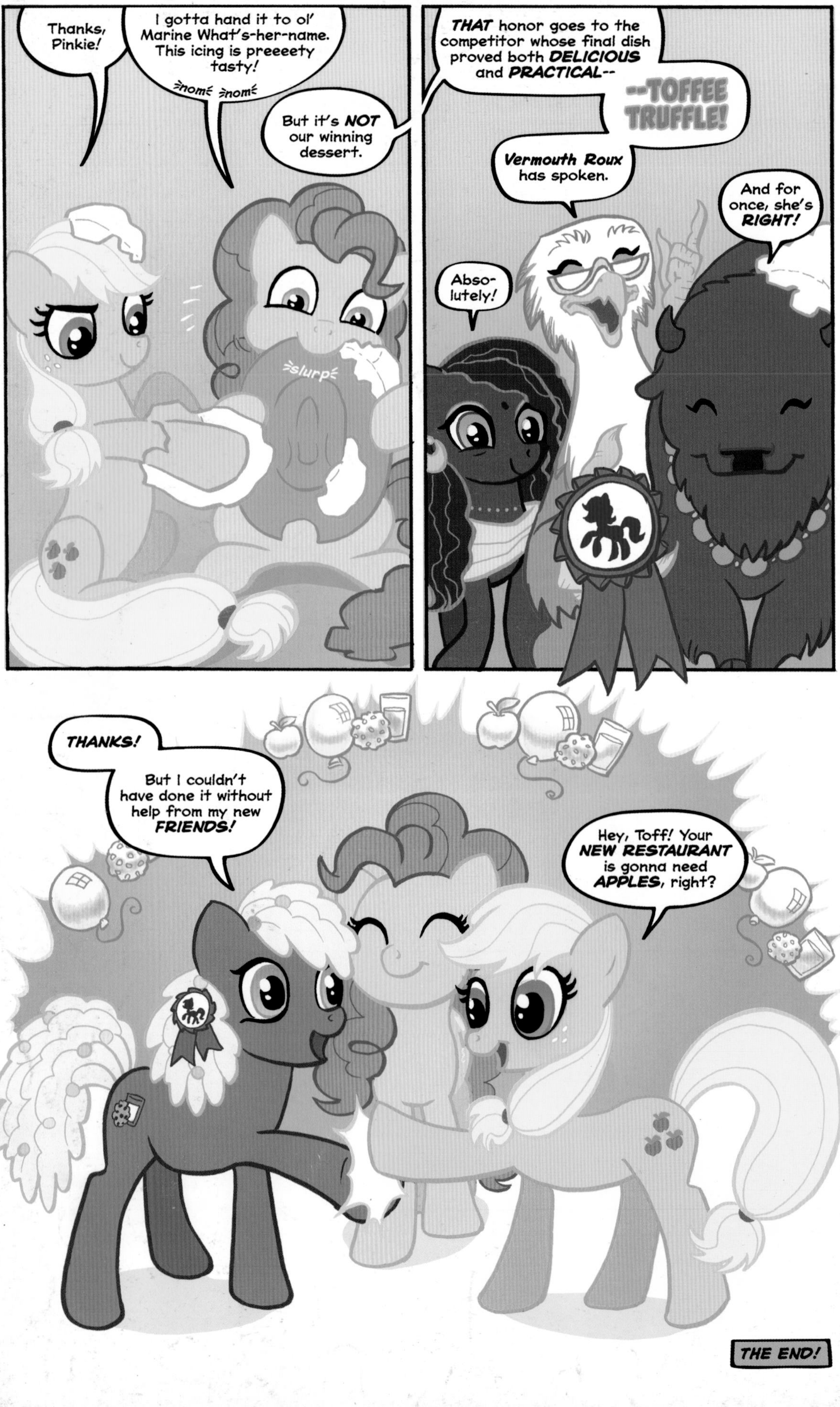

Thanks, Pinkie!
I gotta hand it to ol' Marine What's-her-name. This icing is preeeety tasty!
nom nom
slurp
But it's NOT our winning dessert.
THAT honor goes to the competitor whose final dish proved both DELICIOUS and PRACTICAL--
--TOFFEE TRUFFLE!
Vermouth Roux has spoken.
Abso-lutely!
And for once, she's RIGHT!
THANKS!
But I couldn't have done it without help from my new FRIENDS!
Hey, Toff! Your NEW RESTAURANT is gonna need APPLES, right?
THE END!

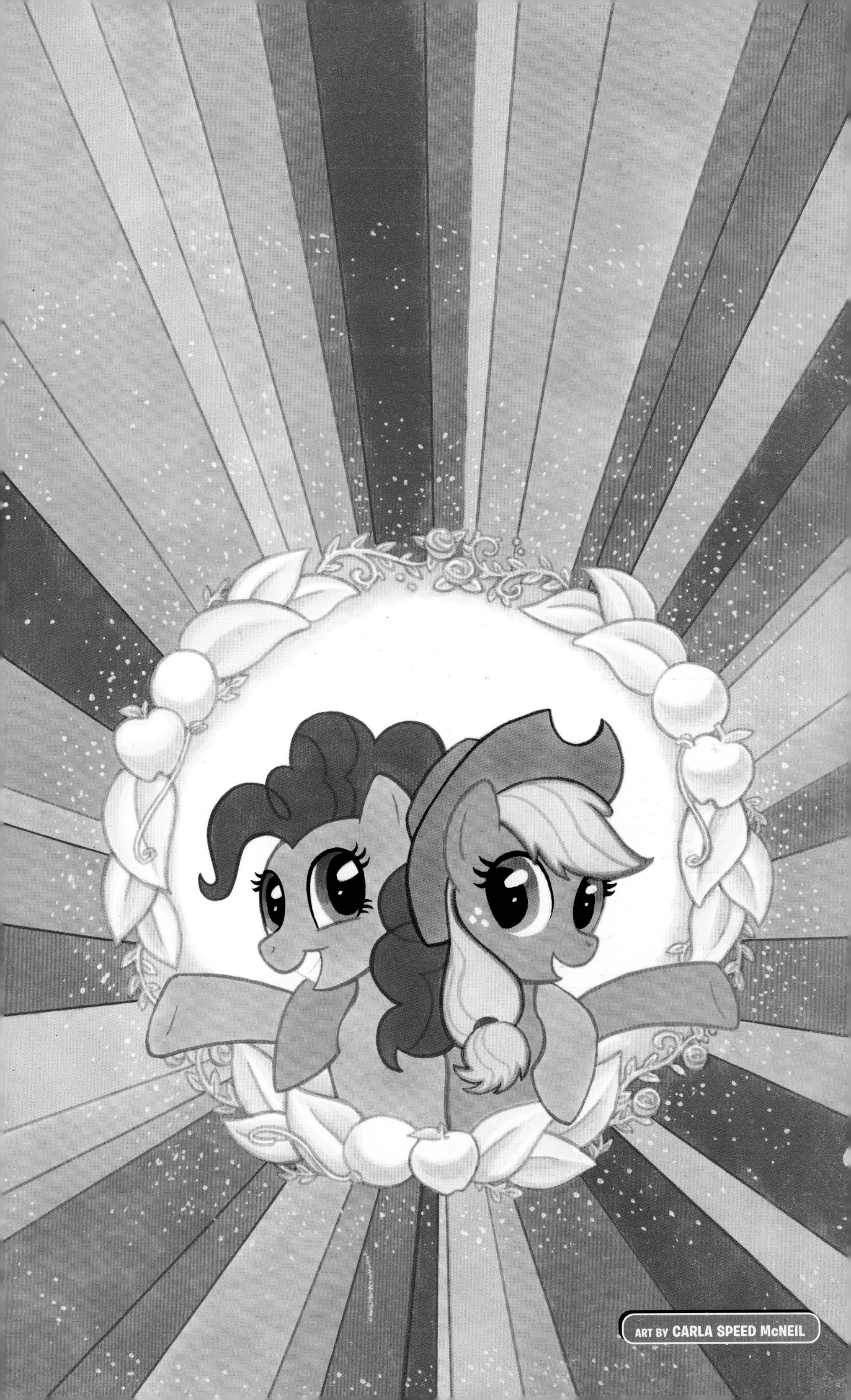
ART BY CARLA SPEED McNEIL

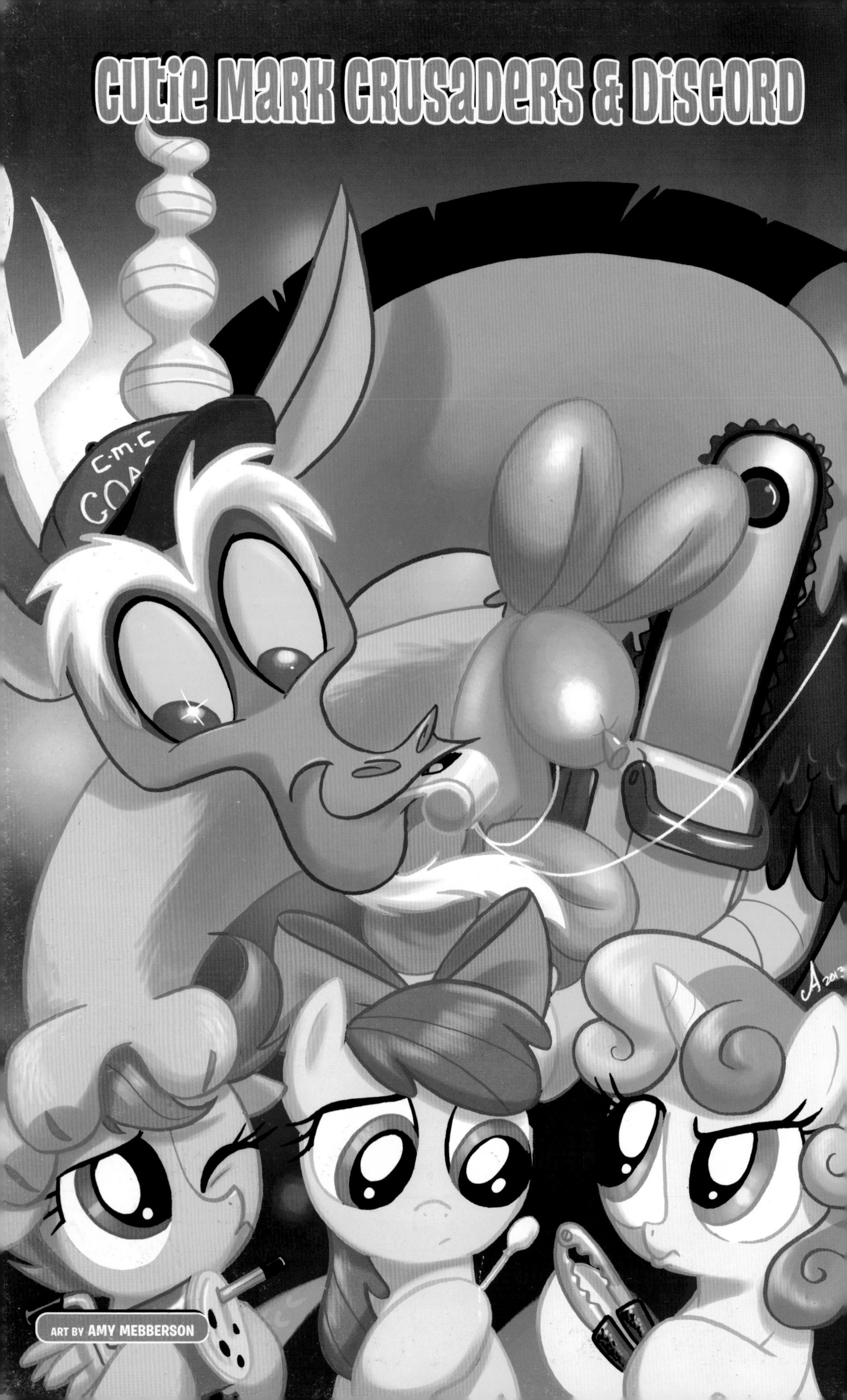
Cutie Mark Crusaders & Discord
ART BY AMY MEBBERSON

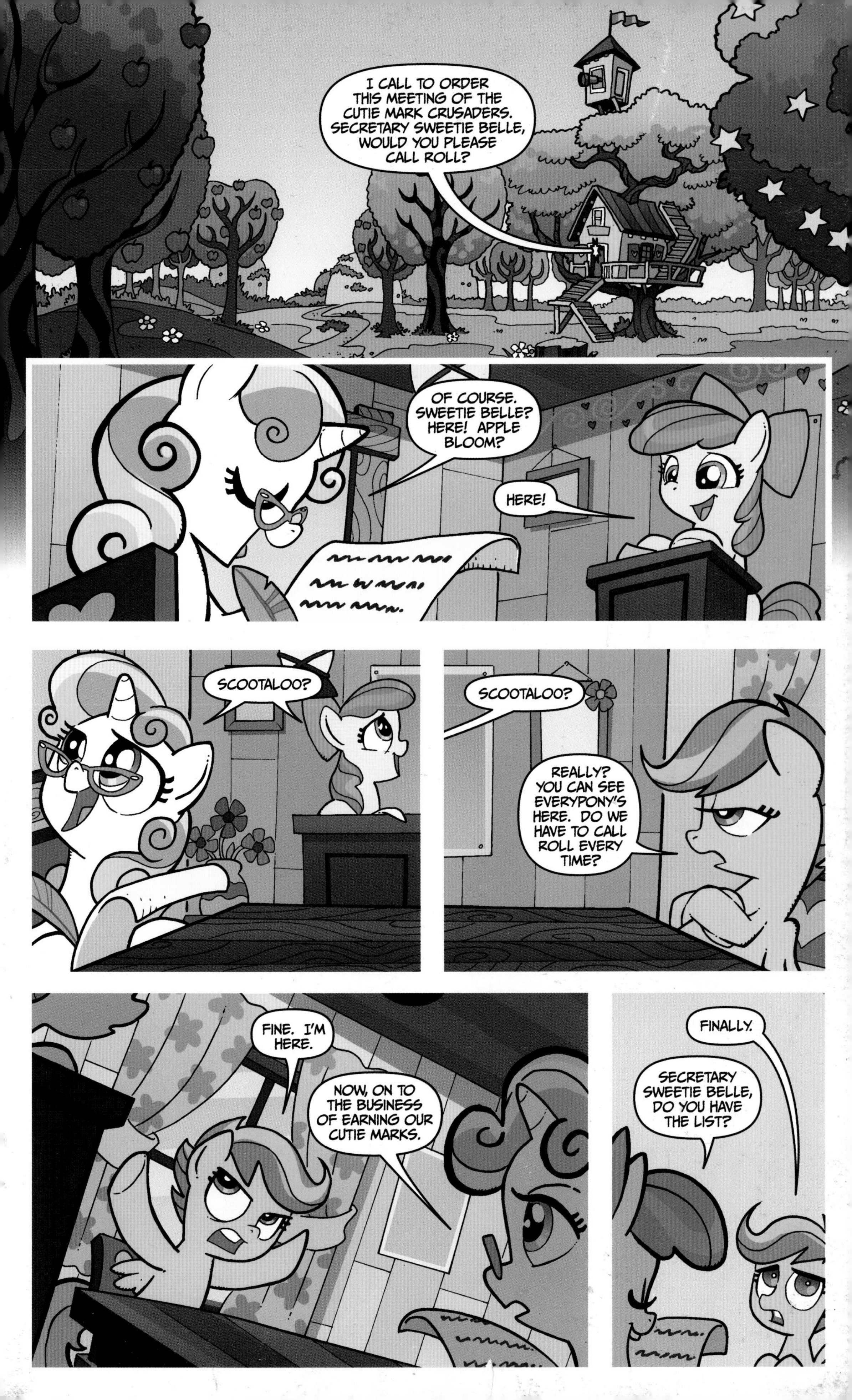
I CALL TO ORDER THIS MEETING OF THE CUTIE MARK CRUSADERS. SECRETARY SWEETIE BELLE, WOULD YOU PLEASE CALL ROLL?
OF COURSE. SWEETIE BELLE? HERE! APPLE BLOOM?
HERE!
SCOOTALOO?
SCOOTALOO?
REALLY? YOU CAN SEE EVERYPONY'S HERE. DO WE HAVE TO CALL ROLL EVERY TIME?
FINE. I'M HERE.
NOW, ON TO THE BUSINESS OF EARNING OUR CUTIE MARKS.
FINALLY.
SECRETARY SWEETIE BELLE, DO YOU HAVE THE LIST?

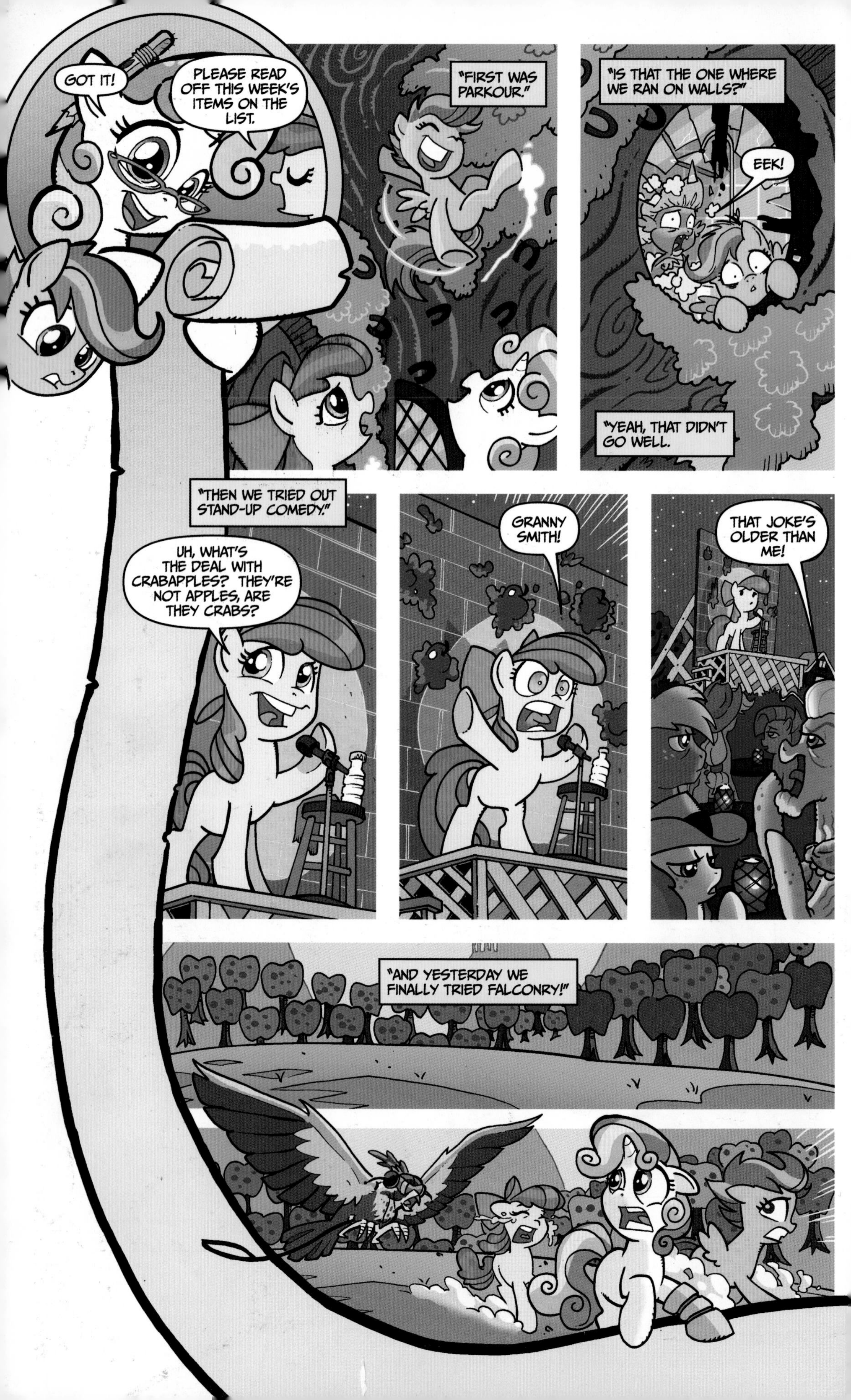
GOT IT!
PLEASE READ OFF THIS WEEK'S ITEMS ON THE LIST.
"FIRST WAS PARKOUR."
"IS THAT THE ONE WHERE WE RAN ON WALLS?"
EEK!
"YEAH, THAT DIDN'T GO WELL.
"THEN WE TRIED OUT STAND-UP COMEDY."
UH, WHAT'S THE DEAL WITH CRABAPPLES? THEY'RE NOT APPLES, ARE THEY CRABS?
GRANNY SMITH!
THAT JOKE'S OLDER THAN ME!
"AND YESTERDAY WE FINALLY TRIED FALCONRY!"

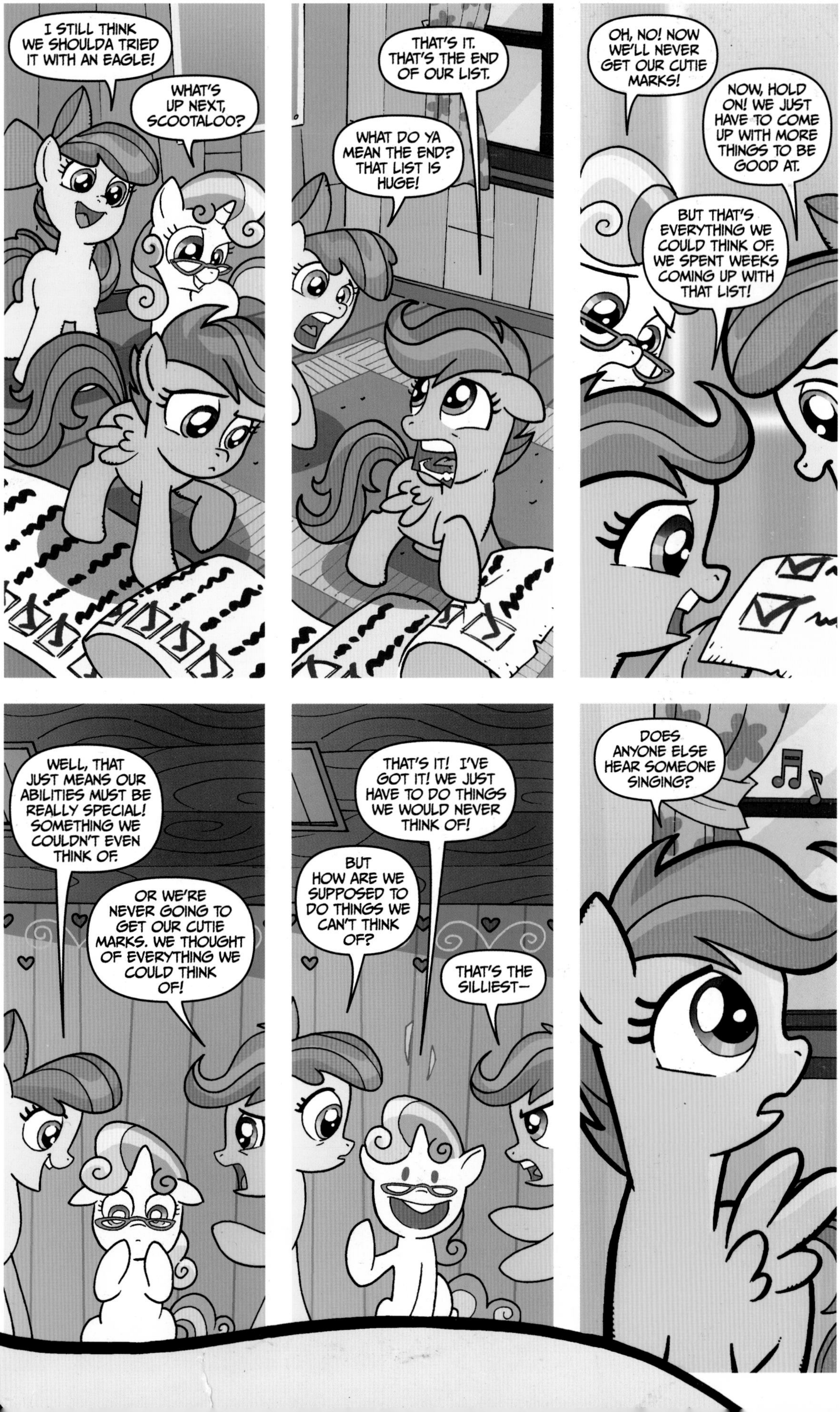
I STILL THINK WE SHOULDA TRIED IT WITH AN EAGLE!
WHAT'S UP NEXT, SCOOTALOO?
THAT'S IT. THAT'S THE END OF OUR LIST.
WHAT DO YA MEAN THE END? THAT LIST IS HUGE!
OH, NO! NOW WE'LL NEVER GET OUR CUTIE MARKS!
NOW, HOLD ON! WE JUST HAVE TO COME UP WITH MORE THINGS TO BE GOOD AT.
BUT THAT'S EVERYTHING WE COULD THINK OF. WE SPENT WEEKS COMING UP WITH THAT LIST!
WELL, THAT JUST MEANS OUR ABILITIES MUST BE REALLY SPECIAL! SOMETHING WE COULDN'T EVEN THINK OF.
OR WE'RE NEVER GOING TO GET OUR CUTIE MARKS. WE THOUGHT OF EVERYTHING WE COULD THINK OF!
THAT'S IT! I'VE GOT IT! WE JUST HAVE TO DO THINGS WE WOULD NEVER THINK OF!
BUT HOW ARE WE SUPPOSED TO DO THINGS WE CAN'T THINK OF?
THAT'S THE SILLIEST—
DOES ANYONE ELSE HEAR SOMEONE SINGING?

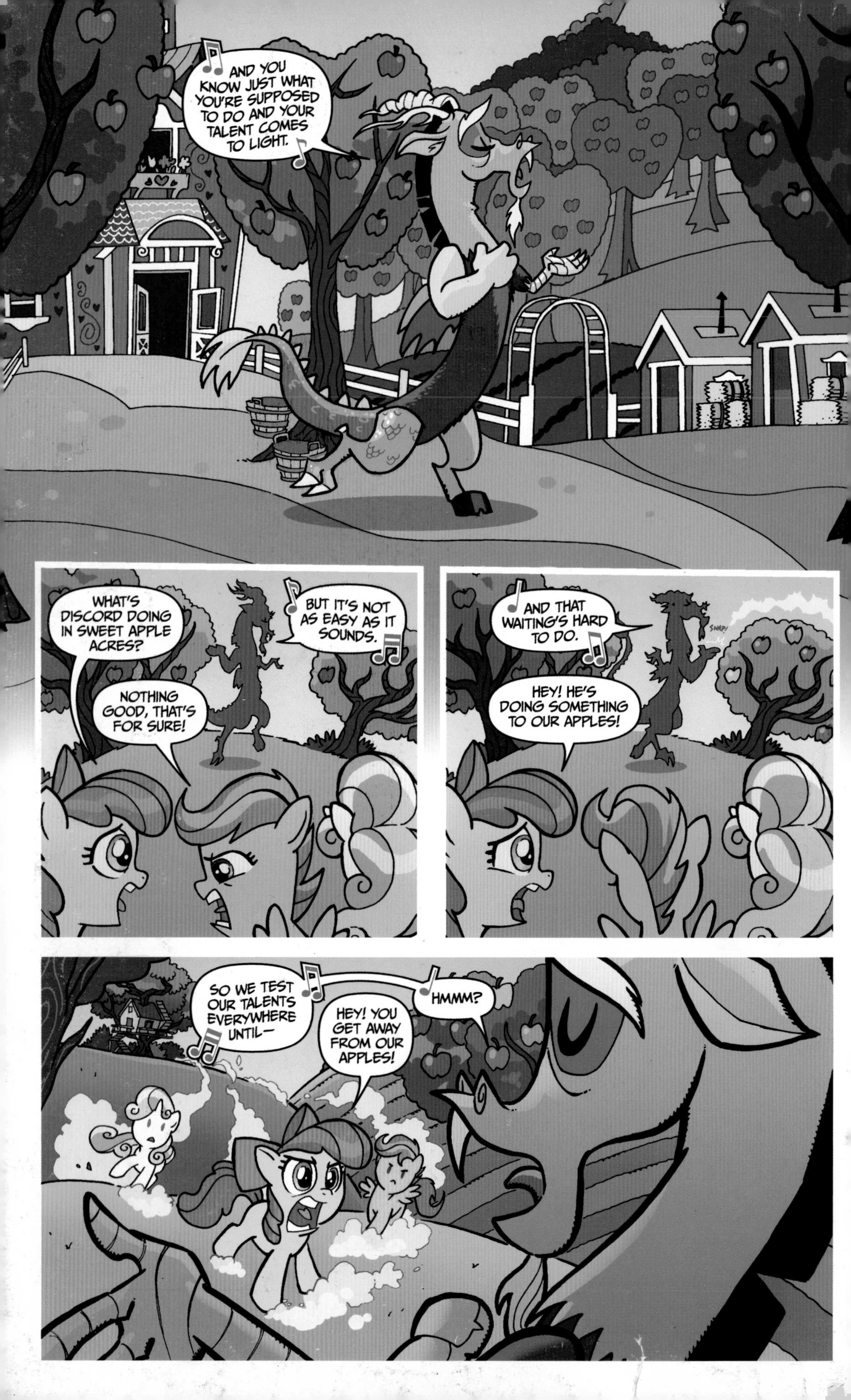
AND YOU KNOW JUST WHAT YOU'RE SUPPOSED TO DO AND YOUR TALENT COMES TO LIGHT.
WHAT'S DISCORD DOING IN SWEET APPLE ACRES?
BUT IT'S NOT AS EASY AS IT SOUNDS.
NOTHING GOOD, THAT'S FOR SURE!
AND THAT WAITING'S HARD TO DO.
SNAP!
HEY! HE'S DOING SOMETHING TO OUR APPLES!
SO WE TEST OUR TALENTS EVERYWHERE UNTIL—
HMMM?
HEY! YOU GET AWAY FROM OUR APPLES!

1446-3235

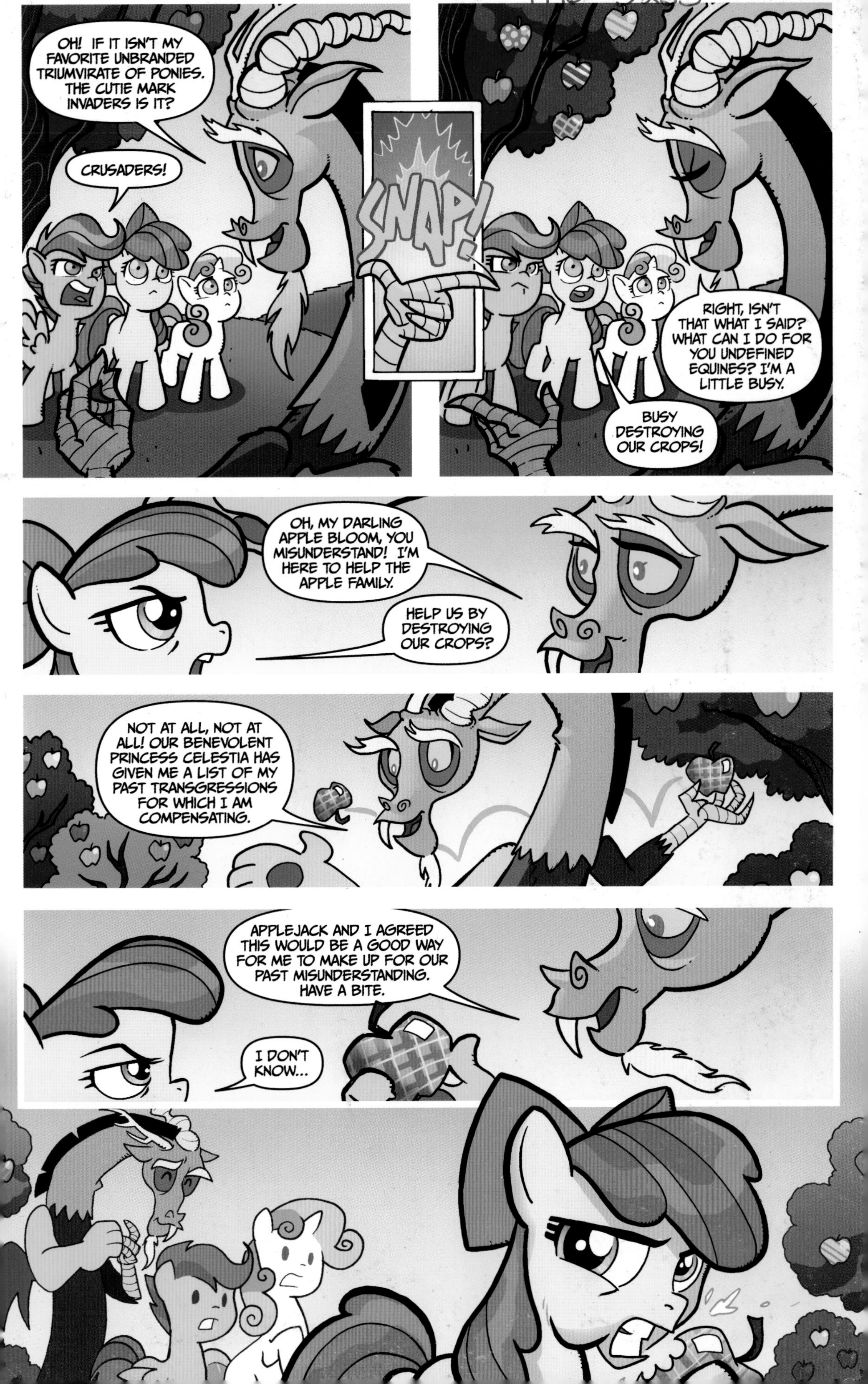

OH! IF IT ISN'T MY FAVORITE UNBRANDED TRIUMVIRATE OF PONIES. THE CUTIE MARK INVADERS IS IT?
CRUSADERS!
SNAP!
RIGHT, ISN'T THAT WHAT I SAID? WHAT CAN I DO FOR YOU UNDEFINED EQUINES? I'M A LITTLE BUSY.
BUSY DESTROYING OUR CROPS!
OH, MY DARLING APPLE BLOOM, YOU MISUNDERSTAND! I'M HERE TO HELP THE APPLE FAMILY.
HELP US BY DESTROYING OUR CROPS?
NOT AT ALL, NOT AT ALL! OUR BENEVOLENT PRINCESS CELESTIA HAS GIVEN ME A LIST OF MY PAST TRANSGRESSIONS FOR WHICH I AM COMPENSATING.
APPLEJACK AND I AGREED THIS WOULD BE A GOOD WAY FOR ME TO MAKE UP FOR OUR PAST MISUNDERSTANDING. HAVE A BITE.
I DON'T KNOW...

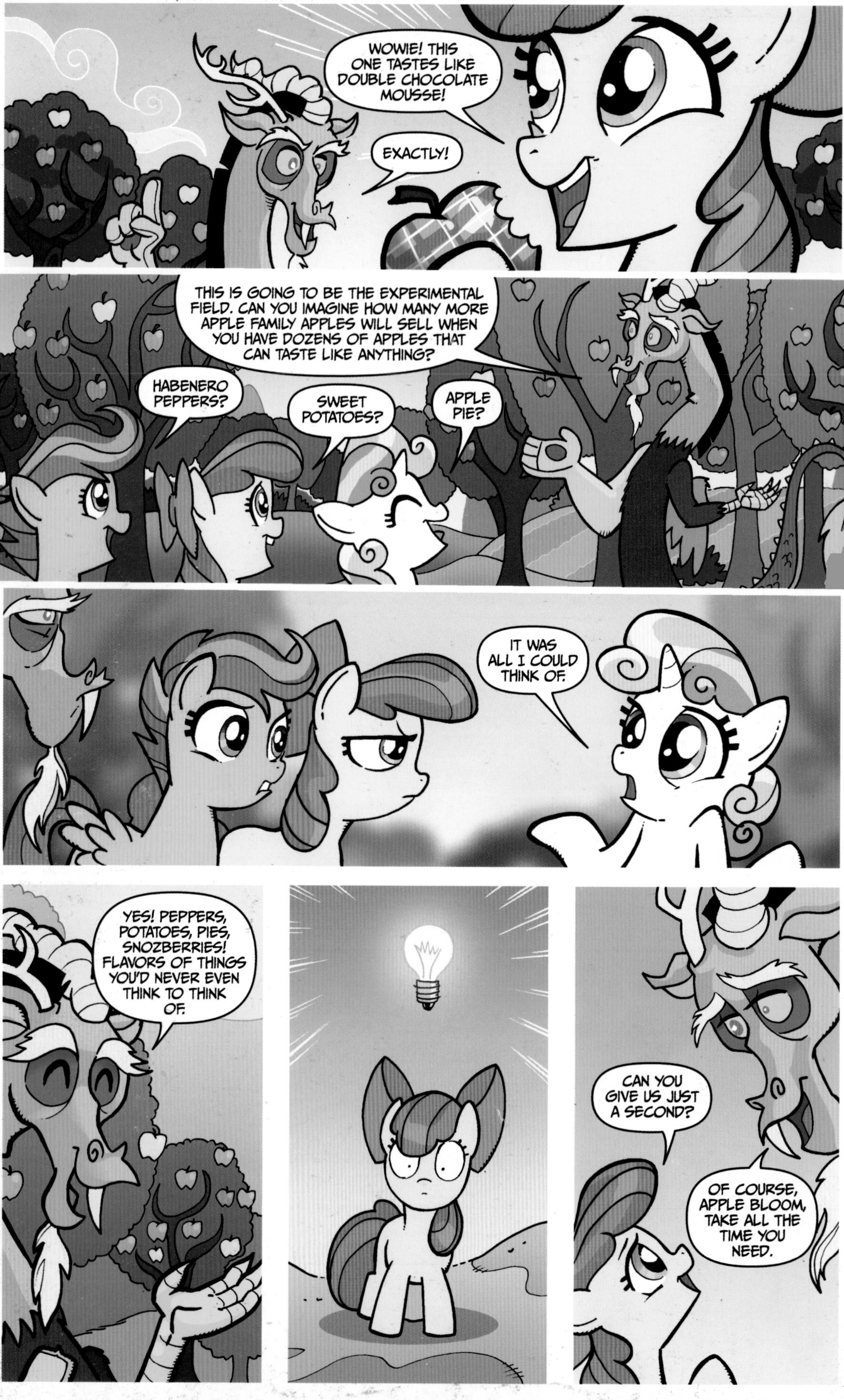
WOWIE! THIS ONE TASTES LIKE DOUBLE CHOCOLATE MOUSSE!
EXACTLY!
THIS IS GOING TO BE THE EXPERIMENTAL FIELD. CAN YOU IMAGINE HOW MANY MORE APPLE FAMILY APPLES WILL SELL WHEN YOU HAVE DOZENS OF APPLES THAT CAN TASTE LIKE ANYTHING?
HABENERO PEPPERS?
SWEET POTATOES?
APPLE PIE?
IT WAS ALL I COULD THINK OF.
YES! PEPPERS, POTATOES, PIES, SNOZBERRIES! FLAVORS OF THINGS YOU'D NEVER EVEN THINK TO THINK OF.
CAN YOU GIVE US JUST A SECOND?
OF COURSE, APPLE BLOOM, TAKE ALL THE TIME YOU NEED.

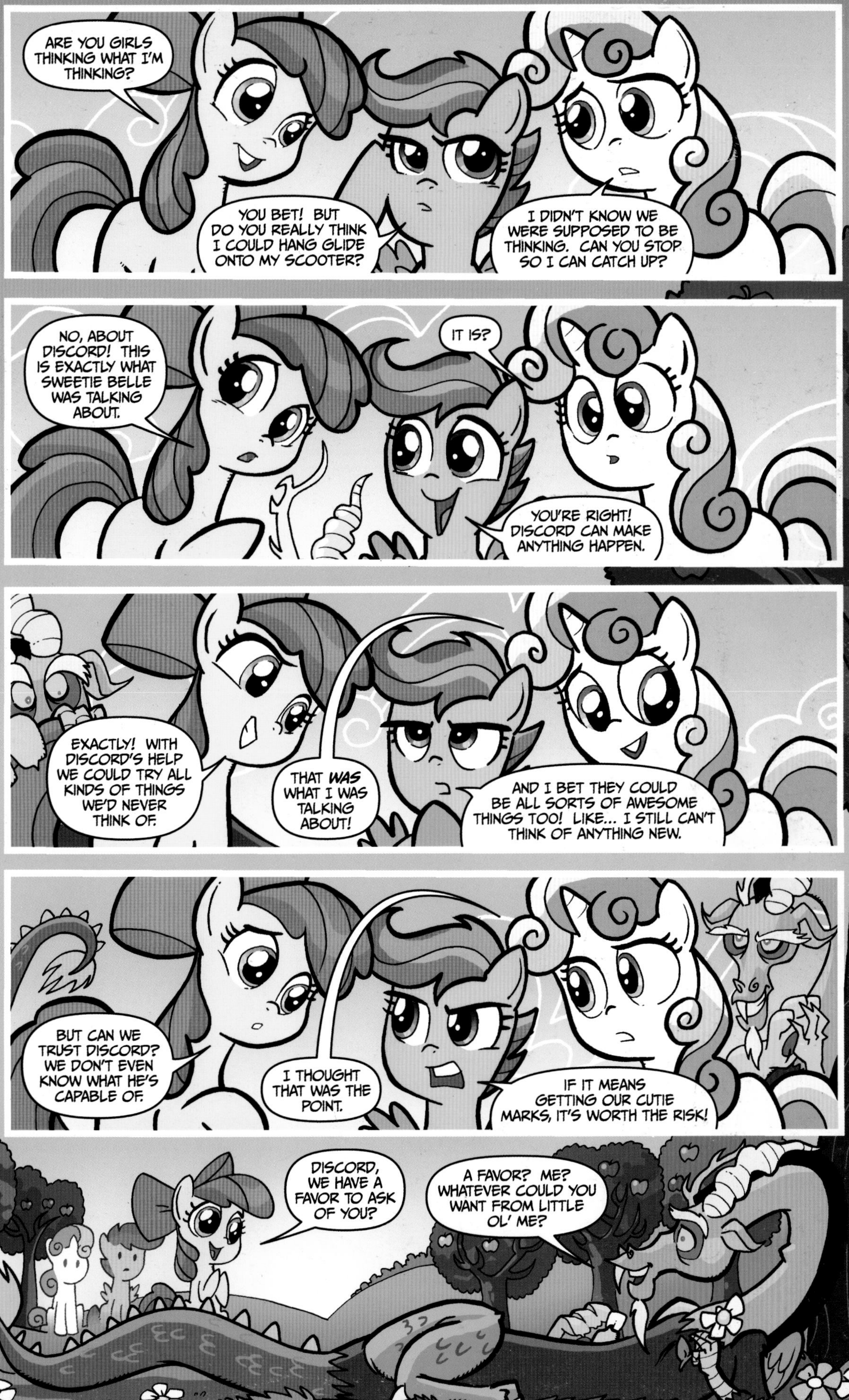
ARE YOU GIRLS THINKING WHAT I'M THINKING?
YOU BET! BUT DO YOU REALLY THINK I COULD HANG GLIDE ONTO MY SCOOTER?
I DIDN'T KNOW WE WERE SUPPOSED TO BE THINKING. CAN YOU STOP SO I CAN CATCH UP?
NO, ABOUT DISCORD! THIS IS EXACTLY WHAT SWEETIE BELLE WAS TALKING ABOUT.
IT IS?
YOU'RE RIGHT! DISCORD CAN MAKE ANYTHING HAPPEN.
EXACTLY! WITH DISCORD'S HELP WE COULD TRY ALL KINDS OF THINGS WE'D NEVER THINK OF.
THAT *WAS* WHAT I WAS TALKING ABOUT!
AND I BET THEY COULD BE ALL SORTS OF AWESOME THINGS TOO! LIKE... I STILL CAN'T THINK OF ANYTHING NEW.
BUT CAN WE TRUST DISCORD? WE DON'T EVEN KNOW WHAT HE'S CAPABLE OF.
I THOUGHT THAT WAS THE POINT.
IF IT MEANS GETTING OUR CUTIE MARKS, IT'S WORTH THE RISK!
DISCORD, WE HAVE A FAVOR TO ASK OF YOU?
A FAVOR? ME? WHATEVER COULD YOU WANT FROM LITTLE OL' ME?

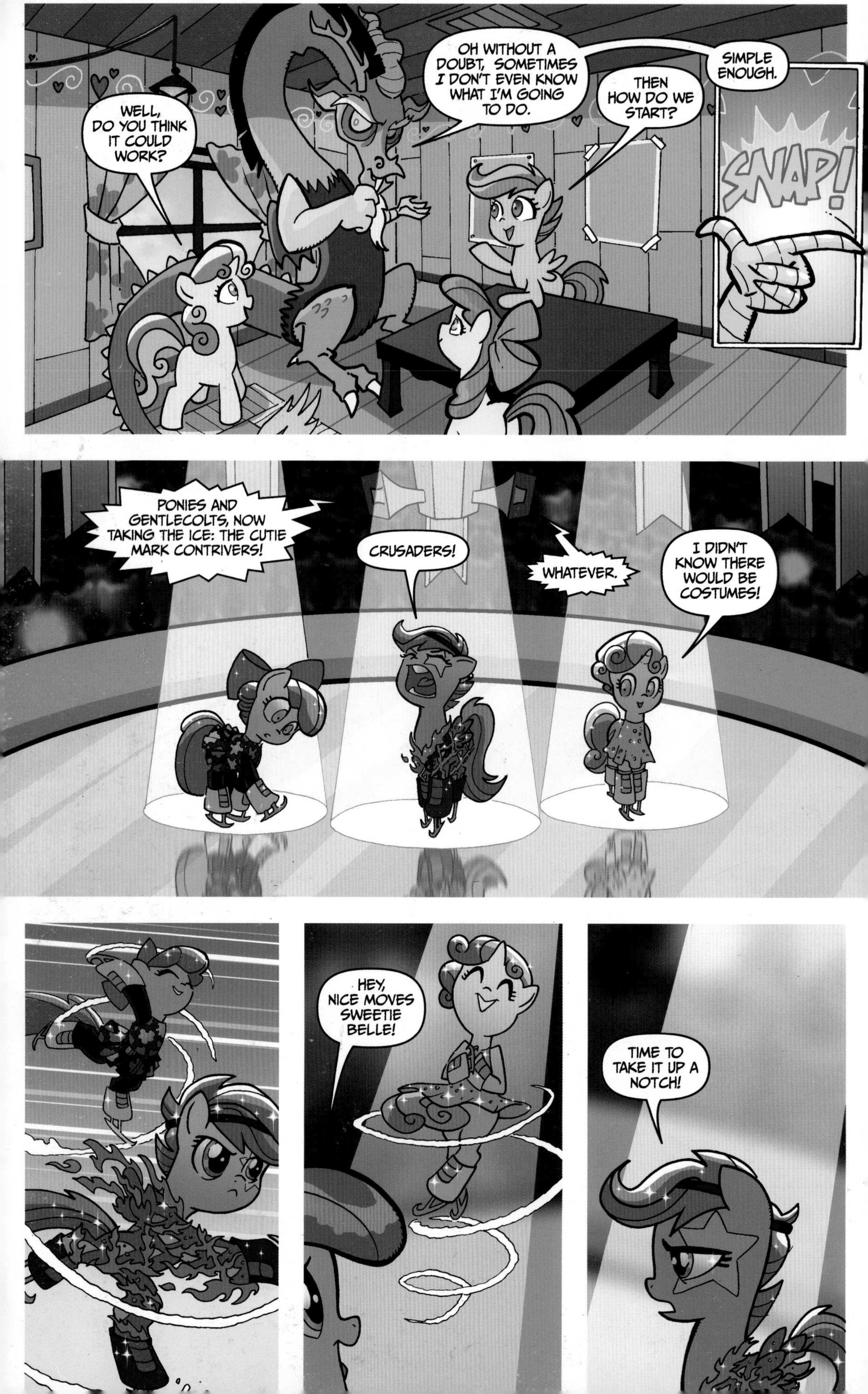
WELL, DO YOU THINK IT COULD WORK?
OH WITHOUT A DOUBT, SOMETIMES I DON'T EVEN KNOW WHAT I'M GOING TO DO.
THEN HOW DO WE START?
SIMPLE ENOUGH.
SNAP!
PONIES AND GENTLECOLTS, NOW TAKING THE ICE: THE CUTIE MARK CONTRIVERS!
CRUSADERS!
WHATEVER.
I DIDN'T KNOW THERE WOULD BE COSTUMES!
HEY, NICE MOVES SWEETIE BELLE!
TIME TO TAKE IT UP A NOTCH!

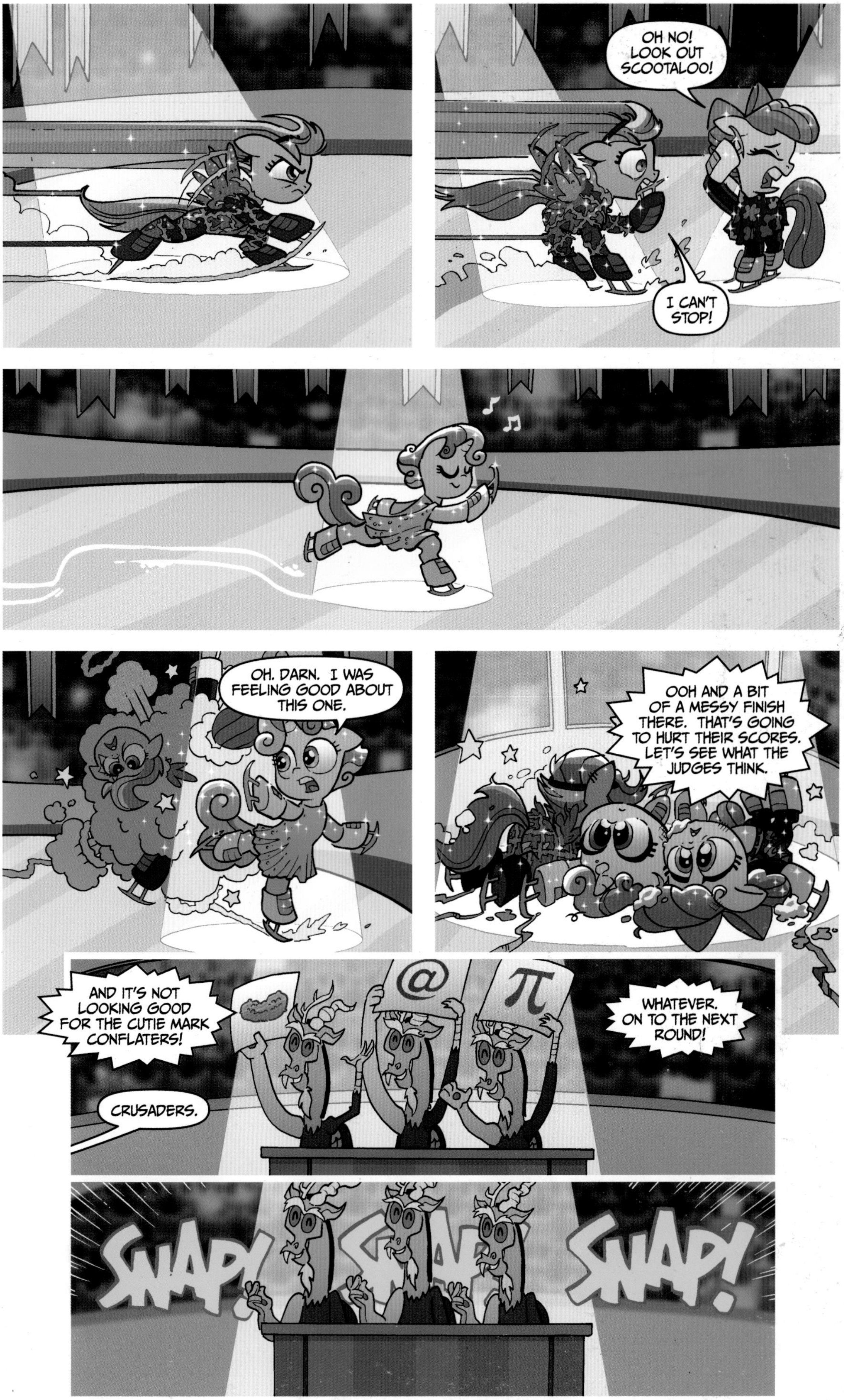
OH NO! LOOK OUT SCOOTALOO!
I CAN'T STOP!
OH. DARN. I WAS FEELING GOOD ABOUT THIS ONE.
OOH AND A BIT OF A MESSY FINISH THERE. THAT'S GOING TO HURT THEIR SCORES. LET'S SEE WHAT THE JUDGES THINK.
AND IT'S NOT LOOKING GOOD FOR THE CUTIE MARK CONFLATERS!
@
π
WHATEVER. ON TO THE NEXT ROUND!
CRUSADERS.
SNAP!
SNAP!
SNAP!

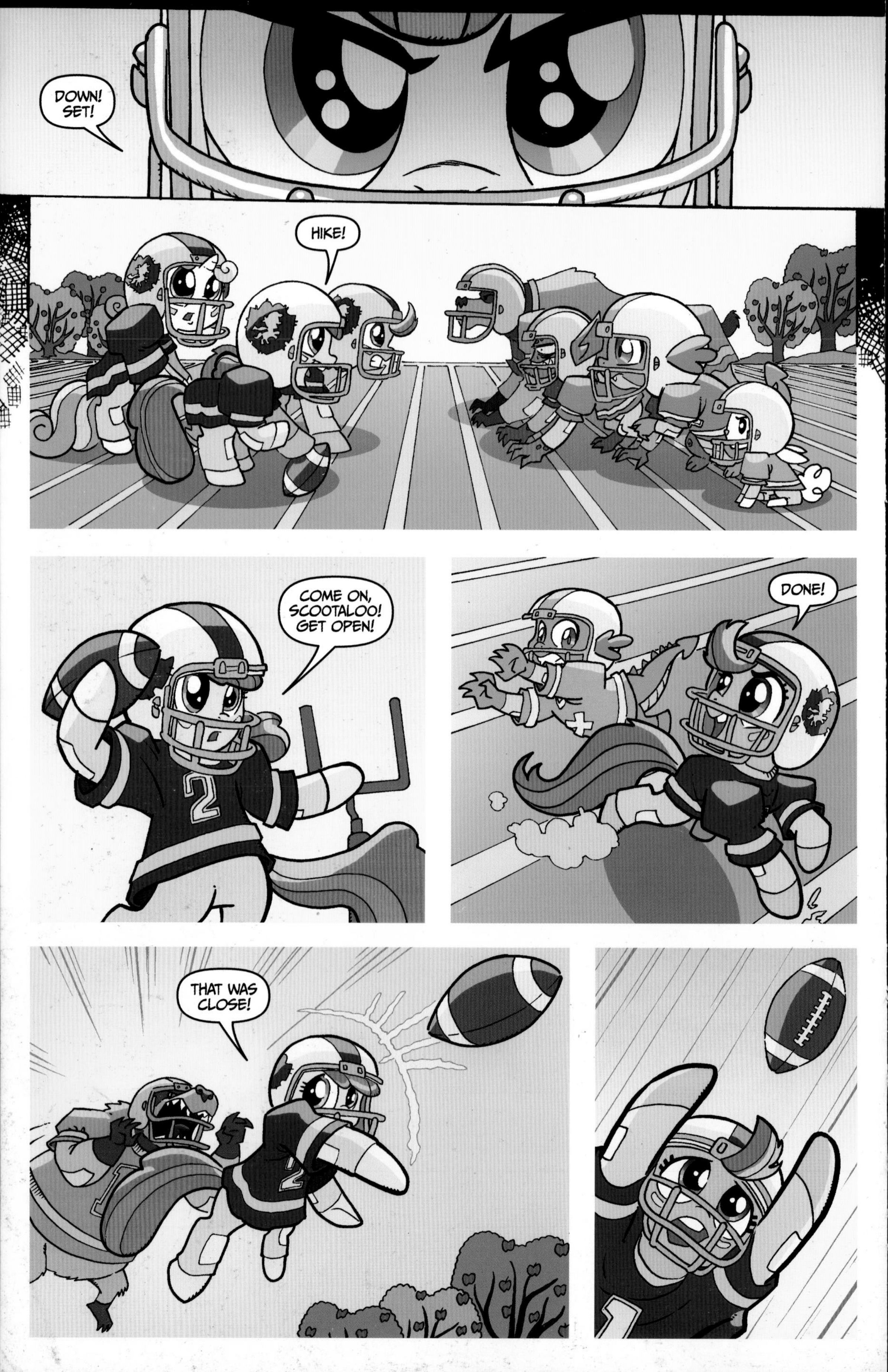
DOWN! SET!
HIKE!
COME ON, SCOOTALOO! GET OPEN!
DONE!
THAT WAS CLOSE!

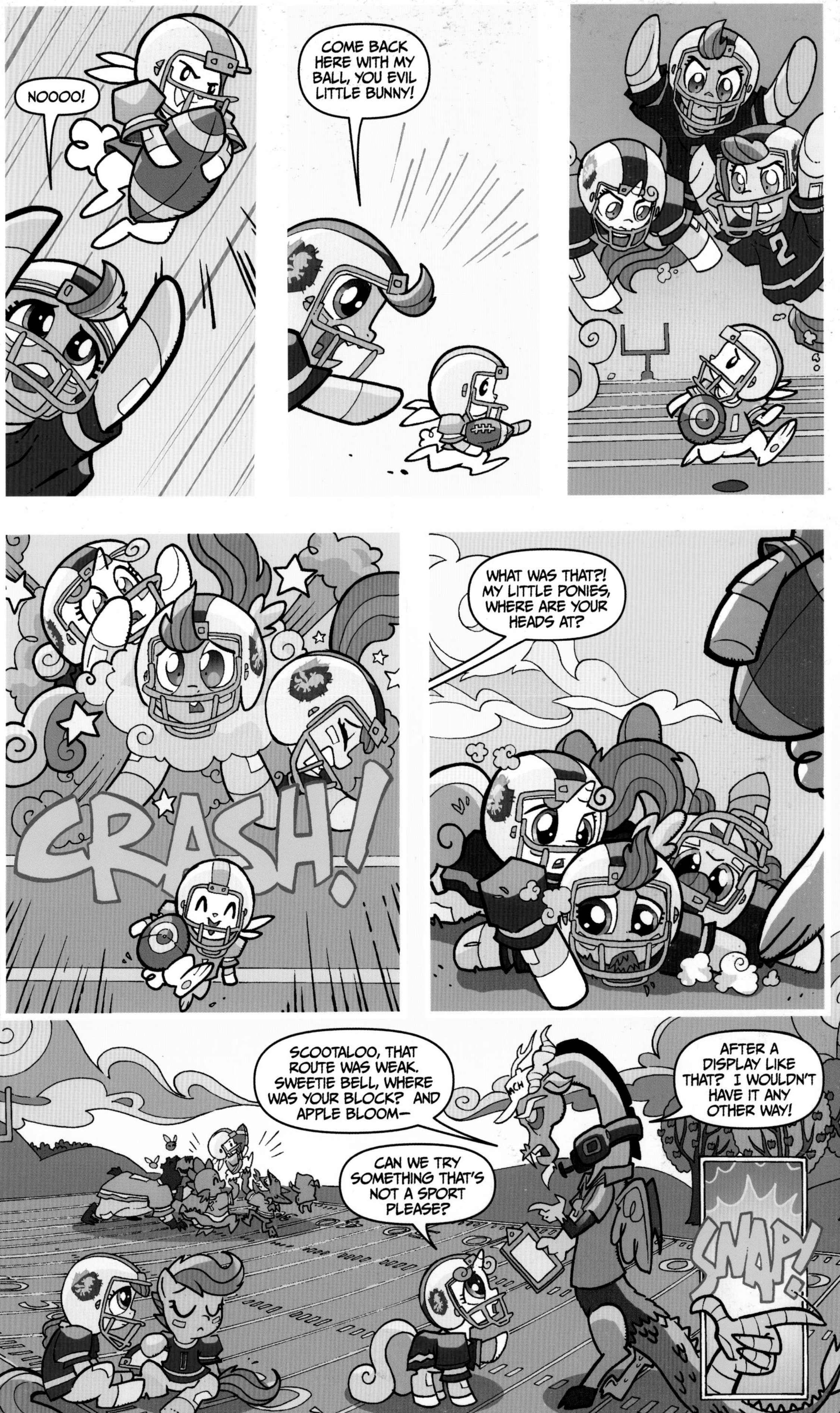
NOOOO!
COME BACK HERE WITH MY BALL, YOU EVIL LITTLE BUNNY!
CRASH!
WHAT WAS THAT?! MY LITTLE PONIES, WHERE ARE YOUR HEADS AT?
SCOOTALOO, THAT ROUTE WAS WEAK. SWEETIE BELL, WHERE WAS YOUR BLOCK? AND APPLE BLOOM—
CAN WE TRY SOMETHING THAT'S NOT A SPORT PLEASE?
AFTER A DISPLAY LIKE THAT? I WOULDN'T HAVE IT ANY OTHER WAY!
SNAP!

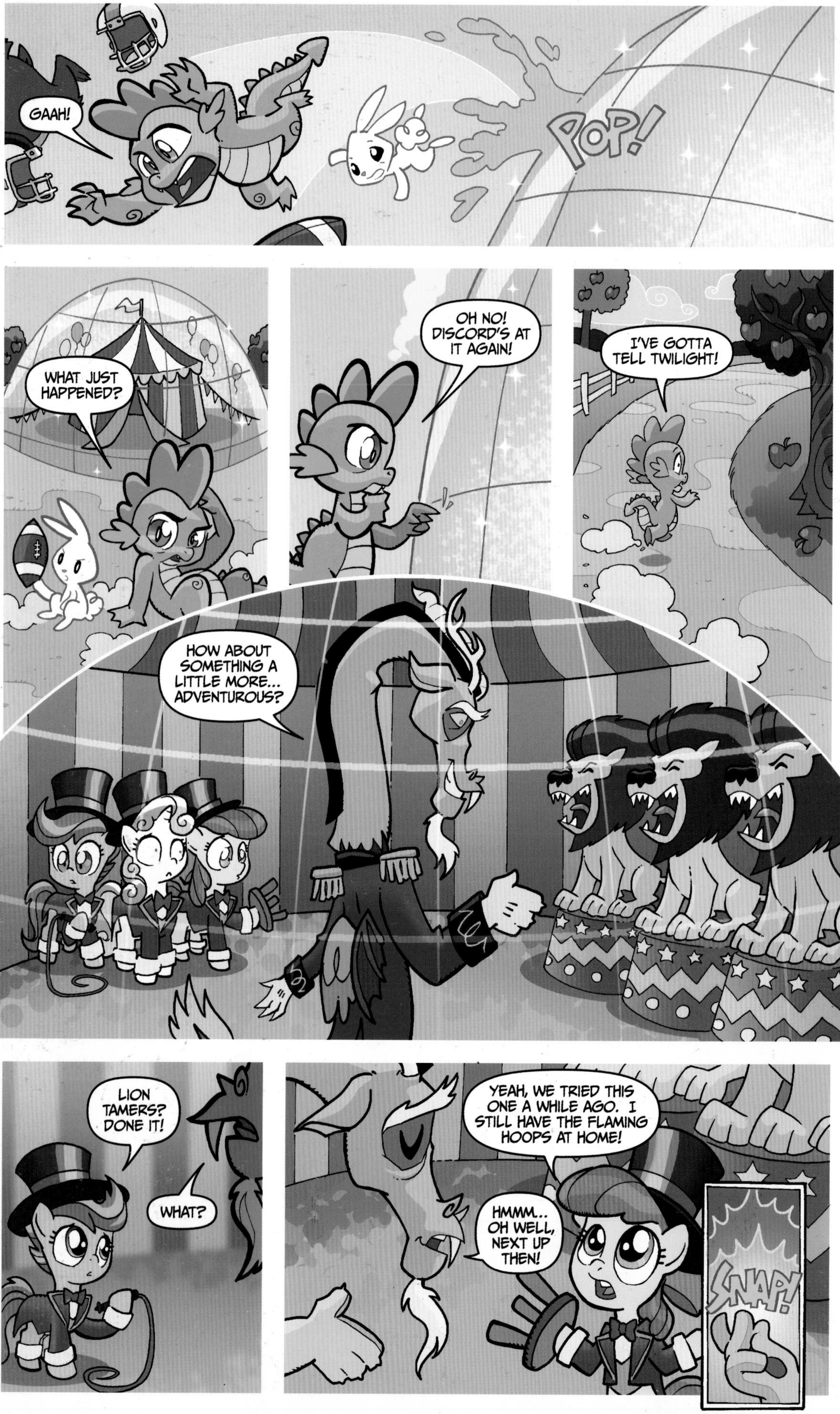
GAAH!
POP!
WHAT JUST HAPPENED?
OH NO! DISCORD'S AT IT AGAIN!
I'VE GOTTA TELL TWILIGHT!
HOW ABOUT SOMETHING A LITTLE MORE... ADVENTUROUS?
LION TAMERS? DONE IT!
WHAT?
YEAH, WE TRIED THIS ONE A WHILE AGO. I STILL HAVE THE FLAMING HOOPS AT HOME!
HMMM... OH WELL, NEXT UP THEN!
SNAP!

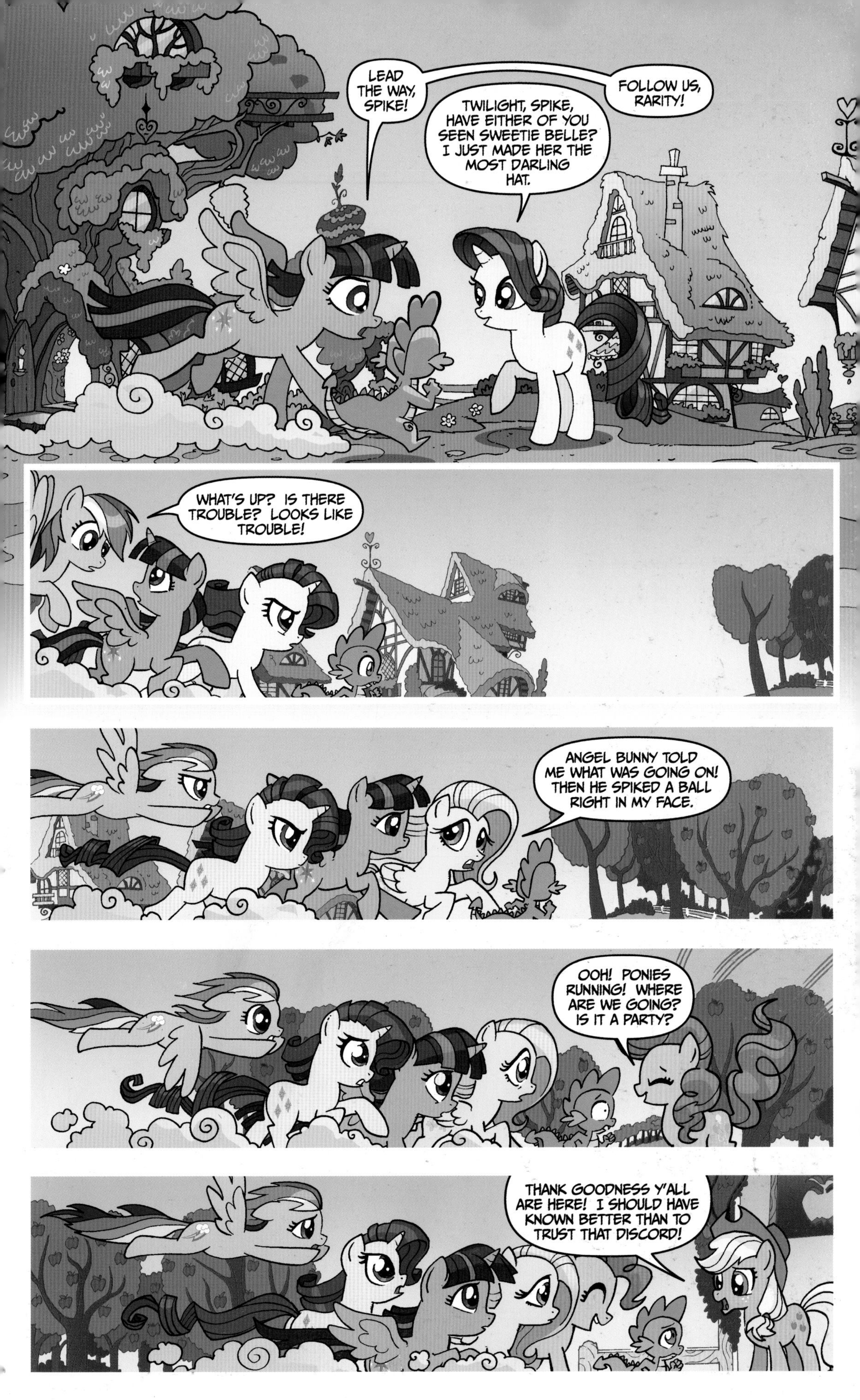
LEAD THE WAY, SPIKE!
FOLLOW US, RARITY!
TWILIGHT, SPIKE, HAVE EITHER OF YOU SEEN SWEETIE BELLE? I JUST MADE HER THE MOST DARLING HAT.
WHAT'S UP? IS THERE TROUBLE? LOOKS LIKE TROUBLE!
ANGEL BUNNY TOLD ME WHAT WAS GOING ON! THEN HE SPIKED A BALL RIGHT IN MY FACE.
OOH! PONIES RUNNING! WHERE ARE WE GOING? IS IT A PARTY?
THANK GOODNESS Y'ALL ARE HERE! I SHOULD HAVE KNOWN BETTER THAN TO TRUST THAT DISCORD!

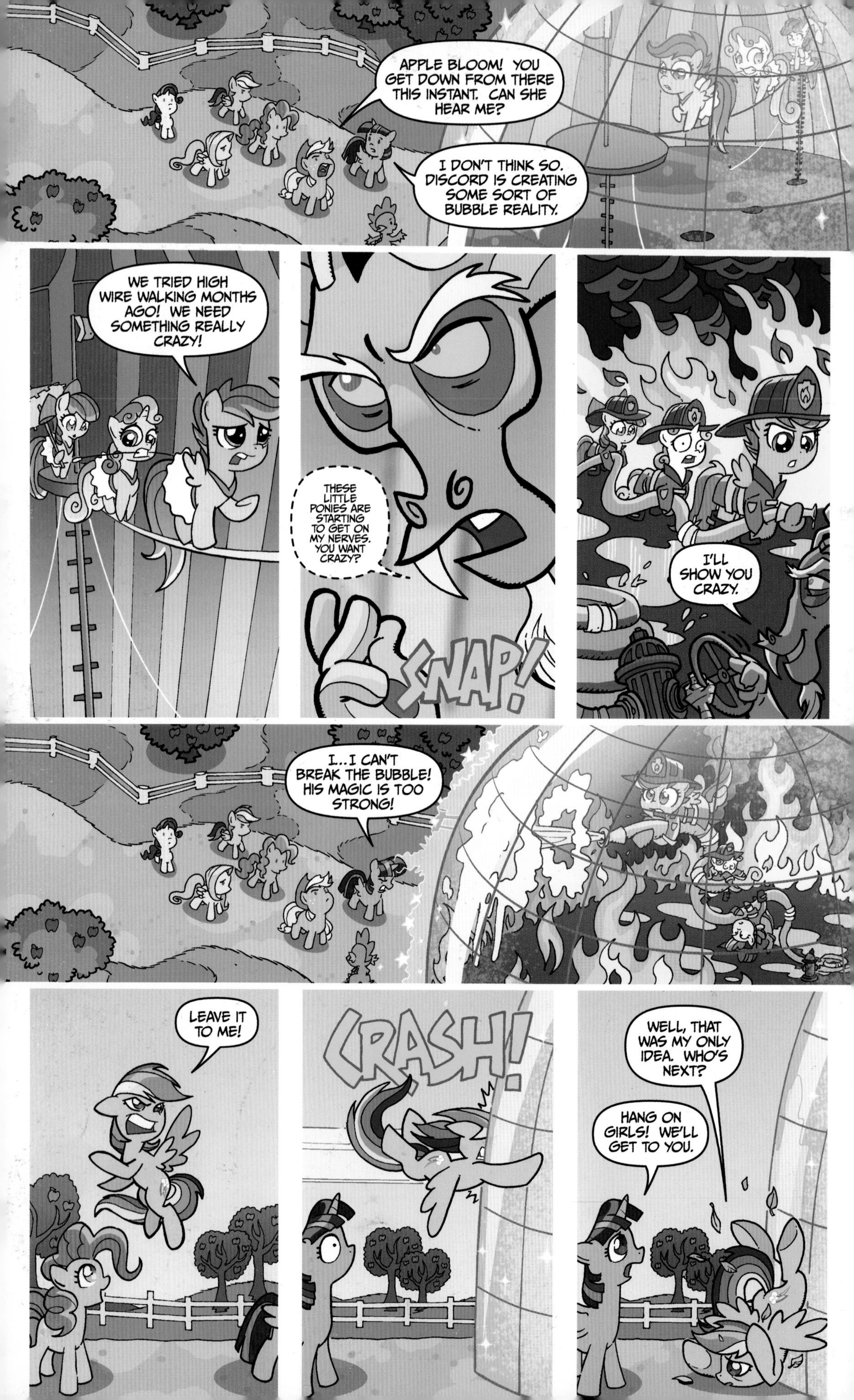
APPLE BLOOM! YOU GET DOWN FROM THERE THIS INSTANT. CAN SHE HEAR ME?
I DON'T THINK SO. DISCORD IS CREATING SOME SORT OF BUBBLE REALITY.
WE TRIED HIGH WIRE WALKING MONTHS AGO! WE NEED SOMETHING REALLY CRAZY!
THESE LITTLE PONIES ARE STARTING TO GET ON MY NERVES. YOU WANT CRAZY?
SNAP!
I'LL SHOW YOU CRAZY.
I...I CAN'T BREAK THE BUBBLE! HIS MAGIC IS TOO STRONG!
LEAVE IT TO ME!
CRASH!
WELL, THAT WAS MY ONLY IDEA. WHO'S NEXT?
HANG ON GIRLS! WE'LL GET TO YOU.

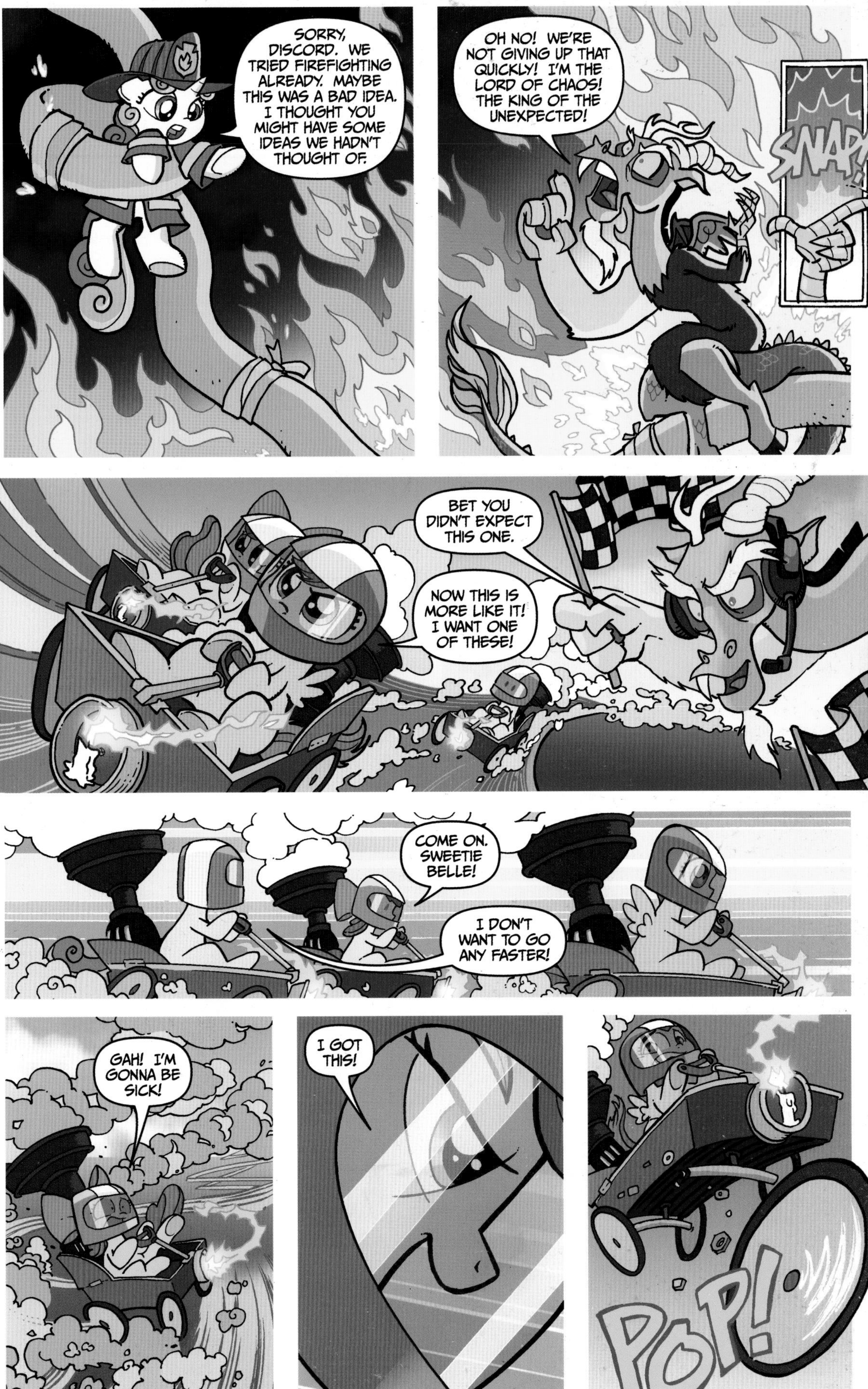
SORRY, DISCORD. WE TRIED FIREFIGHTING ALREADY. MAYBE THIS WAS A BAD IDEA. I THOUGHT YOU MIGHT HAVE SOME IDEAS WE HADN'T THOUGHT OF.
OH NO! WE'RE NOT GIVING UP THAT QUICKLY! I'M THE LORD OF CHAOS! THE KING OF THE UNEXPECTED!
SNAP!
BET YOU DIDN'T EXPECT THIS ONE.
NOW THIS IS MORE LIKE IT! I WANT ONE OF THESE!
COME ON. SWEETIE BELLE!
I DON'T WANT TO GO ANY FASTER!
GAH! I'M GONNA BE SICK!
I GOT THIS!
POP!

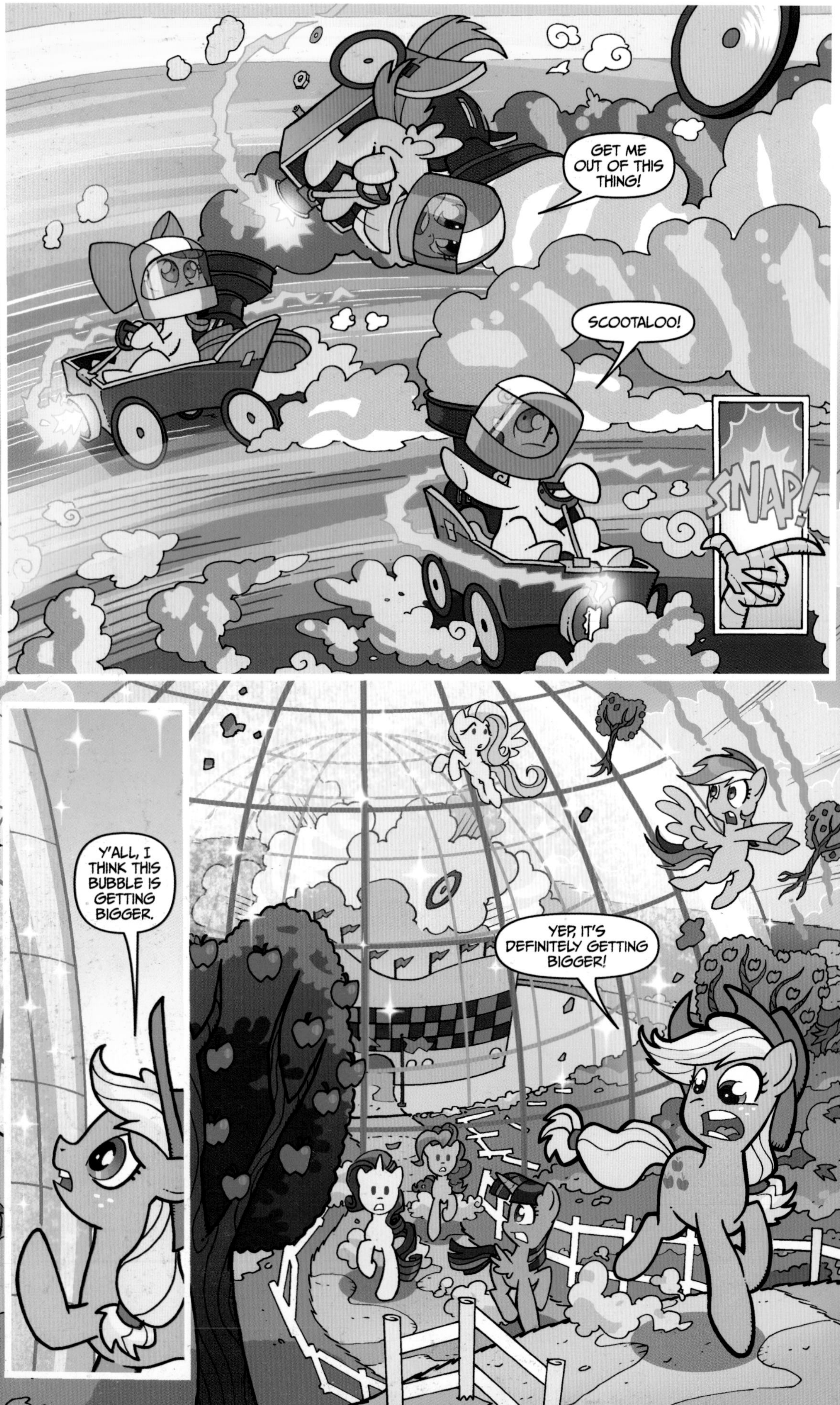

GET ME OUT OF THIS THING!
SCOOTALOO!
SNAP!
Y'ALL, I THINK THIS BUBBLE IS GETTING BIGGER.
YEP, IT'S DEFINITELY GETTING BIGGER!

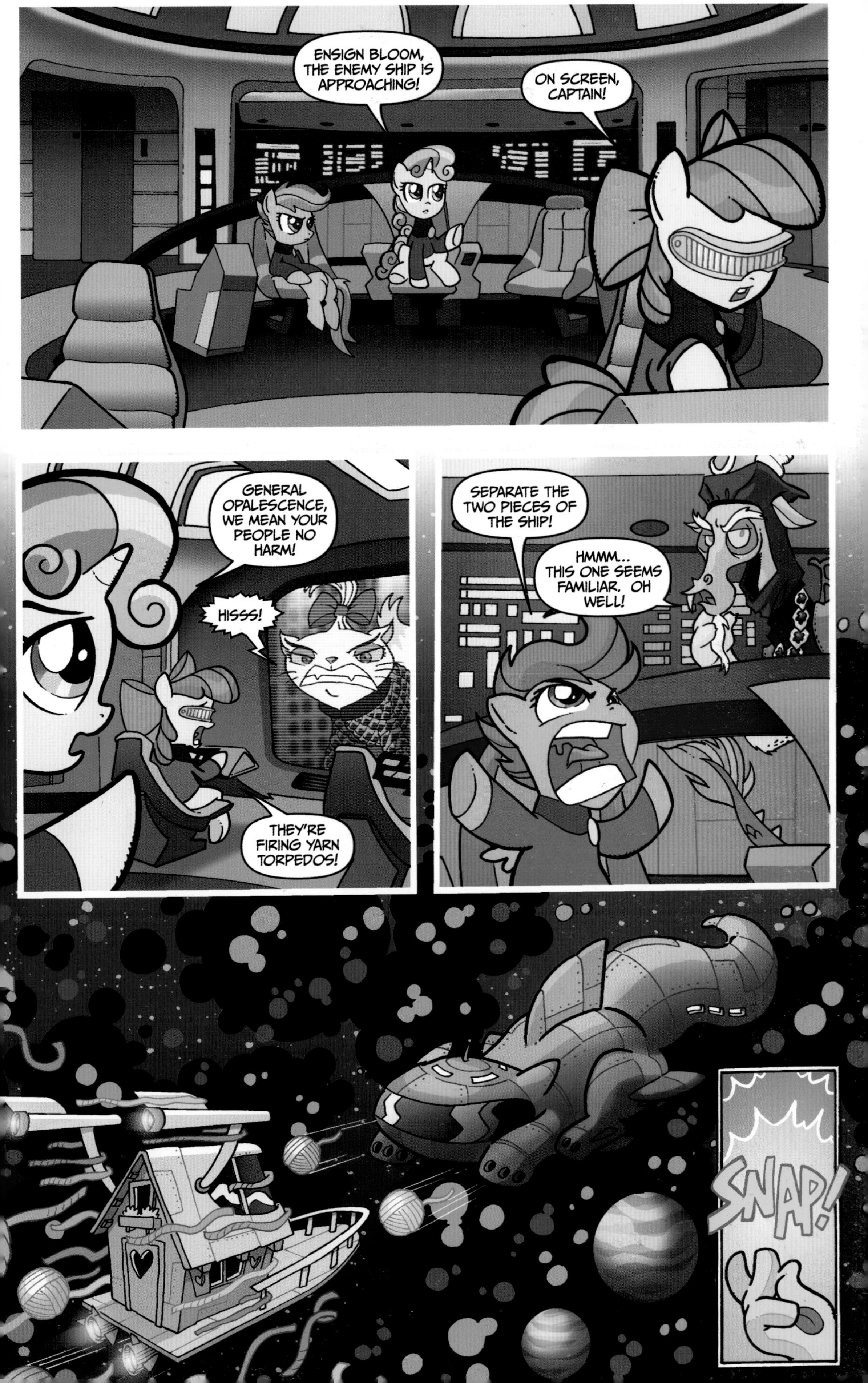

ENSIGN BLOOM, THE ENEMY SHIP IS APPROACHING!
ON SCREEN, CAPTAIN!
GENERAL OPALESCENCE, WE MEAN YOUR PEOPLE NO HARM!
HISSS!
THEY'RE FIRING YARN TORPEDOS!
SEPARATE THE TWO PIECES OF THE SHIP!
HMMM.. THIS ONE SEEMS FAMILIAR. OH WELL!
SNAP!

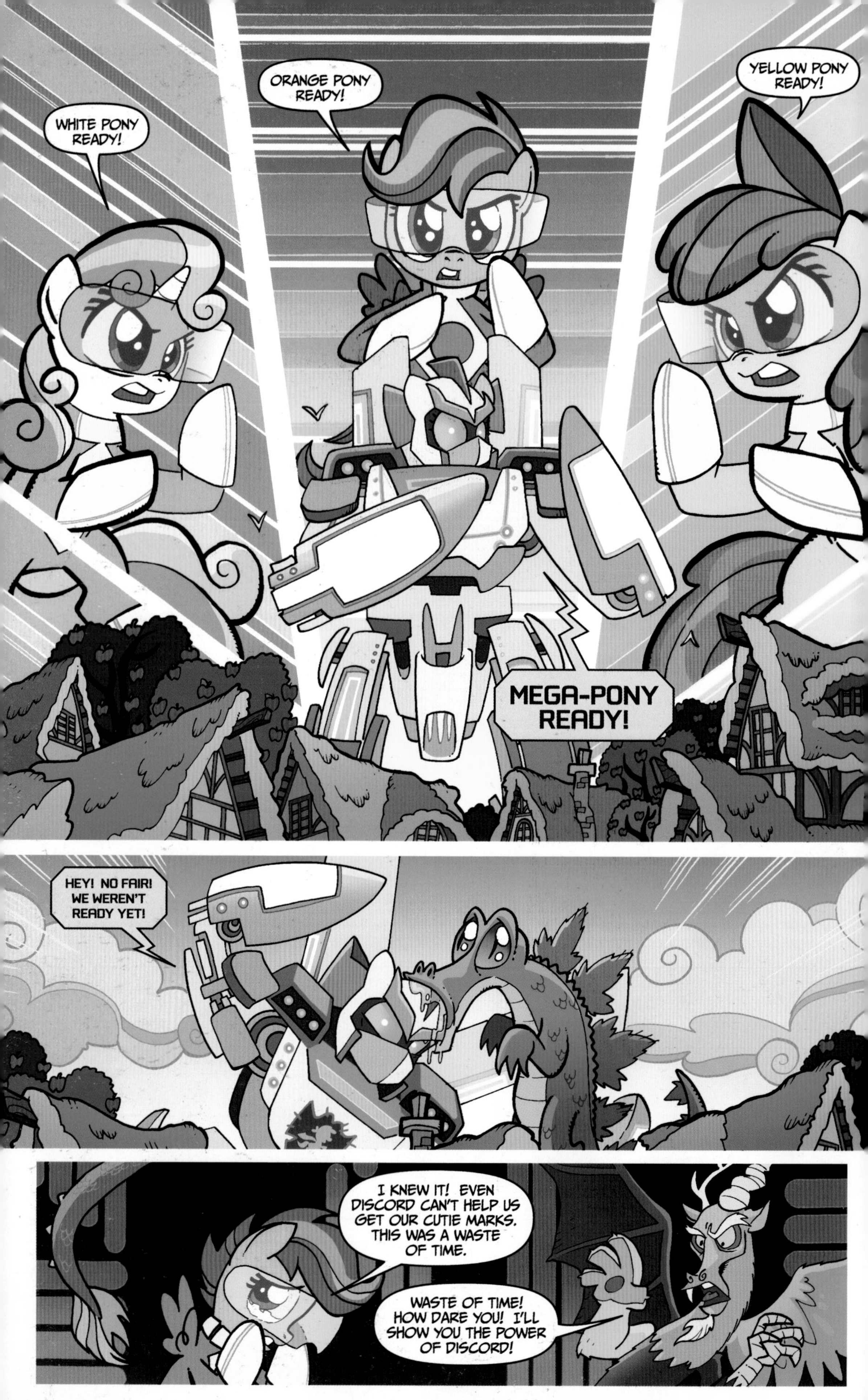
WHITE PONY READY!
ORANGE PONY READY!
YELLOW PONY READY!
MEGA-PONY READY!
HEY! NO FAIR! WE WEREN'T READY YET!
I KNEW IT! EVEN DISCORD CAN'T HELP US GET OUR CUTIE MARKS. THIS WAS A WASTE OF TIME.
WASTE OF TIME! HOW DARE YOU! I'LL SHOW YOU THE POWER OF DISCORD!

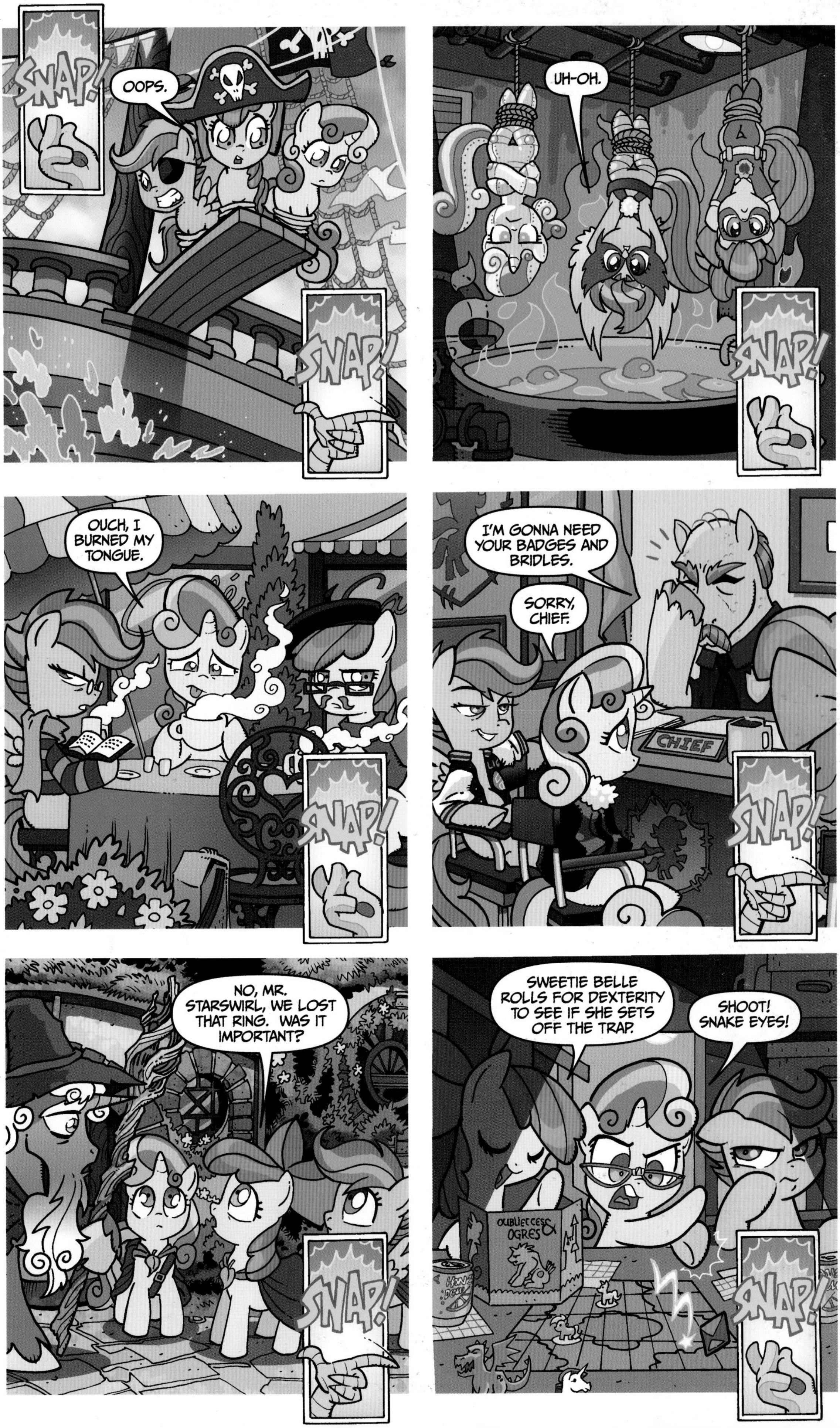
SNAP!
OOPS.
SNAP!
UH-OH.
SNAP!
OUCH, I BURNED MY TONGUE.
SNAP!
I'M GONNA NEED YOUR BADGES AND BRIDLES.
SORRY, CHIEF.
CHIEF
SNAP!
NO, MR. STARSWIRL, WE LOST THAT RING. WAS IT IMPORTANT?
SNAP!
SWEETIE BELLE ROLLS FOR DEXTERITY TO SEE IF SHE SETS OFF THE TRAP.
SHOOT! SNAKE EYES!
OUBLIETTES & OGRES
SNAP!

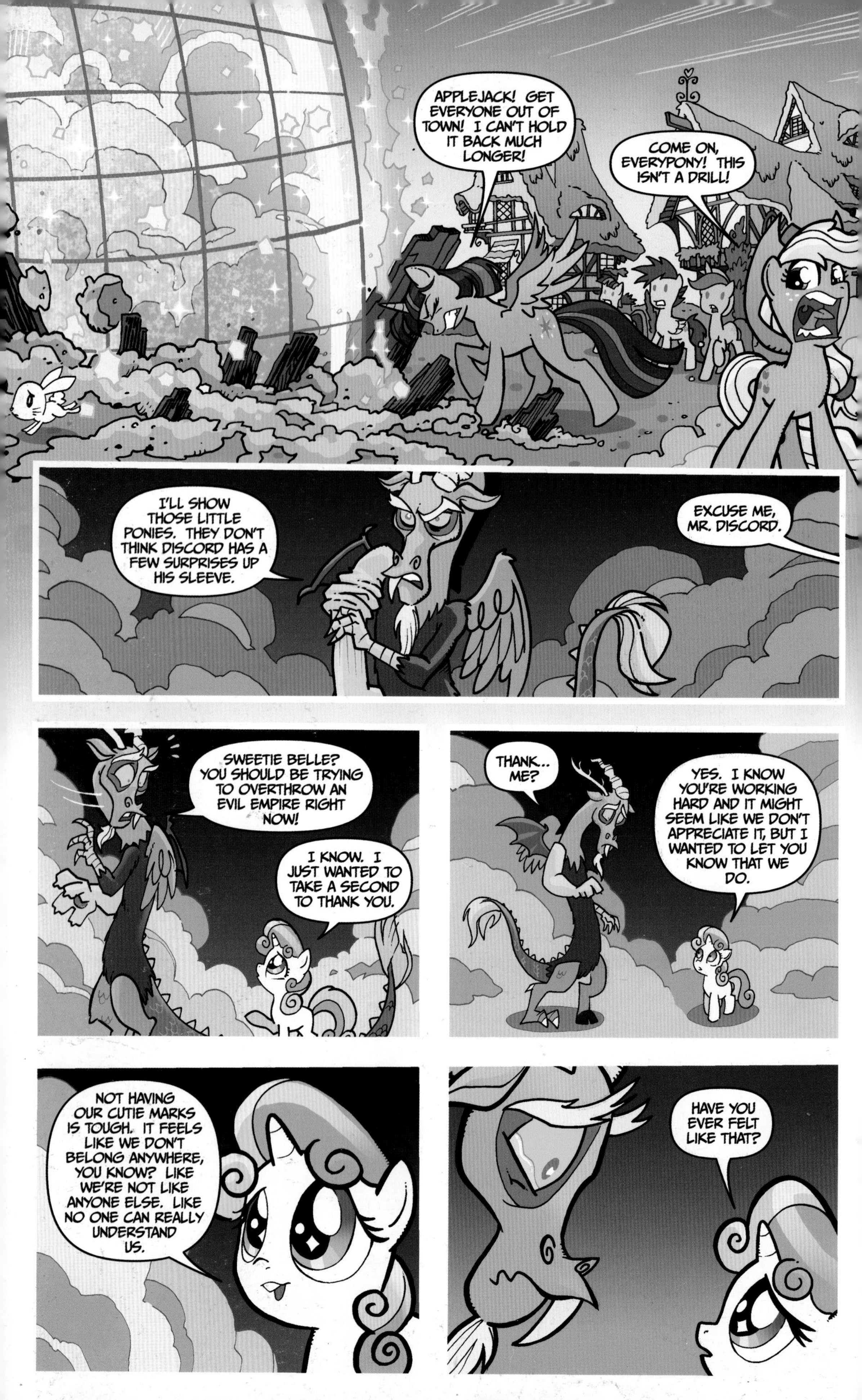
APPLEJACK! GET EVERYONE OUT OF TOWN! I CAN'T HOLD IT BACK MUCH LONGER!
COME ON, EVERYPONY! THIS ISN'T A DRILL!
I'LL SHOW THOSE LITTLE PONIES. THEY DON'T THINK DISCORD HAS A FEW SURPRISES UP HIS SLEEVE.
EXCUSE ME, MR. DISCORD.
SWEETIE BELLE? YOU SHOULD BE TRYING TO OVERTHROW AN EVIL EMPIRE RIGHT NOW!
I KNOW. I JUST WANTED TO TAKE A SECOND TO THANK YOU.
THANK... ME?
YES. I KNOW YOU'RE WORKING HARD AND IT MIGHT SEEM LIKE WE DON'T APPRECIATE IT, BUT I WANTED TO LET YOU KNOW THAT WE DO.
NOT HAVING OUR CUTIE MARKS IS TOUGH. IT FEELS LIKE WE DON'T BELONG ANYWHERE, YOU KNOW? LIKE WE'RE NOT LIKE ANYONE ELSE. LIKE NO ONE CAN REALLY UNDERSTAND US.
HAVE YOU EVER FELT LIKE THAT?

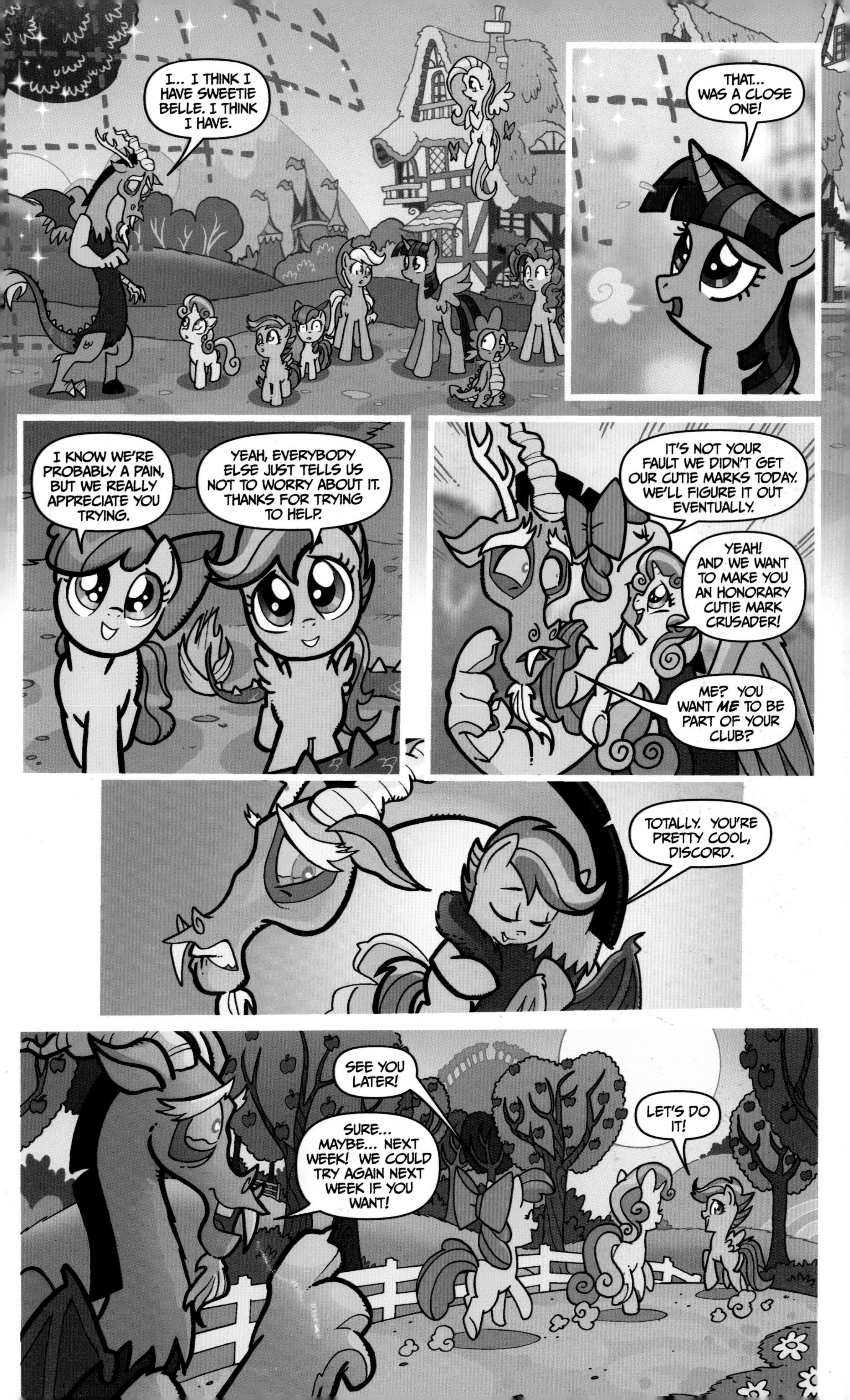
I... I THINK I HAVE SWEETIE BELLE. I THINK I HAVE.
THAT... WAS A CLOSE ONE!
I KNOW WE'RE PROBABLY A PAIN, BUT WE REALLY APPRECIATE YOU TRYING.
YEAH, EVERYBODY ELSE JUST TELLS US NOT TO WORRY ABOUT IT. THANKS FOR TRYING TO HELP.
IT'S NOT YOUR FAULT WE DIDN'T GET OUR CUTIE MARKS TODAY. WE'LL FIGURE IT OUT EVENTUALLY.
YEAH! AND WE WANT TO MAKE YOU AN HONORARY CUTIE MARK CRUSADER!
ME? YOU WANT *ME* TO BE PART OF YOUR CLUB?
TOTALLY. YOU'RE PRETTY COOL, DISCORD.
SEE YOU LATER!
SURE... MAYBE... NEXT WEEK! WE COULD TRY AGAIN NEXT WEEK IF YOU WANT!
LET'S DO IT!

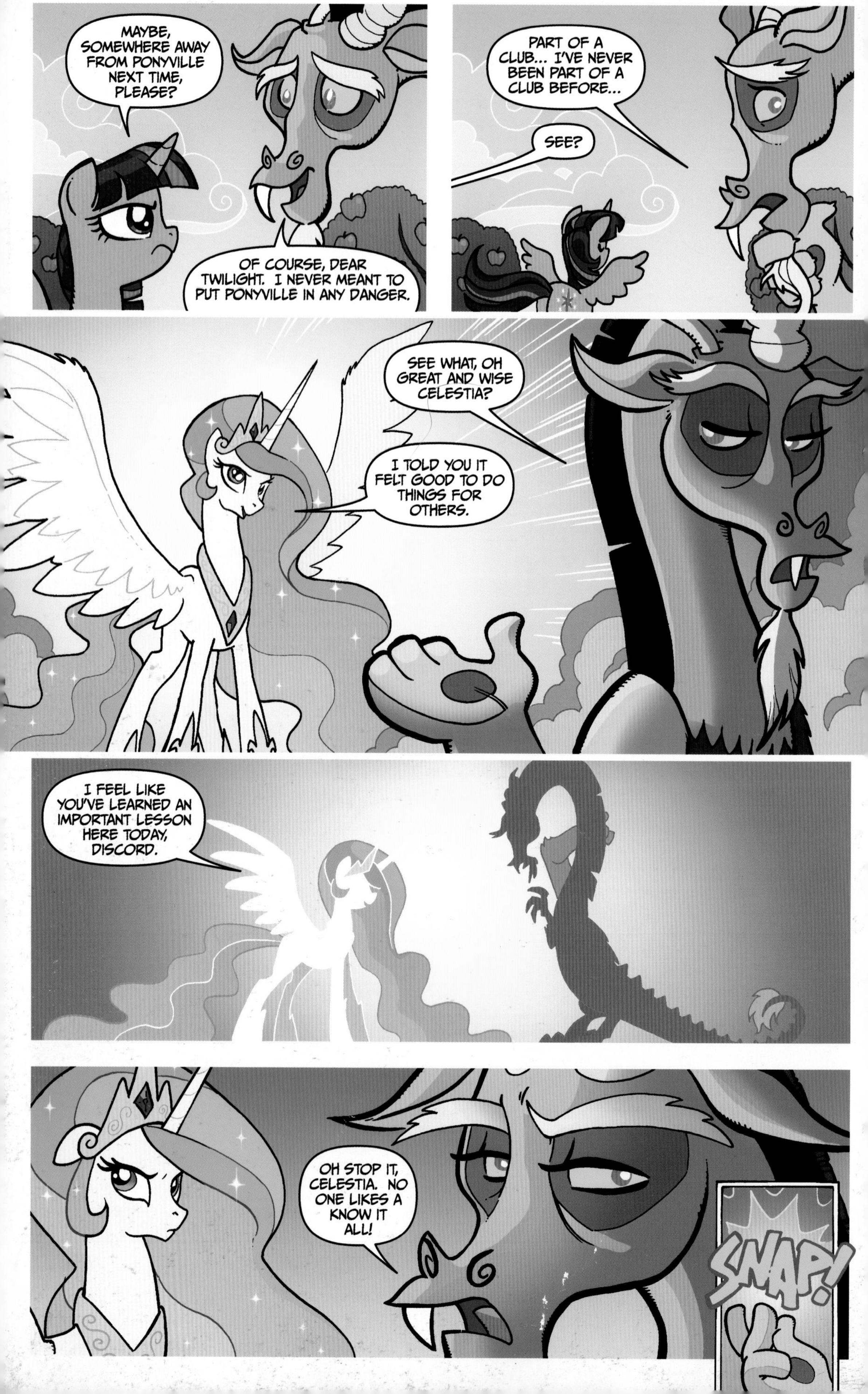
MAYBE, SOMEWHERE AWAY FROM PONYVILLE NEXT TIME, PLEASE?
OF COURSE, DEAR TWILIGHT. I NEVER MEANT TO PUT PONYVILLE IN ANY DANGER.
PART OF A CLUB... I'VE NEVER BEEN PART OF A CLUB BEFORE...
SEE?
SEE WHAT, OH GREAT AND WISE CELESTIA?
I TOLD YOU IT FELT GOOD TO DO THINGS FOR OTHERS.
I FEEL LIKE YOU'VE LEARNED AN IMPORTANT LESSON HERE TODAY, DISCORD.
OH STOP IT, CELESTIA. NO ONE LIKES A KNOW IT ALL!
SNAP!

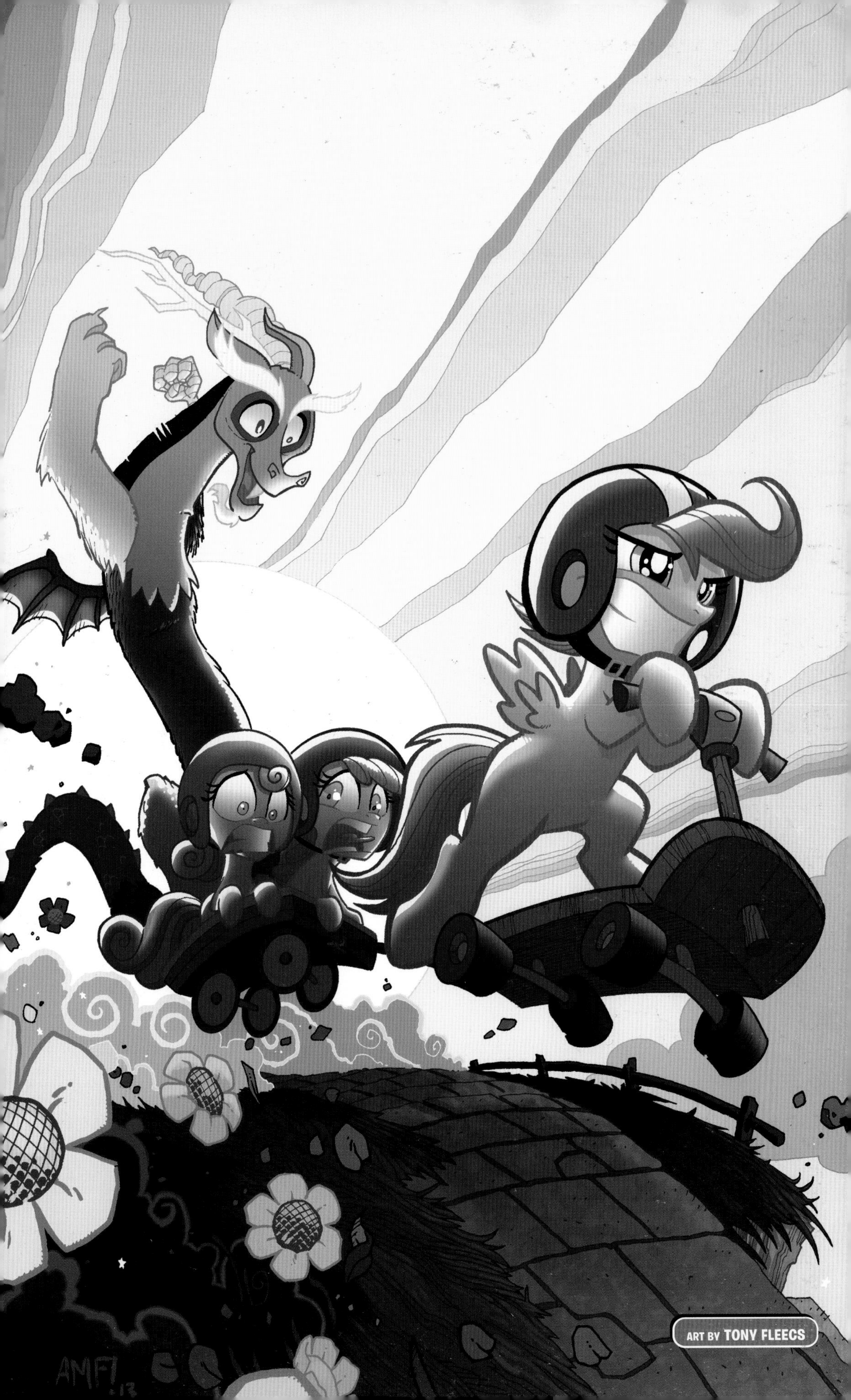

ART BY TONY FLEECS

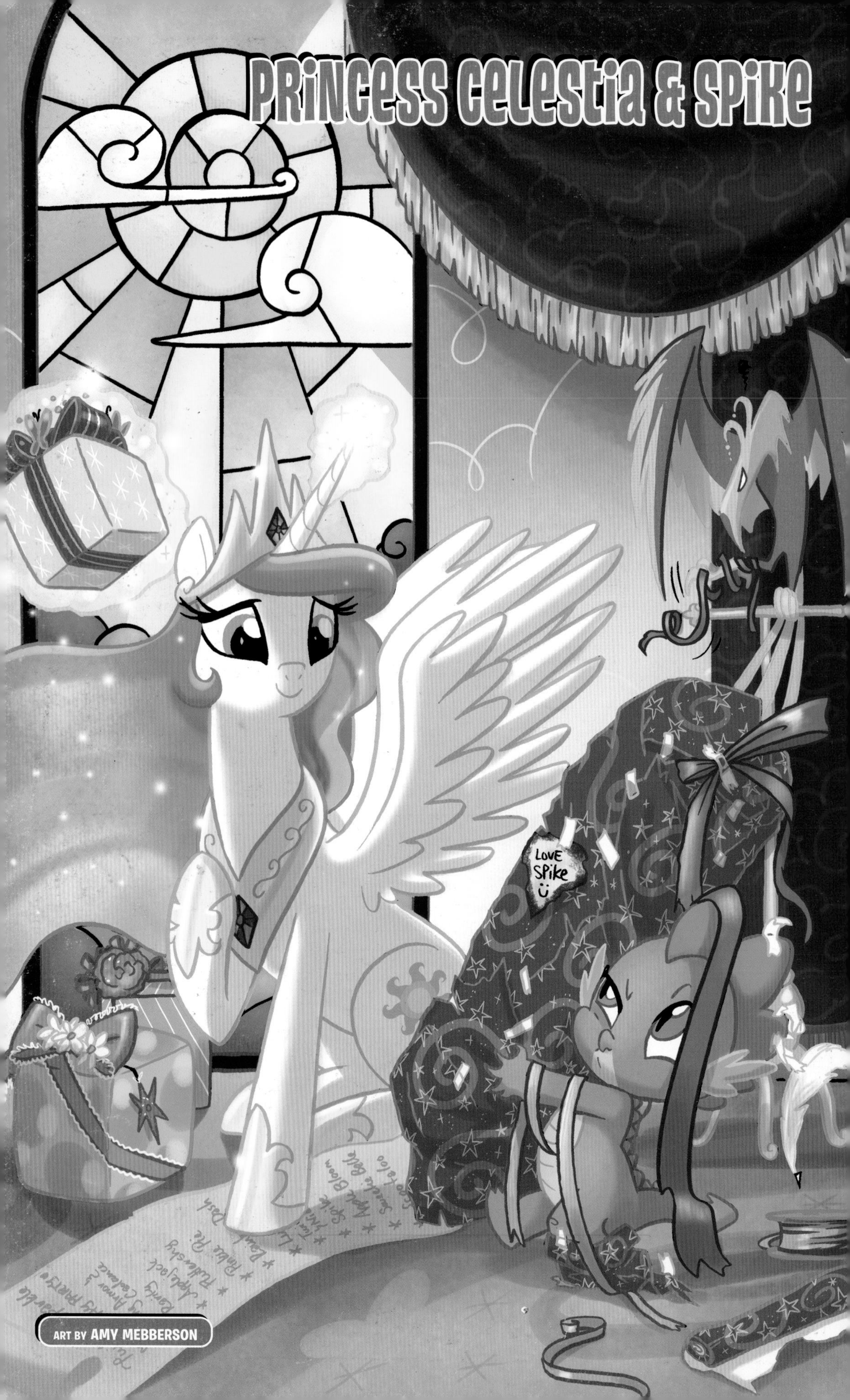
PRINCESS CELESTIA & SPIKE
LOVE
SPIKE
ART BY AMY MEBBERSON

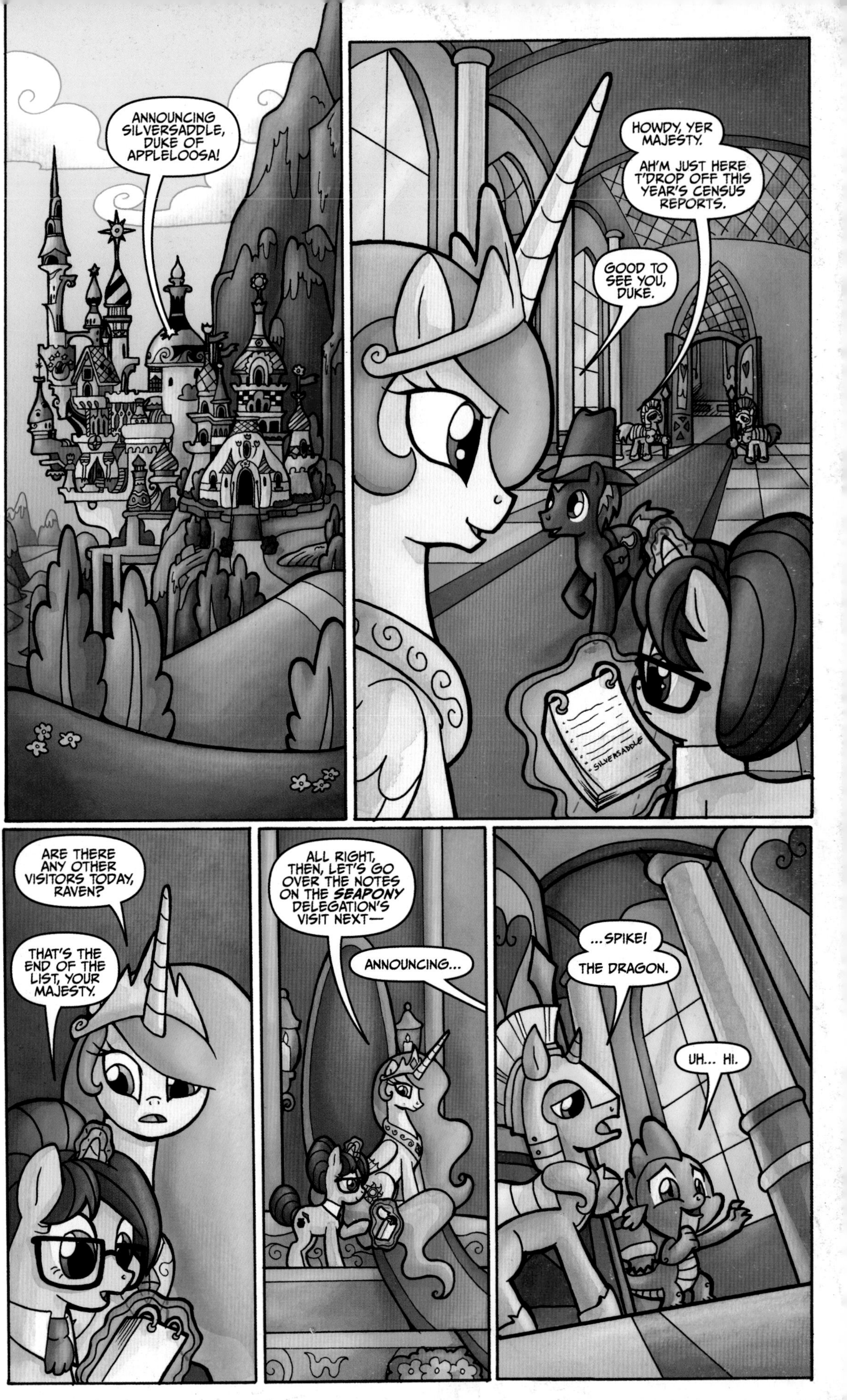
ANNOUNCING SILVERSADDLE, DUKE OF APPLELOOSA!
HOWDY, YER MAJESTY.
AH'M JUST HERE T'DROP OFF THIS YEAR'S CENSUS REPORTS.
GOOD TO SEE YOU, DUKE.
SILVERSADDLE
ARE THERE ANY OTHER VISITORS TODAY, RAVEN?
THAT'S THE END OF THE LIST, YOUR MAJESTY.
ALL RIGHT, THEN, LET'S GO OVER THE NOTES ON THE SEAPONY DELEGATION'S VISIT NEXT—
ANNOUNCING...
...SPIKE!
THE DRAGON.
UH... HI.

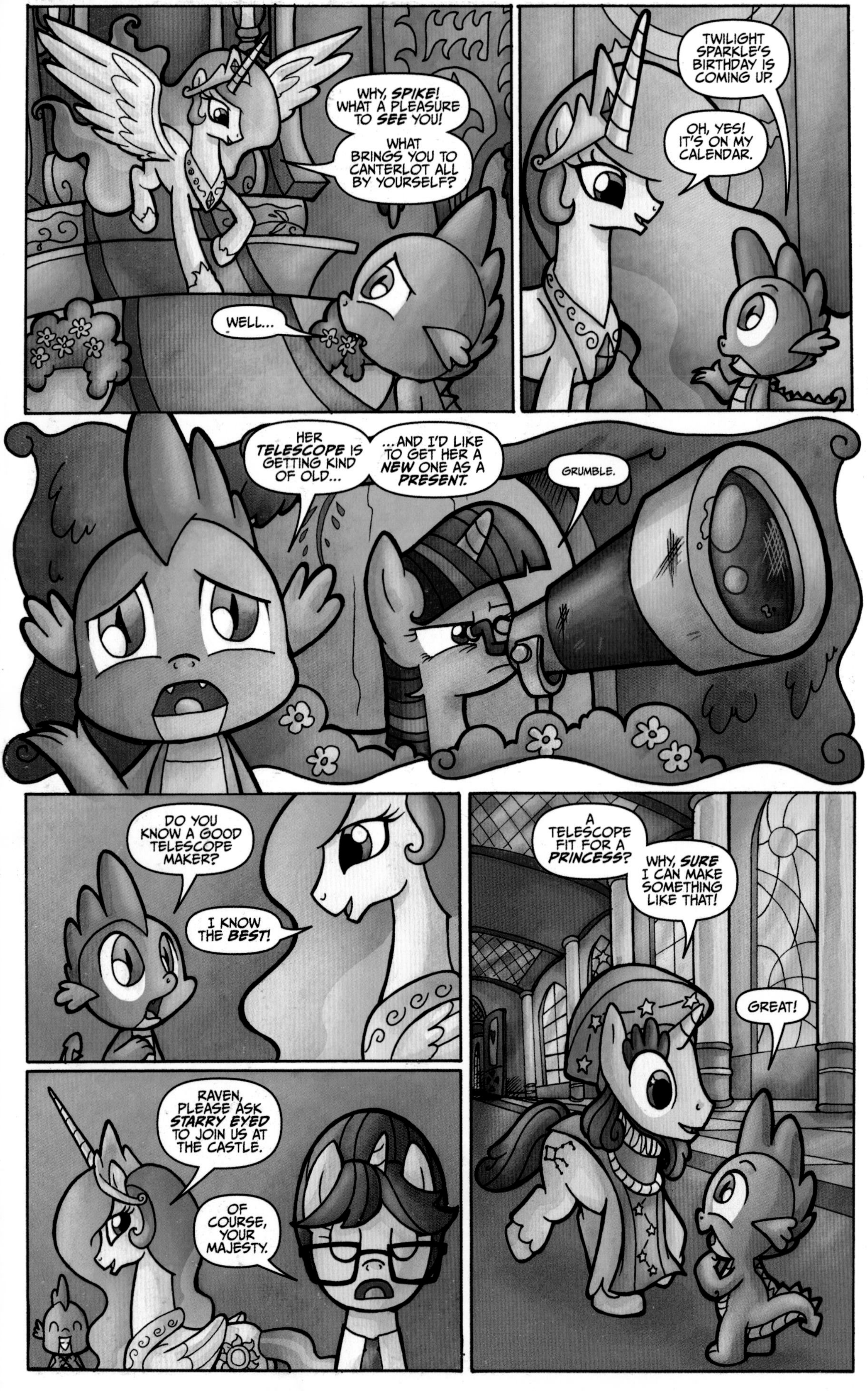
WHY, SPIKE! WHAT A PLEASURE TO SEE YOU!
WHAT BRINGS YOU TO CANTERLOT ALL BY YOURSELF?
WELL...
TWILIGHT SPARKLE'S BIRTHDAY IS COMING UP.
OH, YES! IT'S ON MY CALENDAR.
HER TELESCOPE IS GETTING KIND OF OLD...
...AND I'D LIKE TO GET HER A NEW ONE AS A PRESENT.
GRUMBLE.
DO YOU KNOW A GOOD TELESCOPE MAKER?
I KNOW THE BEST!
RAVEN, PLEASE ASK STARRY EYED TO JOIN US AT THE CASTLE.
OF COURSE, YOUR MAJESTY.
A TELESCOPE FIT FOR A PRINCESS?
WHY, SURE I CAN MAKE SOMETHING LIKE THAT!
GREAT!

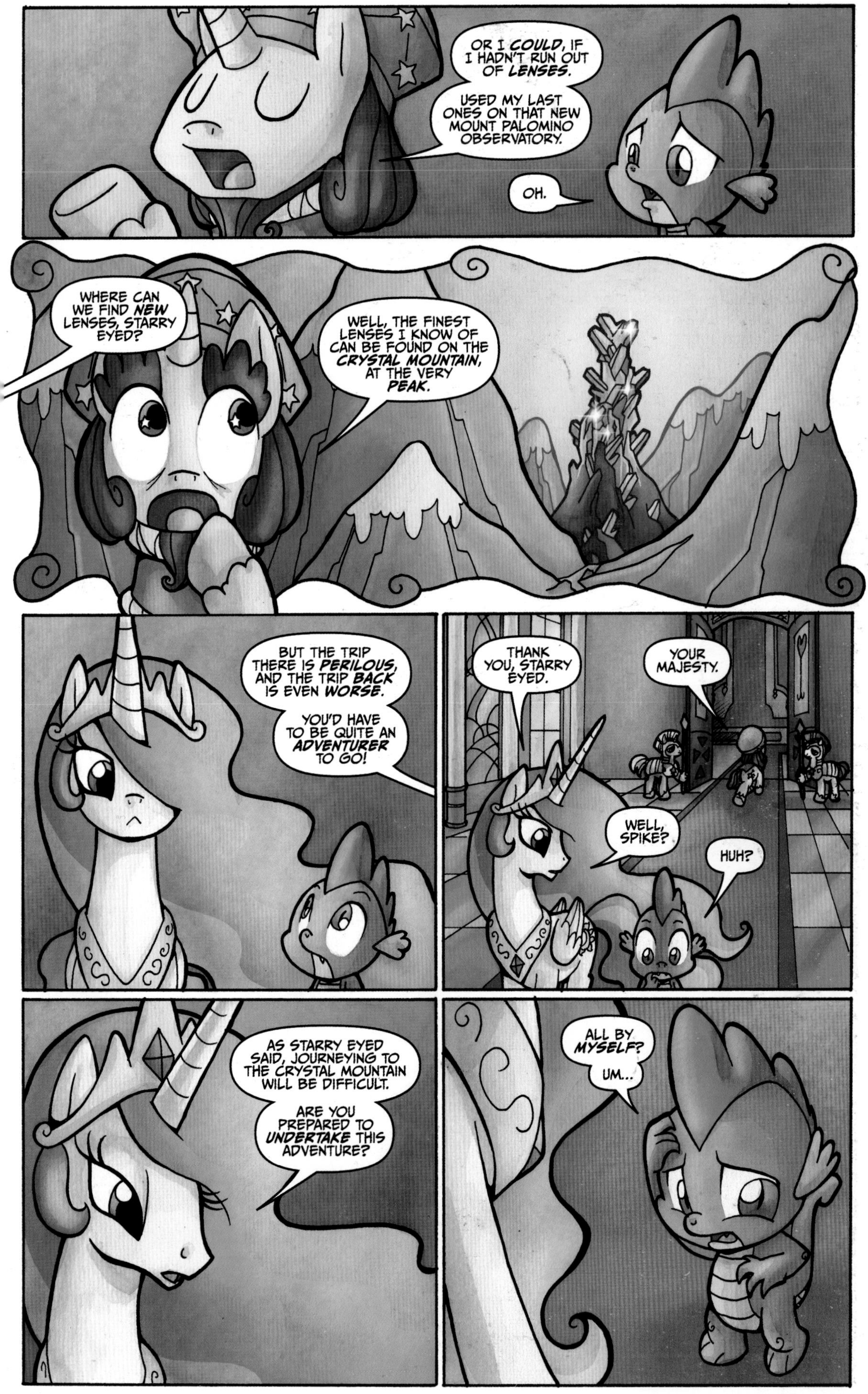
OR I COULD, IF I HADN'T RUN OUT OF LENSES.
USED MY LAST ONES ON THAT NEW MOUNT PALOMINO OBSERVATORY.
OH.
WHERE CAN WE FIND NEW LENSES, STARRY EYED?
WELL, THE FINEST LENSES I KNOW OF CAN BE FOUND ON THE CRYSTAL MOUNTAIN, AT THE VERY PEAK.
BUT THE TRIP THERE IS PERILOUS, AND THE TRIP BACK IS EVEN WORSE.
YOU'D HAVE TO BE QUITE AN ADVENTURER TO GO!
THANK YOU, STARRY EYED.
YOUR MAJESTY.
WELL, SPIKE?
HUH?
AS STARRY EYED SAID, JOURNEYING TO THE CRYSTAL MOUNTAIN WILL BE DIFFICULT.
ARE YOU PREPARED TO UNDERTAKE THIS ADVENTURE?
ALL BY MYSELF?
UM...

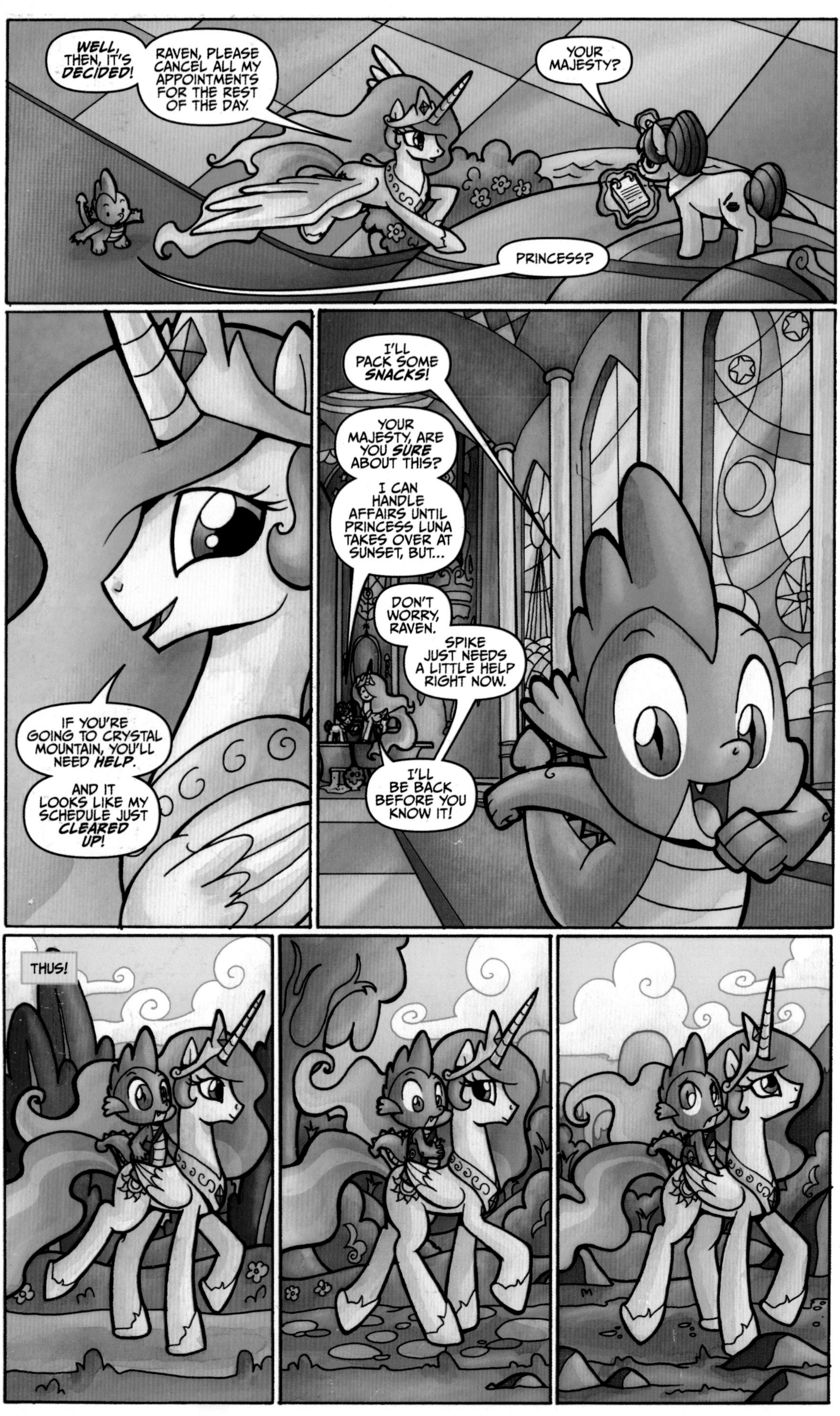

WELL, THEN, IT'S DECIDED!
RAVEN, PLEASE CANCEL ALL MY APPOINTMENTS FOR THE REST OF THE DAY.
YOUR MAJESTY?
PRINCESS?
IF YOU'RE GOING TO CRYSTAL MOUNTAIN, YOU'LL NEED HELP.
AND IT LOOKS LIKE MY SCHEDULE JUST CLEARED UP!
I'LL PACK SOME SNACKS!
YOUR MAJESTY, ARE YOU SURE ABOUT THIS?
I CAN HANDLE AFFAIRS UNTIL PRINCESS LUNA TAKES OVER AT SUNSET, BUT...
DON'T WORRY, RAVEN.
SPIKE JUST NEEDS A LITTLE HELP RIGHT NOW.
I'LL BE BACK BEFORE YOU KNOW IT!
THUS!

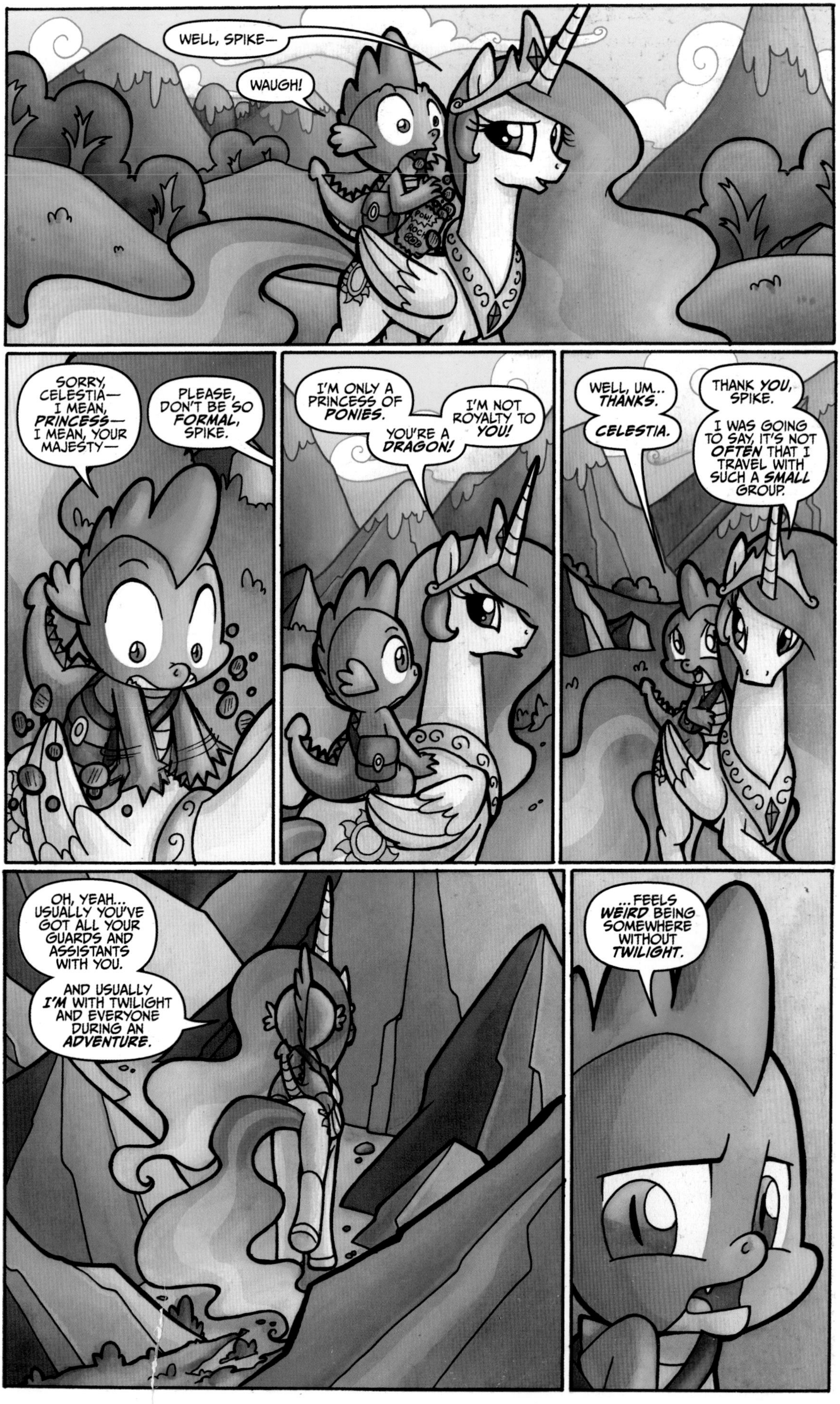
WELL, SPIKE—
WAUGH!
SORRY, CELESTIA— I MEAN, PRINCESS— I MEAN, YOUR MAJESTY—
PLEASE, DON'T BE SO FORMAL, SPIKE.
I'M ONLY A PRINCESS OF PONIES.
I'M NOT ROYALTY TO YOU!
YOU'RE A DRAGON!
WELL, UM... THANKS.
CELESTIA.
THANK YOU, SPIKE.
I WAS GOING TO SAY, IT'S NOT OFTEN THAT I TRAVEL WITH SUCH A SMALL GROUP.
OH, YEAH... USUALLY YOU'VE GOT ALL YOUR GUARDS AND ASSISTANTS WITH YOU.
AND USUALLY I'M WITH TWILIGHT AND EVERYONE DURING AN ADVENTURE.
...FEELS WEIRD BEING SOMEWHERE WITHOUT TWILIGHT.

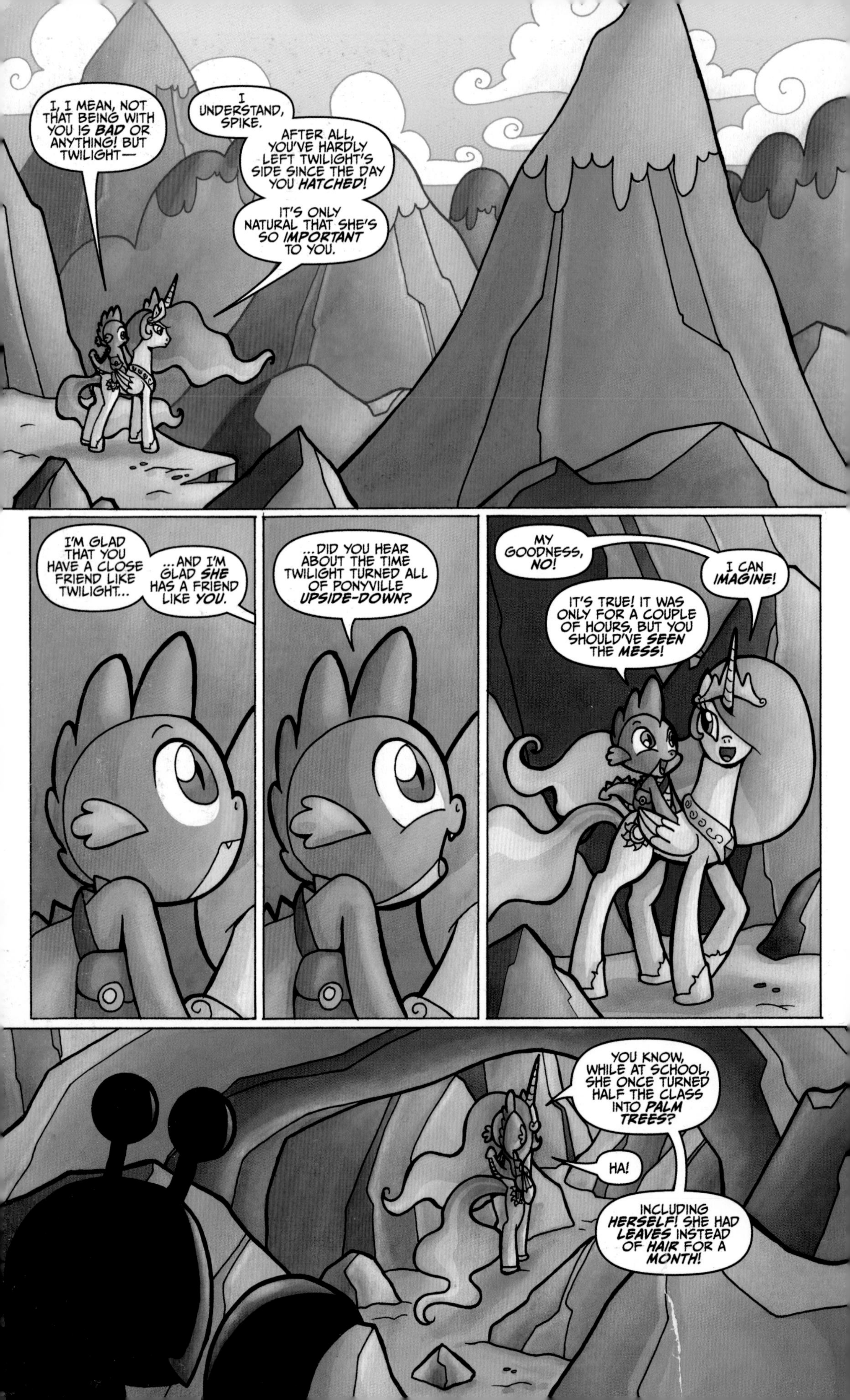
I, I MEAN, NOT THAT BEING WITH YOU IS BAD OR ANYTHING! BUT TWILIGHT—
I UNDERSTAND, SPIKE.
AFTER ALL, YOU'VE HARDLY LEFT TWILIGHT'S SIDE SINCE THE DAY YOU HATCHED!
IT'S ONLY NATURAL THAT SHE'S SO IMPORTANT TO YOU.
I'M GLAD THAT YOU HAVE A CLOSE FRIEND LIKE TWILIGHT...
...AND I'M GLAD SHE HAS A FRIEND LIKE YOU.
...DID YOU HEAR ABOUT THE TIME TWILIGHT TURNED ALL OF PONYVILLE UPSIDE-DOWN?
MY GOODNESS, NO!
IT'S TRUE! IT WAS ONLY FOR A COUPLE OF HOURS, BUT YOU SHOULD'VE SEEN THE MESS!
I CAN IMAGINE!
YOU KNOW, WHILE AT SCHOOL, SHE ONCE TURNED HALF THE CLASS INTO PALM TREES?
HA!
INCLUDING HERSELF! SHE HAD LEAVES INSTEAD OF HAIR FOR A MONTH!

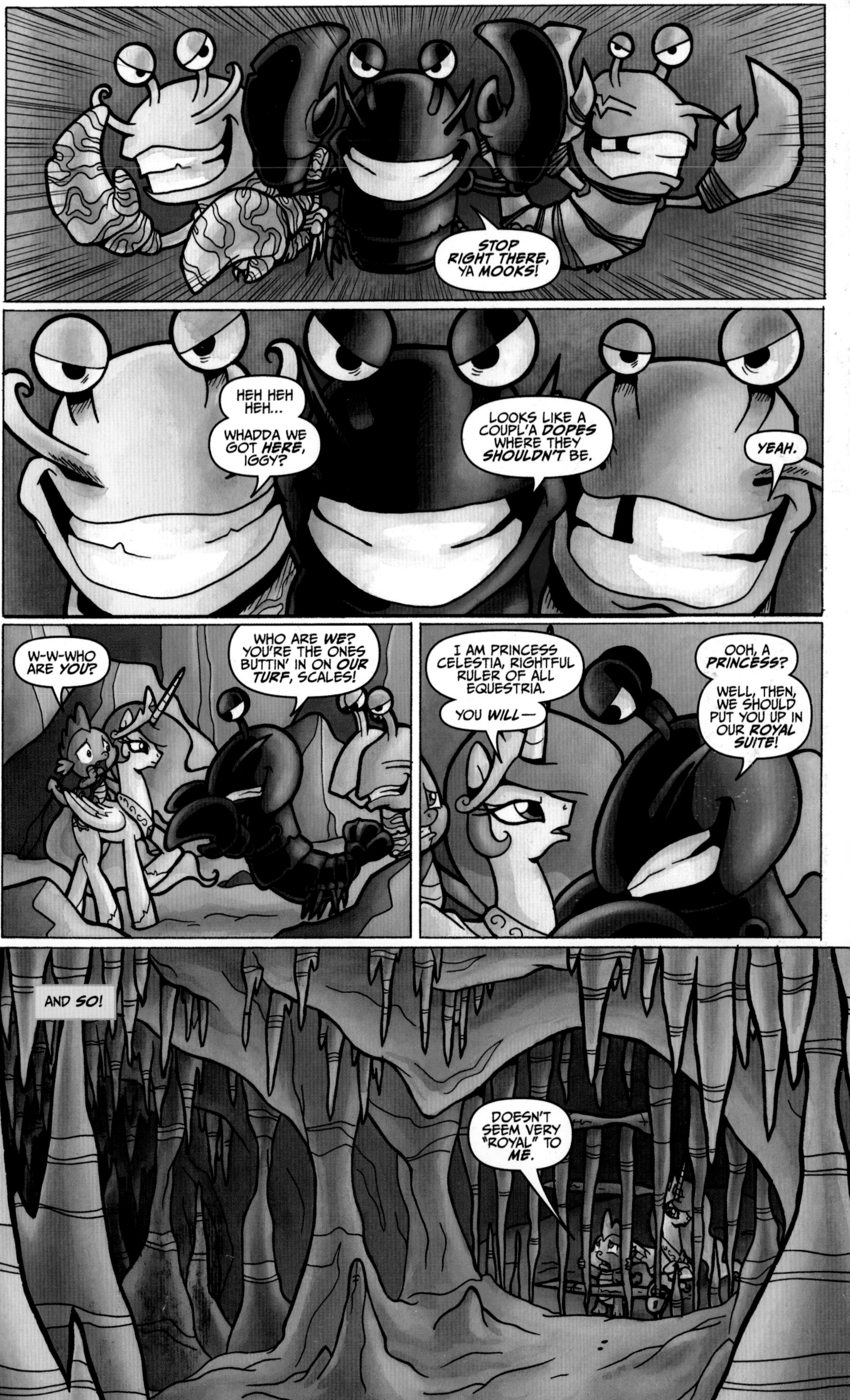
STOP RIGHT THERE, YA MOOKS!
HEH HEH HEH...
WHADDA WE GOT HERE, IGGY?
LOOKS LIKE A COUPL'A DOPES WHERE THEY SHOULDN'T BE.
YEAH.
W-W-WHO ARE YOU?
WHO ARE WE? YOU'RE THE ONES BUTTIN' IN ON OUR TURF, SCALES!
I AM PRINCESS CELESTIA, RIGHTFUL RULER OF ALL EQUESTRIA.
YOU WILL—
OOH, A PRINCESS?
WELL, THEN, WE SHOULD PUT YOU UP IN OUR ROYAL SUITE!
AND SO!
DOESN'T SEEM VERY "ROYAL" TO ME.

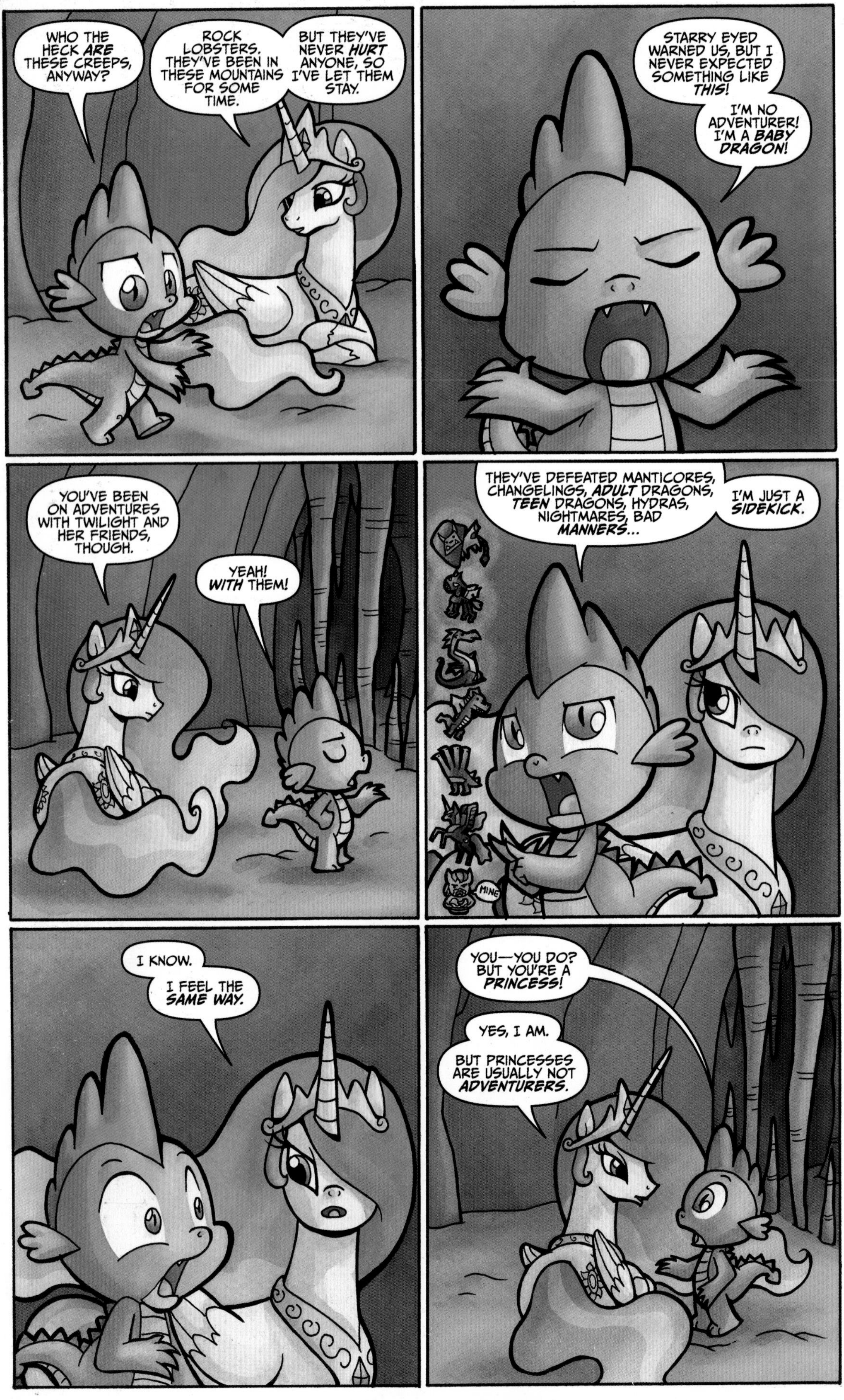
WHO THE HECK **ARE** THESE CREEPS, ANYWAY?
ROCK LOBSTERS. THEY'VE BEEN IN THESE MOUNTAINS FOR SOME TIME.
BUT THEY'VE NEVER **HURT** ANYONE, SO I'VE LET THEM STAY.
STARRY EYED WARNED US, BUT I NEVER EXPECTED SOMETHING LIKE **THIS**!
I'M NO ADVENTURER! I'M A **BABY DRAGON**!
YOU'VE BEEN ON ADVENTURES WITH TWILIGHT AND HER FRIENDS, THOUGH.
YEAH! **WITH** THEM!
THEY'VE DEFEATED MANTICORES, CHANGELINGS, **ADULT** DRAGONS, **TEEN** DRAGONS, HYDRAS, NIGHTMARES, BAD **MANNERS**...
I'M JUST A **SIDEKICK**.
MINE
I KNOW.
I FEEL THE **SAME WAY**.
YOU—YOU DO? BUT YOU'RE A **PRINCESS**!
YES, I AM.
BUT PRINCESSES ARE USUALLY NOT **ADVENTURERS**.

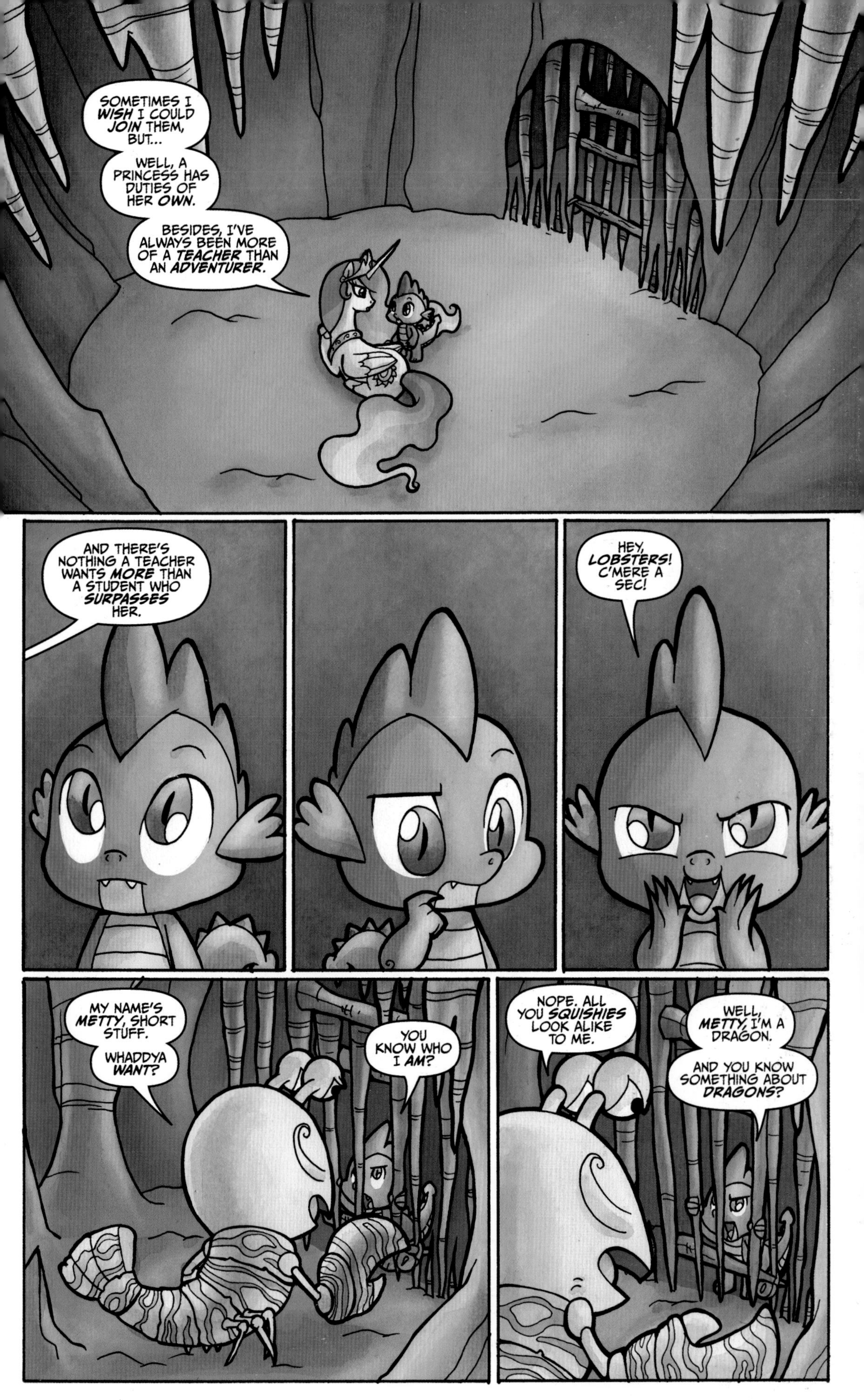
SOMETIMES I WISH I COULD JOIN THEM, BUT...
WELL, A PRINCESS HAS DUTIES OF HER OWN.
BESIDES, I'VE ALWAYS BEEN MORE OF A TEACHER THAN AN ADVENTURER.
AND THERE'S NOTHING A TEACHER WANTS MORE THAN A STUDENT WHO SURPASSES HER.
HEY, LOBSTERS! C'MERE A SEC!
MY NAME'S METTY, SHORT STUFF.
WHADDYA WANT?
YOU KNOW WHO I AM?
NOPE. ALL YOU SQUISHIES LOOK ALIKE TO ME.
WELL, METTY, I'M A DRAGON.
AND YOU KNOW SOMETHING ABOUT DRAGONS?

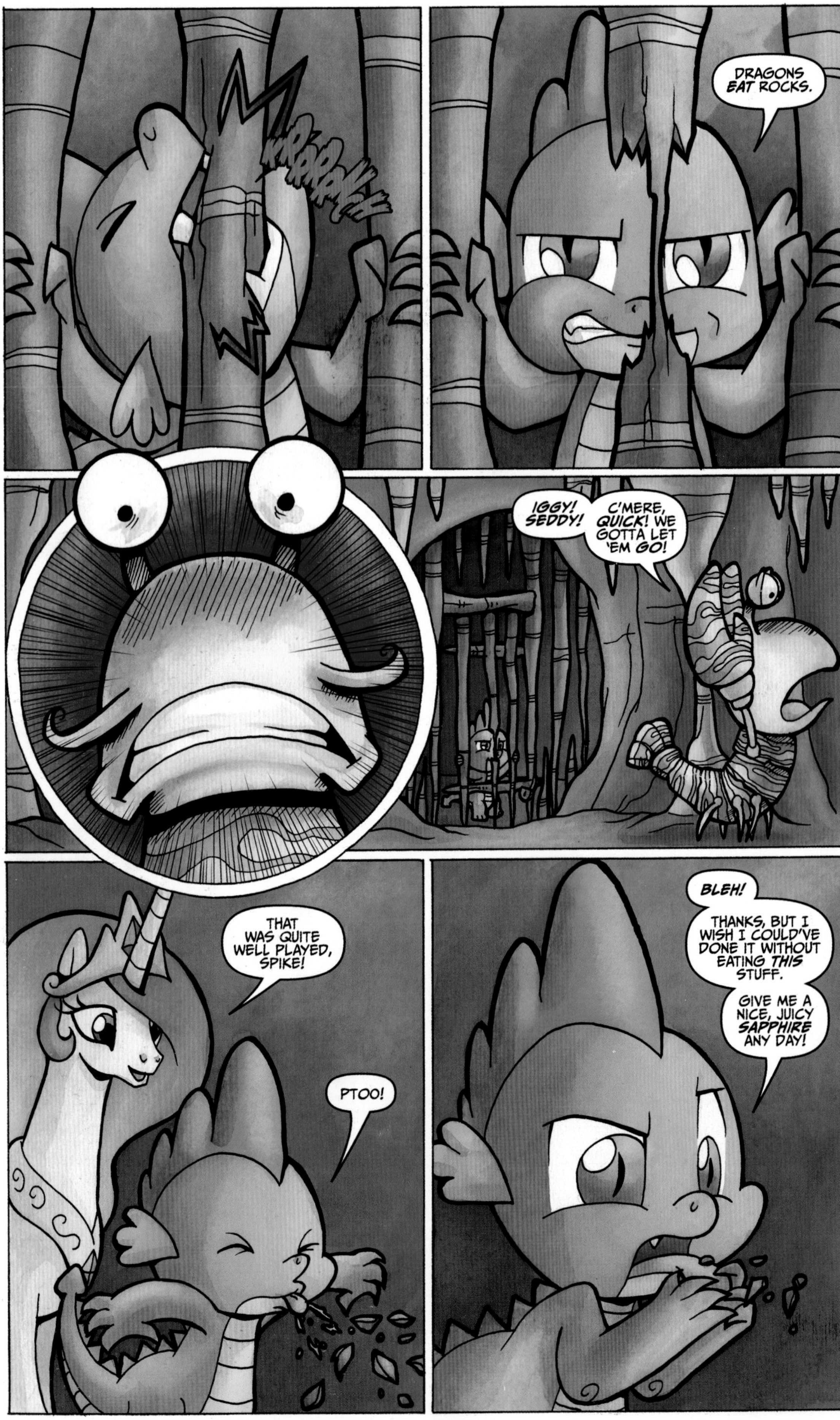
DRAGONS EAT ROCKS.
IGGY! SEDDY!
C'MERE, QUICK! WE GOTTA LET 'EM GO!
THAT WAS QUITE WELL PLAYED, SPIKE!
PTOO!
BLEH!
THANKS, BUT I WISH I COULD'VE DONE IT WITHOUT EATING THIS STUFF.
GIVE ME A NICE, JUICY SAPPHIRE ANY DAY!

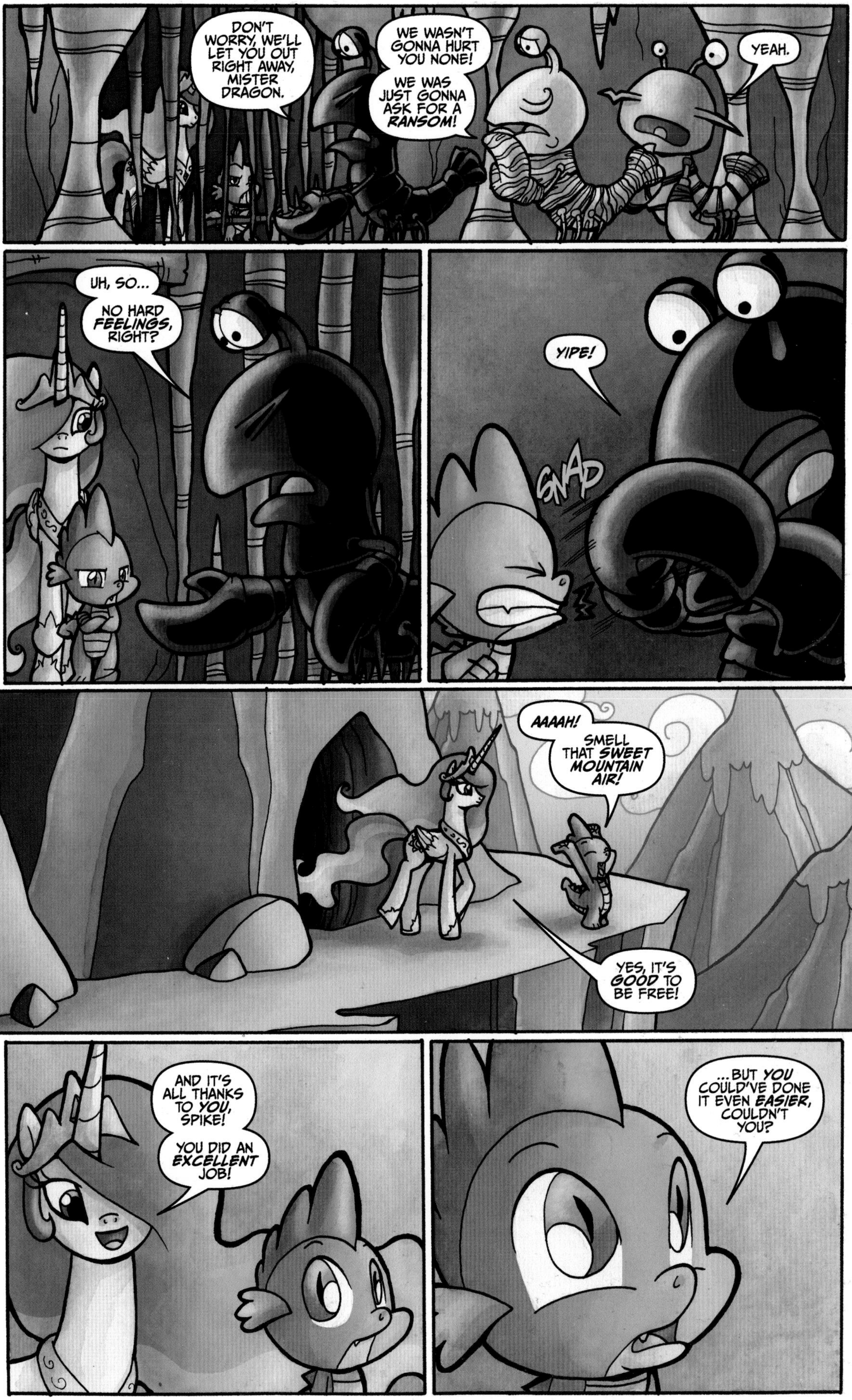
DON'T WORRY, WE'LL LET YOU OUT RIGHT AWAY, MISTER DRAGON.
WE WASN'T GONNA HURT YOU NONE!
WE WAS JUST GONNA ASK FOR A RANSOM!
YEAH.
UH, SO... NO HARD FEELINGS, RIGHT?
YIPE!
SNAP
AAAAH! SMELL THAT SWEET MOUNTAIN AIR!
YES, IT'S GOOD TO BE FREE!
AND IT'S ALL THANKS TO YOU, SPIKE!
YOU DID AN EXCELLENT JOB!
...BUT YOU COULD'VE DONE IT EVEN EASIER, COULDN'T YOU?

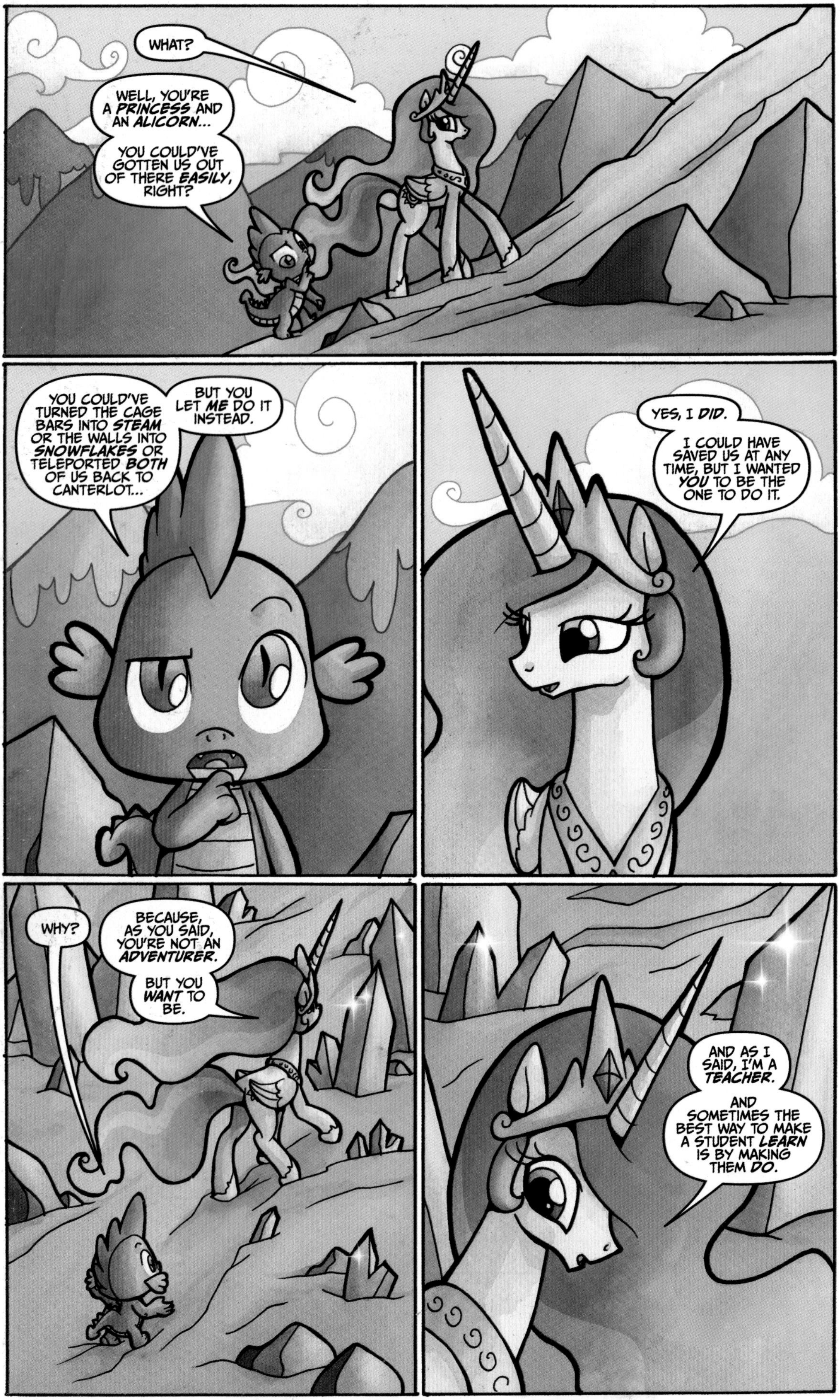
WHAT?
WELL, YOU'RE A PRINCESS AND AN ALICORN...
YOU COULD'VE GOTTEN US OUT OF THERE EASILY, RIGHT?
YOU COULD'VE TURNED THE CAGE BARS INTO STEAM OR THE WALLS INTO SNOWFLAKES OR TELEPORTED BOTH OF US BACK TO CANTERLOT...
BUT YOU LET ME DO IT INSTEAD.
YES, I DID.
I COULD HAVE SAVED US AT ANY TIME, BUT I WANTED YOU TO BE THE ONE TO DO IT.
WHY?
BECAUSE, AS YOU SAID, YOU'RE NOT AN ADVENTURER.
BUT YOU WANT TO BE.
AND AS I SAID, I'M A TEACHER.
AND SOMETIMES THE BEST WAY TO MAKE A STUDENT LEARN IS BY MAKING THEM DO.

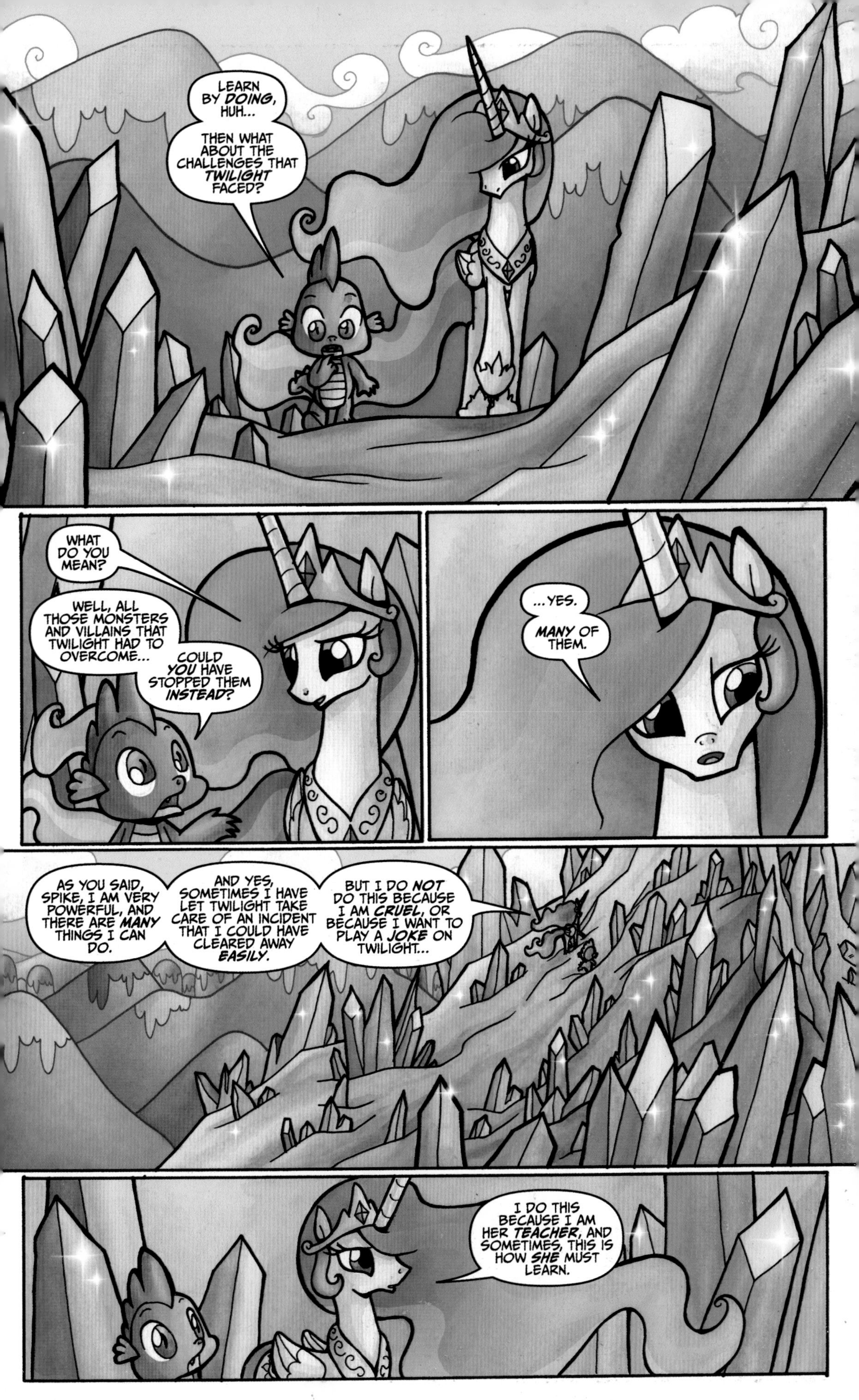
LEARN BY DOING, HUH...
THEN WHAT ABOUT THE CHALLENGES THAT TWILIGHT FACED?
WHAT DO YOU MEAN?
WELL, ALL THOSE MONSTERS AND VILLAINS THAT TWILIGHT HAD TO OVERCOME...
COULD YOU HAVE STOPPED THEM INSTEAD?
...YES.
MANY OF THEM.
AS YOU SAID, SPIKE, I AM VERY POWERFUL, AND THERE ARE MANY THINGS I CAN DO.
AND YES, SOMETIMES I HAVE LET TWILIGHT TAKE CARE OF AN INCIDENT THAT I COULD HAVE CLEARED AWAY EASILY.
BUT I DO NOT DO THIS BECAUSE I AM CRUEL, OR BECAUSE I WANT TO PLAY A JOKE ON TWILIGHT...
I DO THIS BECAUSE I AM HER TEACHER, AND SOMETIMES, THIS IS HOW SHE MUST LEARN.

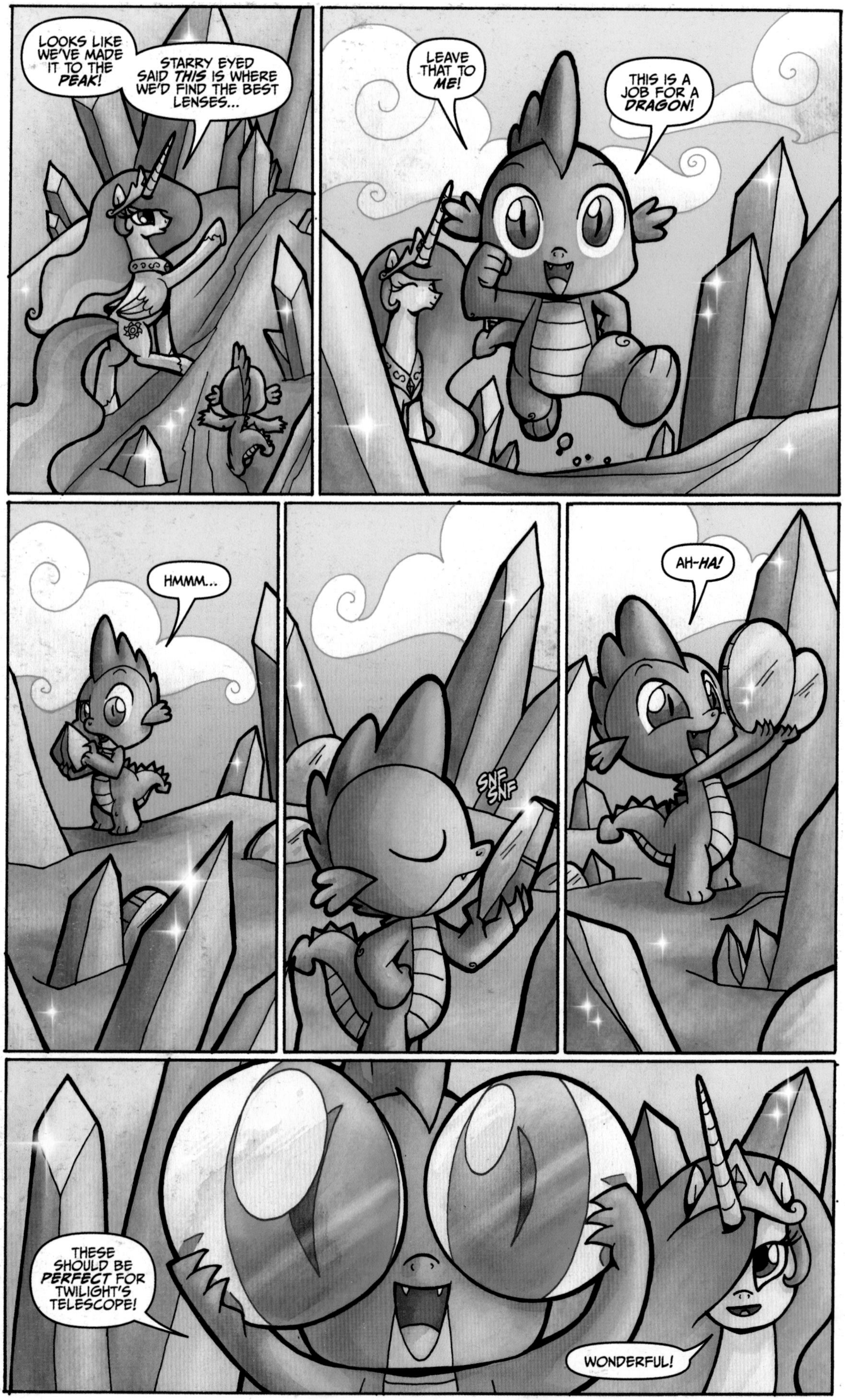
LOOKS LIKE WE'VE MADE IT TO THE PEAK!
STARRY EYED SAID THIS IS WHERE WE'D FIND THE BEST LENSES...
LEAVE THAT TO ME!
THIS IS A JOB FOR A DRAGON!
HMMM...
SNF SNF
AH-HA!
THESE SHOULD BE PERFECT FOR TWILIGHT'S TELESCOPE!
WONDERFUL!

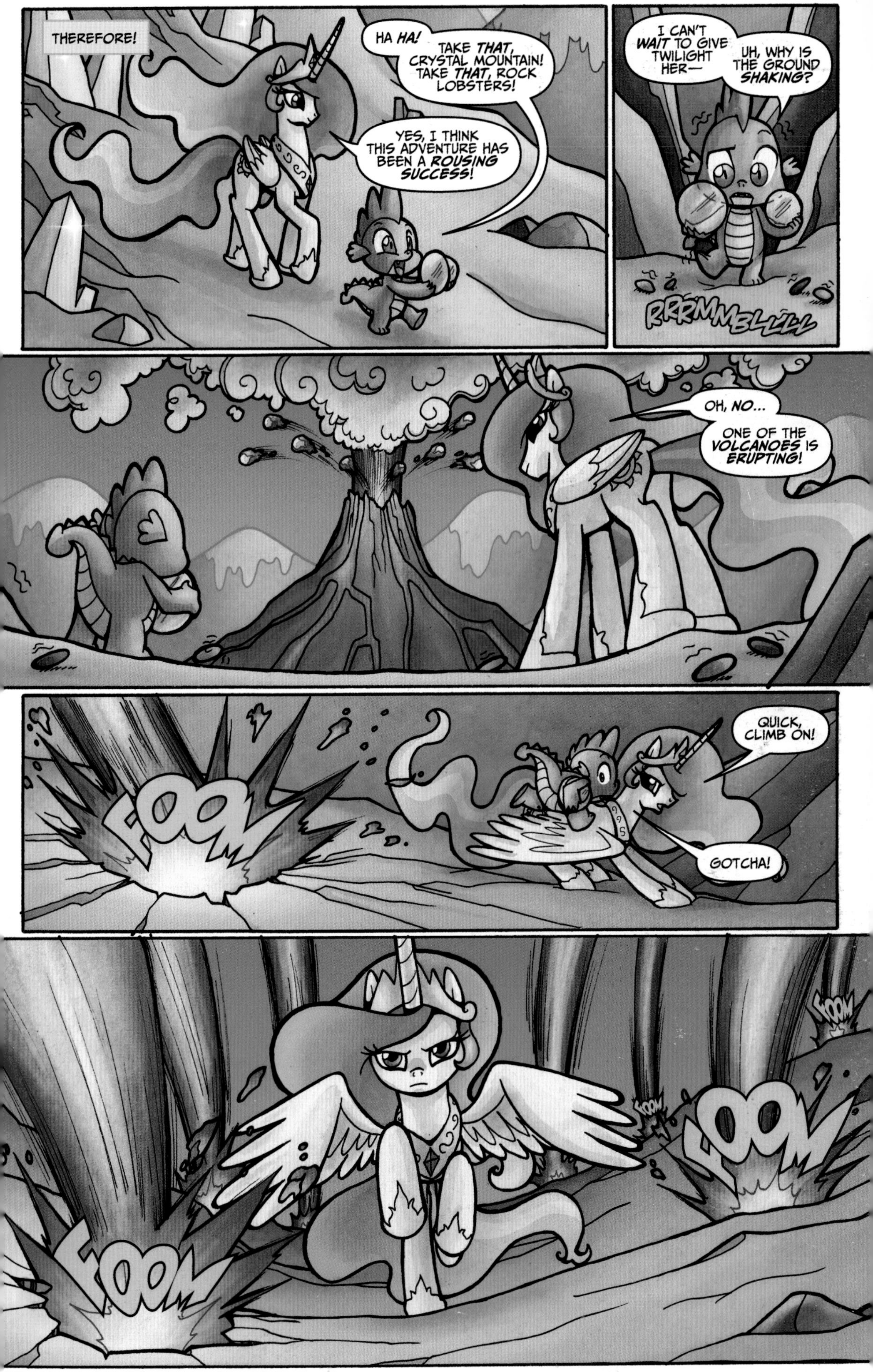
THEREFORE!
HA HA! TAKE THAT, CRYSTAL MOUNTAIN! TAKE THAT, ROCK LOBSTERS!
YES, I THINK THIS ADVENTURE HAS BEEN A ROUSING SUCCESS!
I CAN'T WAIT TO GIVE TWILIGHT HER—
UH, WHY IS THE GROUND SHAKING?
RRRMMBLLLL
OH, NO...
ONE OF THE VOLCANOES IS ERUPTING!
FOOM
QUICK, CLIMB ON!
GOTCHA!
FOOM
FOOM
FOOM
FOOM

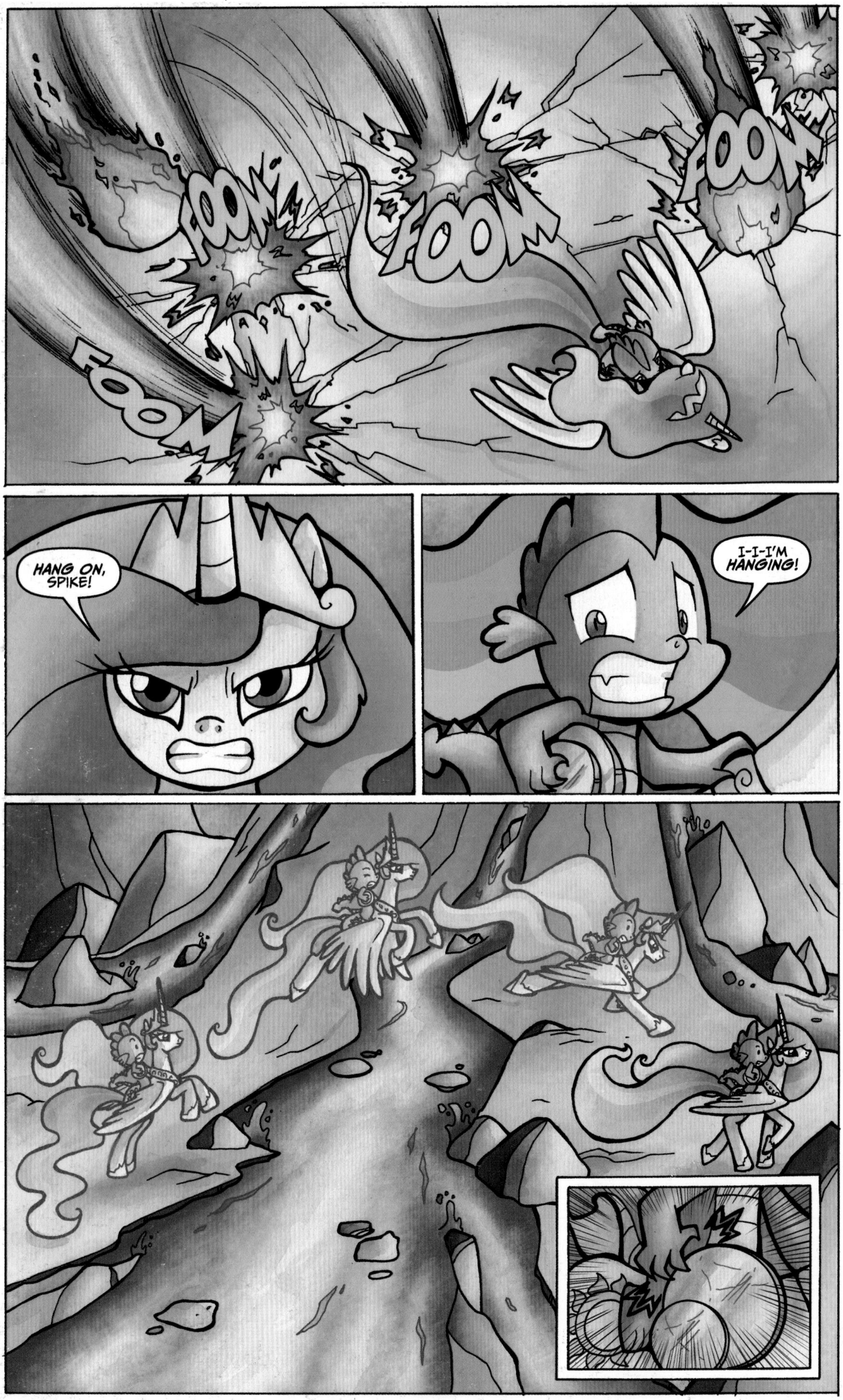
FOOM
FOOM
FOOM
FOOM
HANG ON, SPIKE!
I-I-I'M HANGING!

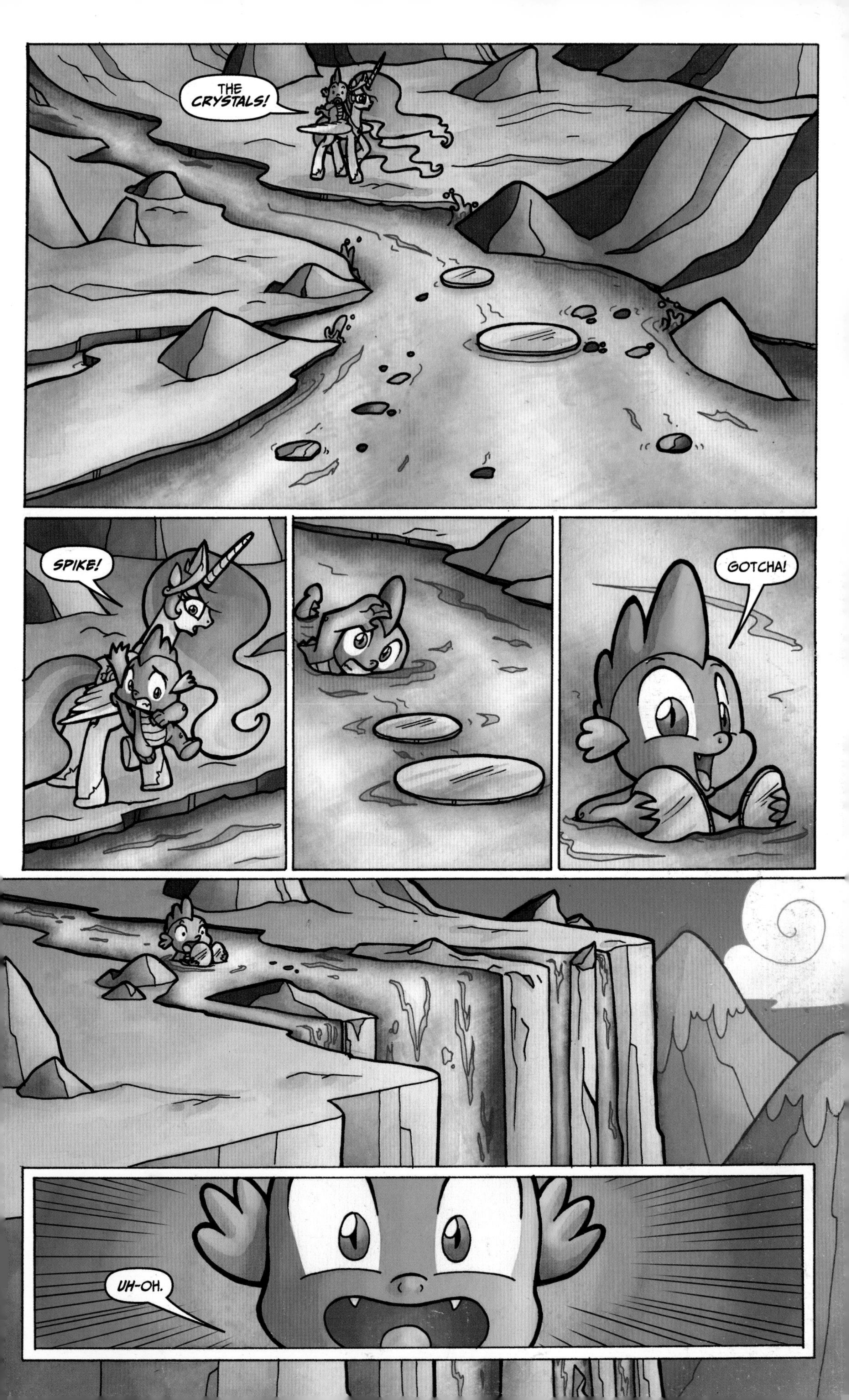
THE CRYSTALS!
SPIKE!
GOTCHA!
UH-OH.

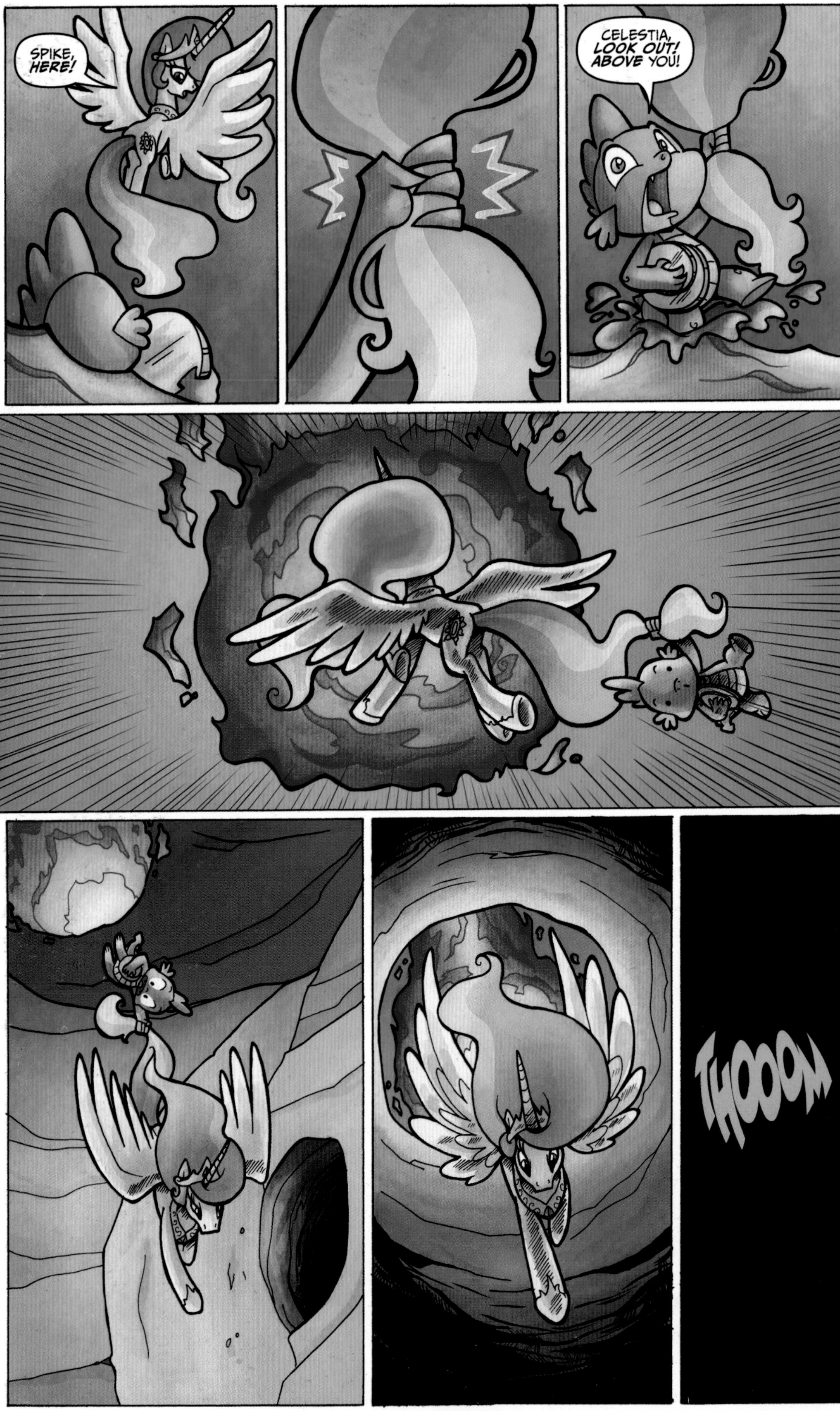
SPIKE, HERE!
CELESTIA, LOOK OUT! ABOVE YOU!
THOOOM

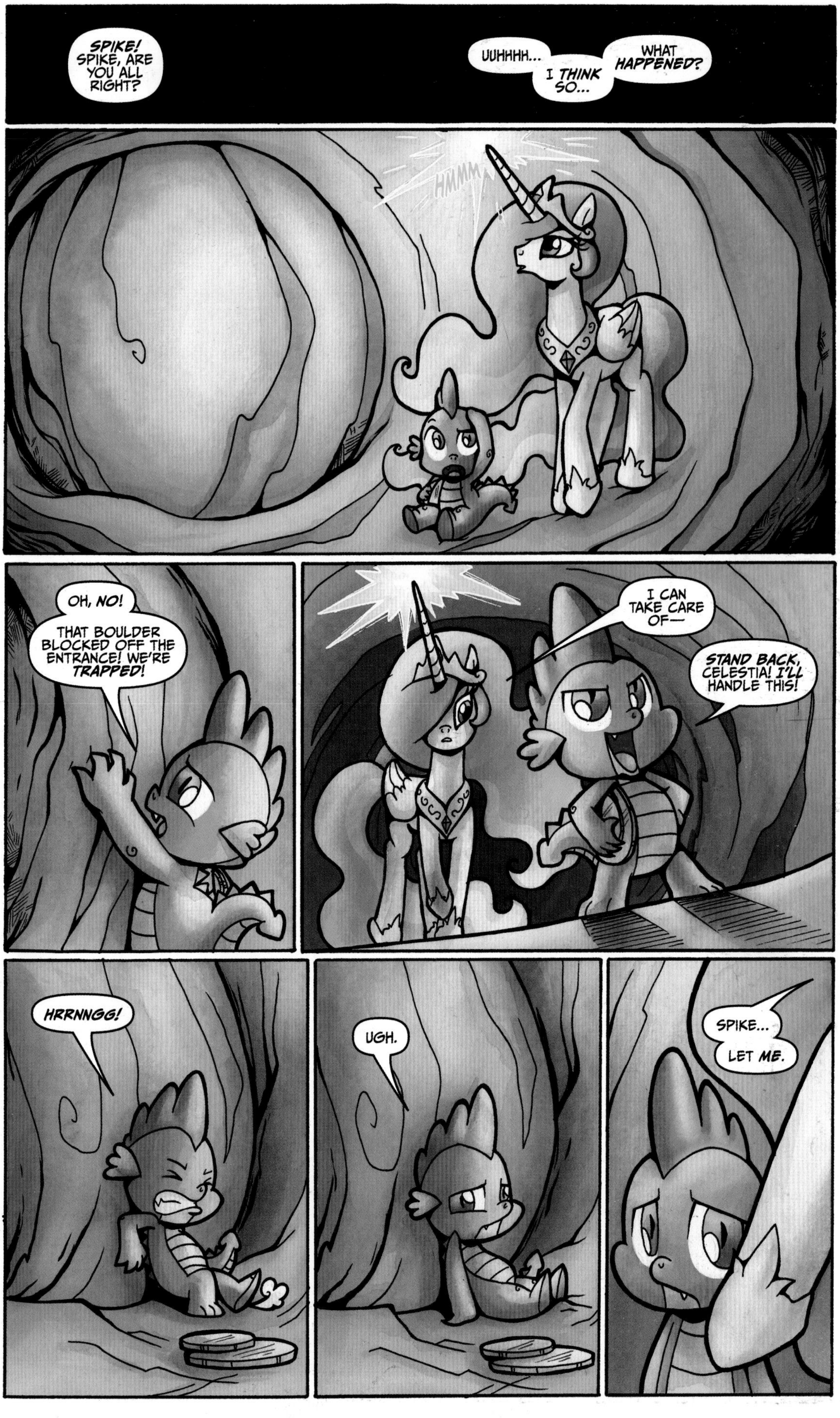
SPIKE! SPIKE, ARE YOU ALL RIGHT?
UUHHHH...
I THINK SO...
WHAT HAPPENED?
HMMM
OH, NO!
THAT BOULDER BLOCKED OFF THE ENTRANCE! WE'RE TRAPPED!
I CAN TAKE CARE OF—
STAND BACK, CELESTIA! I'LL HANDLE THIS!
HRRNNGG!
UGH.
SPIKE...
LET ME.

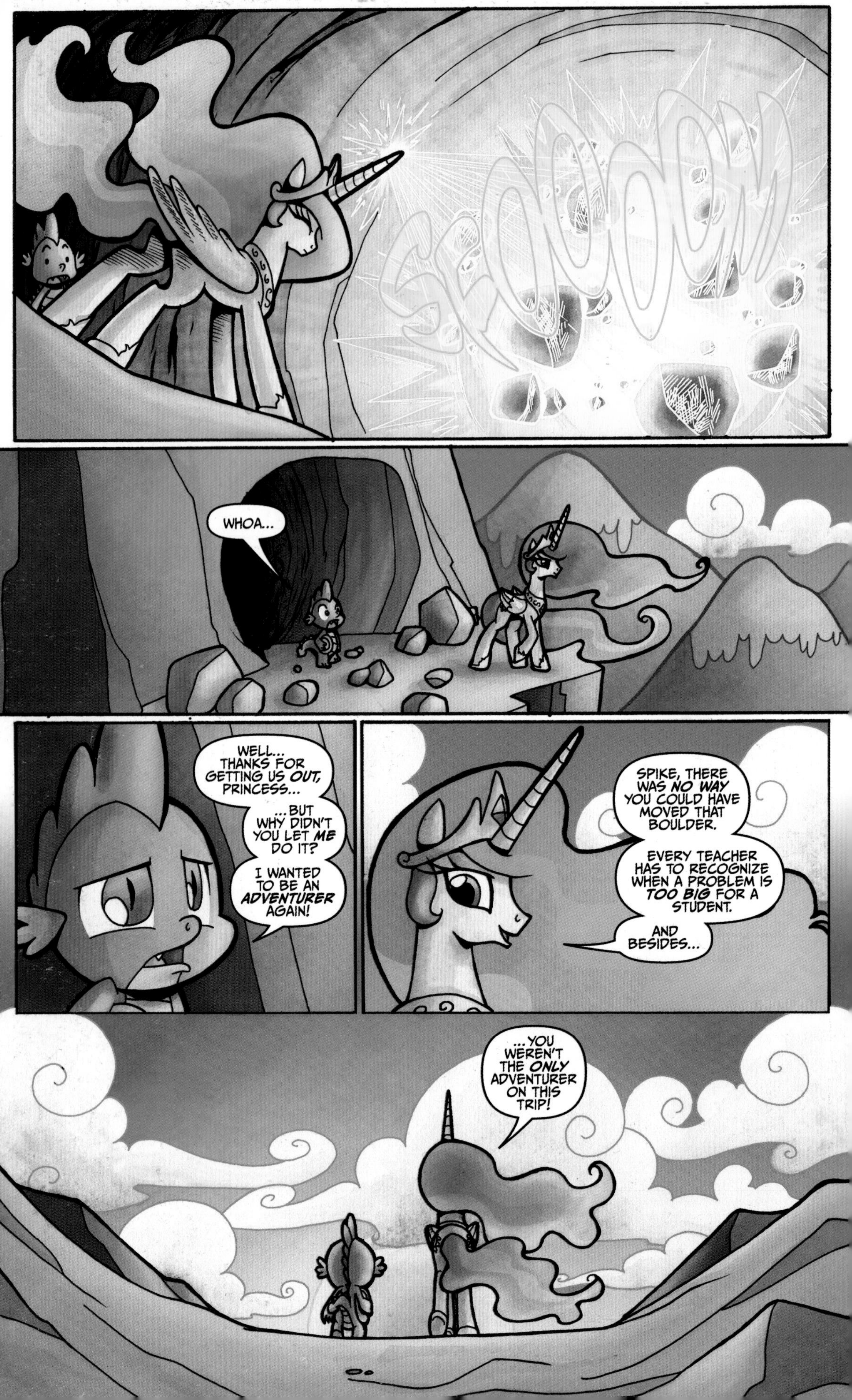
SKOOOOM
WHOA...
WELL... THANKS FOR GETTING US OUT, PRINCESS...
...BUT WHY DIDN'T YOU LET ME DO IT?
I WANTED TO BE AN ADVENTURER AGAIN!
SPIKE, THERE WAS NO WAY YOU COULD HAVE MOVED THAT BOULDER.
EVERY TEACHER HAS TO RECOGNIZE WHEN A PROBLEM IS TOO BIG FOR A STUDENT.
AND BESIDES...
...YOU WEREN'T THE ONLY ADVENTURER ON THIS TRIP!

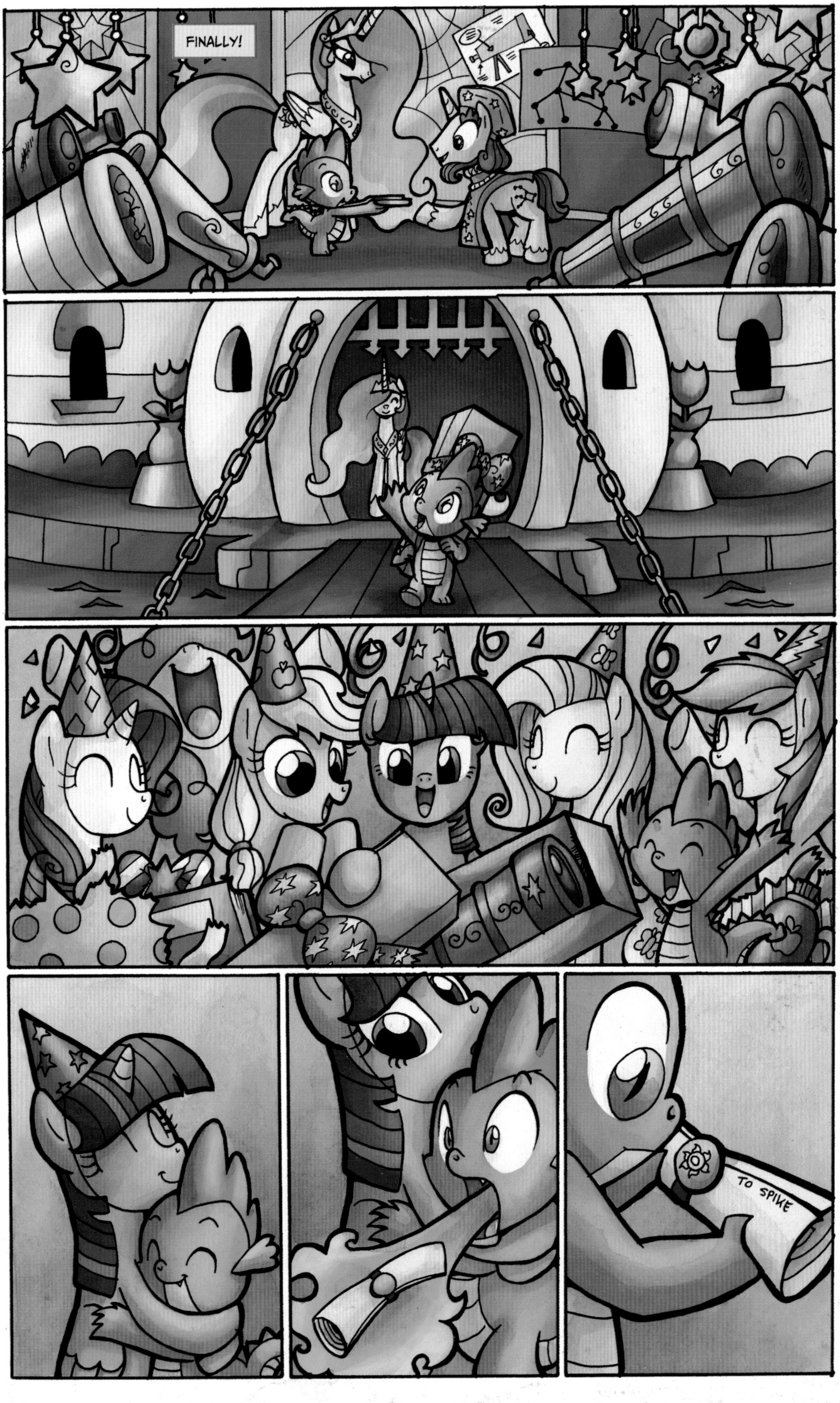
FINALLY!
TO SPIKE

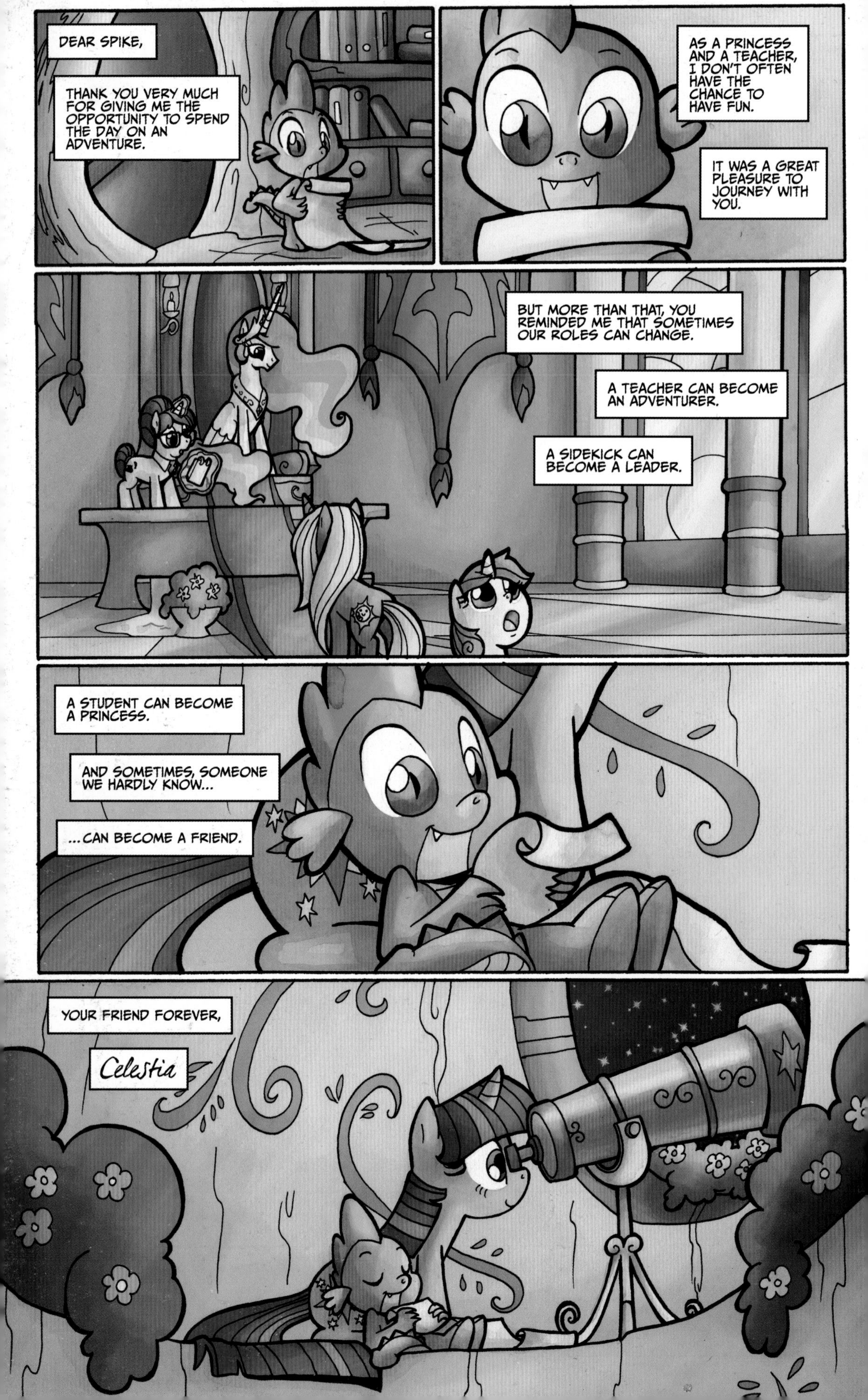
DEAR SPIKE,
THANK YOU VERY MUCH FOR GIVING ME THE OPPORTUNITY TO SPEND THE DAY ON AN ADVENTURE.
AS A PRINCESS AND A TEACHER, I DON'T OFTEN HAVE THE CHANCE TO HAVE FUN.
IT WAS A GREAT PLEASURE TO JOURNEY WITH YOU.
BUT MORE THAN THAT, YOU REMINDED ME THAT SOMETIMES OUR ROLES CAN CHANGE.
A TEACHER CAN BECOME AN ADVENTURER.
A SIDEKICK CAN BECOME A LEADER.
A STUDENT CAN BECOME A PRINCESS.
AND SOMETIMES, SOMEONE WE HARDLY KNOW...
...CAN BECOME A FRIEND.
YOUR FRIEND FOREVER,
Celestia

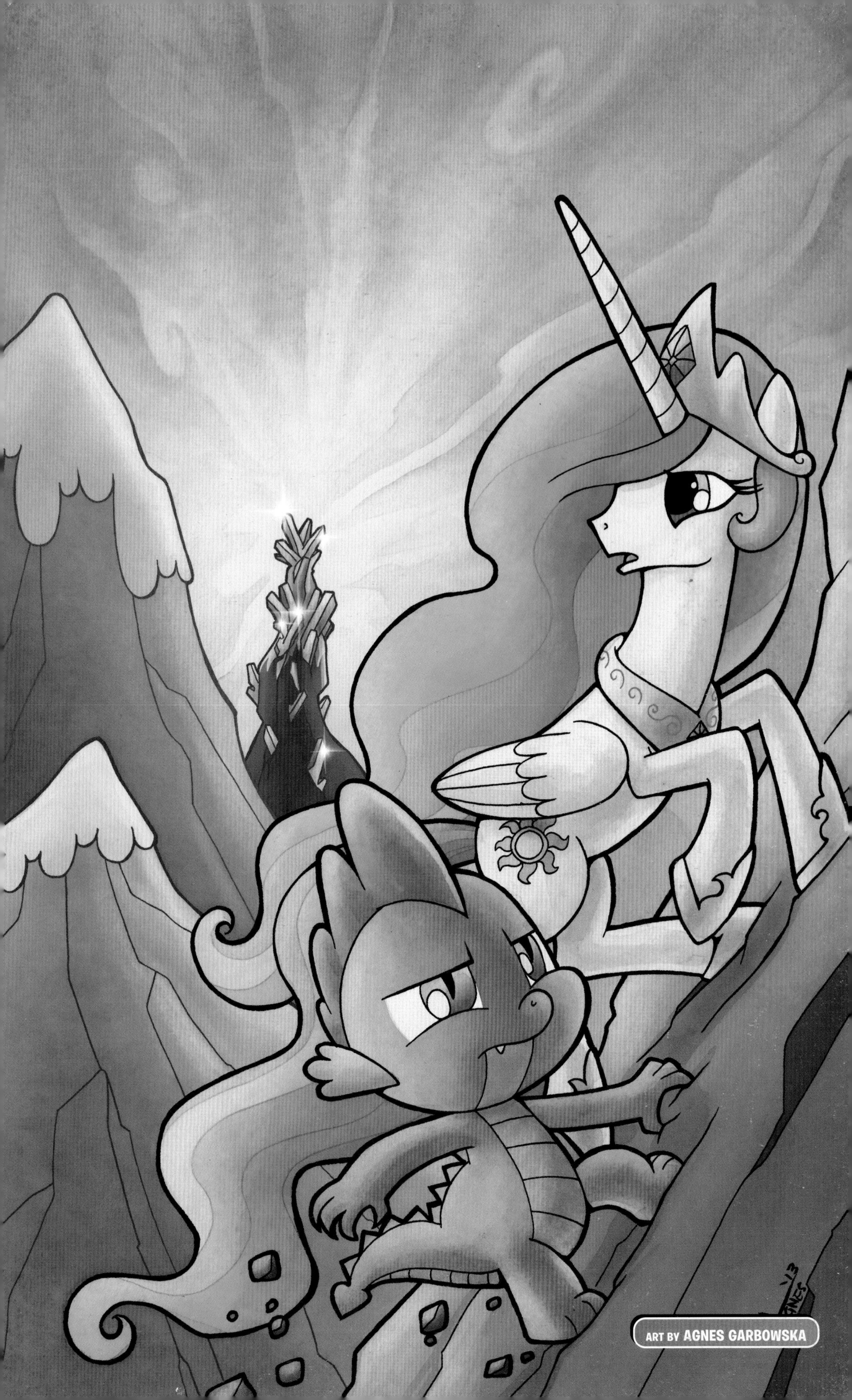

ART BY **AGNES GARBOWSKA**

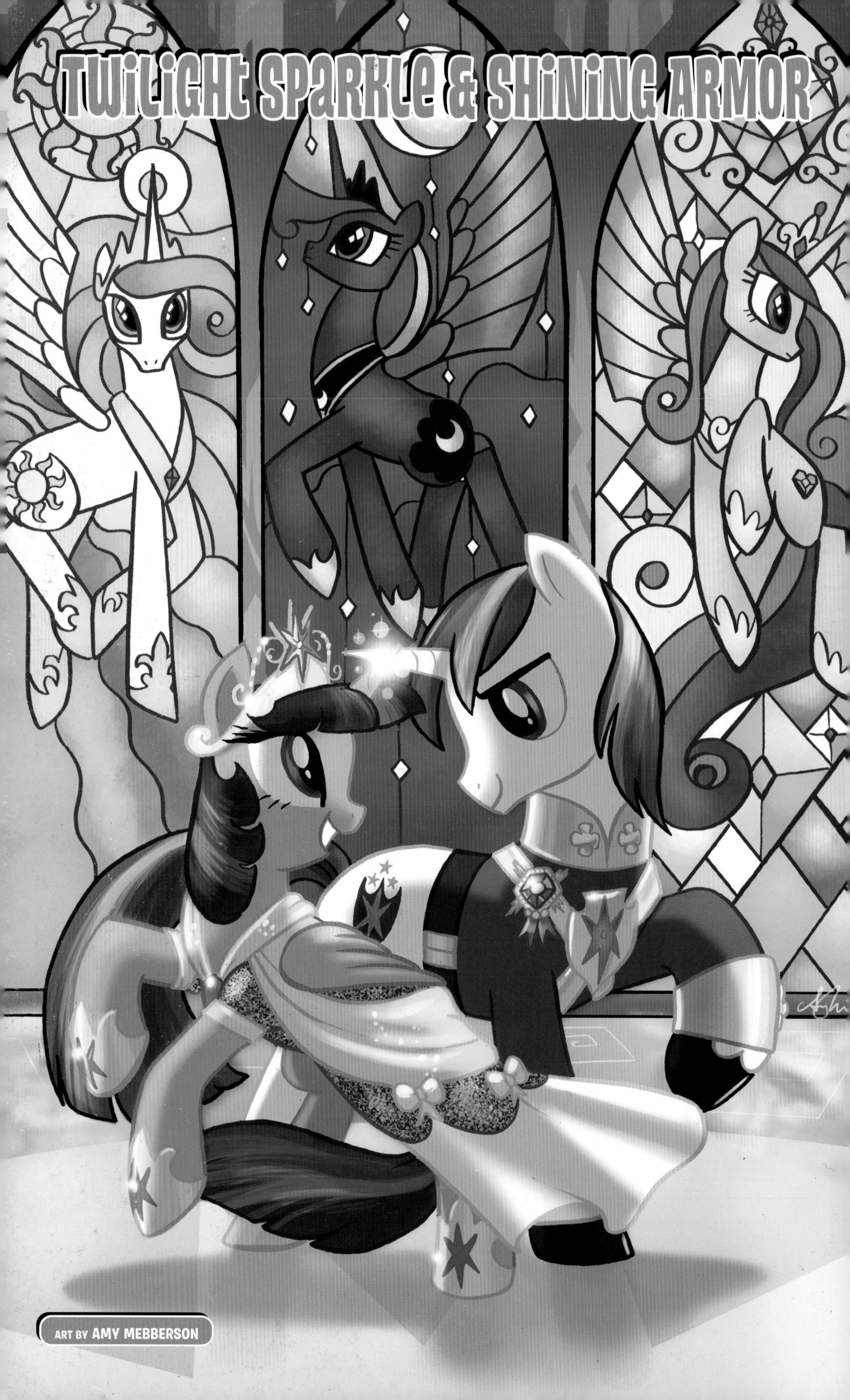
TWILIGHT SPARKLE & SHINING ARMOR
ART BY AMY MEBBERSON

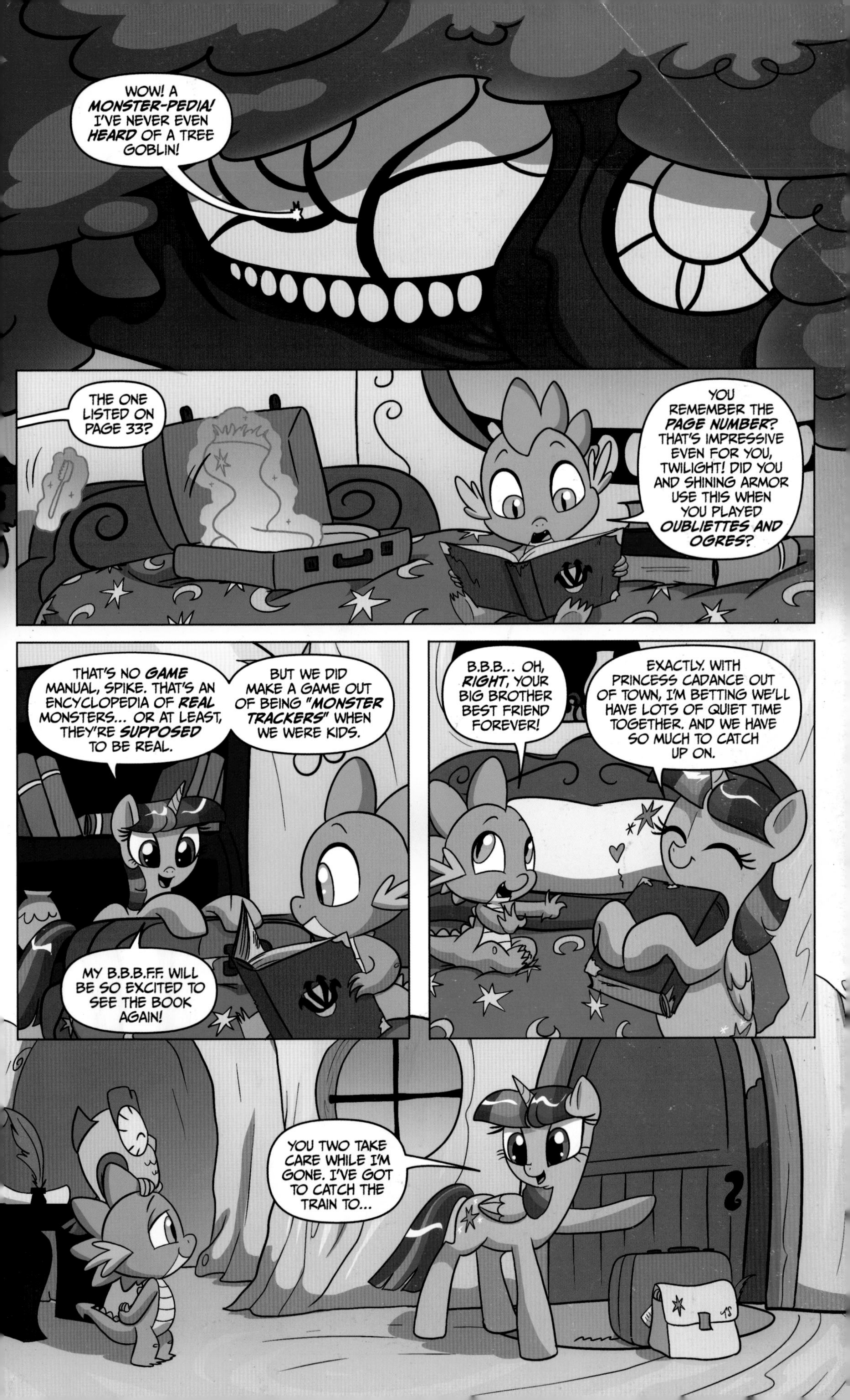
WOW! A MONSTER-PEDIA! I'VE NEVER EVEN HEARD OF A TREE GOBLIN!
THE ONE LISTED ON PAGE 33?
YOU REMEMBER THE PAGE NUMBER? THAT'S IMPRESSIVE EVEN FOR YOU, TWILIGHT! DID YOU AND SHINING ARMOR USE THIS WHEN YOU PLAYED OUBLIETTES AND OGRES?
THAT'S NO GAME MANUAL, SPIKE. THAT'S AN ENCYCLOPEDIA OF REAL MONSTERS... OR AT LEAST, THEY'RE SUPPOSED TO BE REAL.
BUT WE DID MAKE A GAME OUT OF BEING "MONSTER TRACKERS" WHEN WE WERE KIDS.
MY B.B.B.F.F. WILL BE SO EXCITED TO SEE THE BOOK AGAIN!
B.B.B... OH, RIGHT, YOUR BIG BROTHER BEST FRIEND FOREVER!
EXACTLY. WITH PRINCESS CADANCE OUT OF TOWN, I'M BETTING WE'LL HAVE LOTS OF QUIET TIME TOGETHER. AND WE HAVE SO MUCH TO CATCH UP ON.
YOU TWO TAKE CARE WHILE I'M GONE. I'VE GOT TO CATCH THE TRAIN TO...

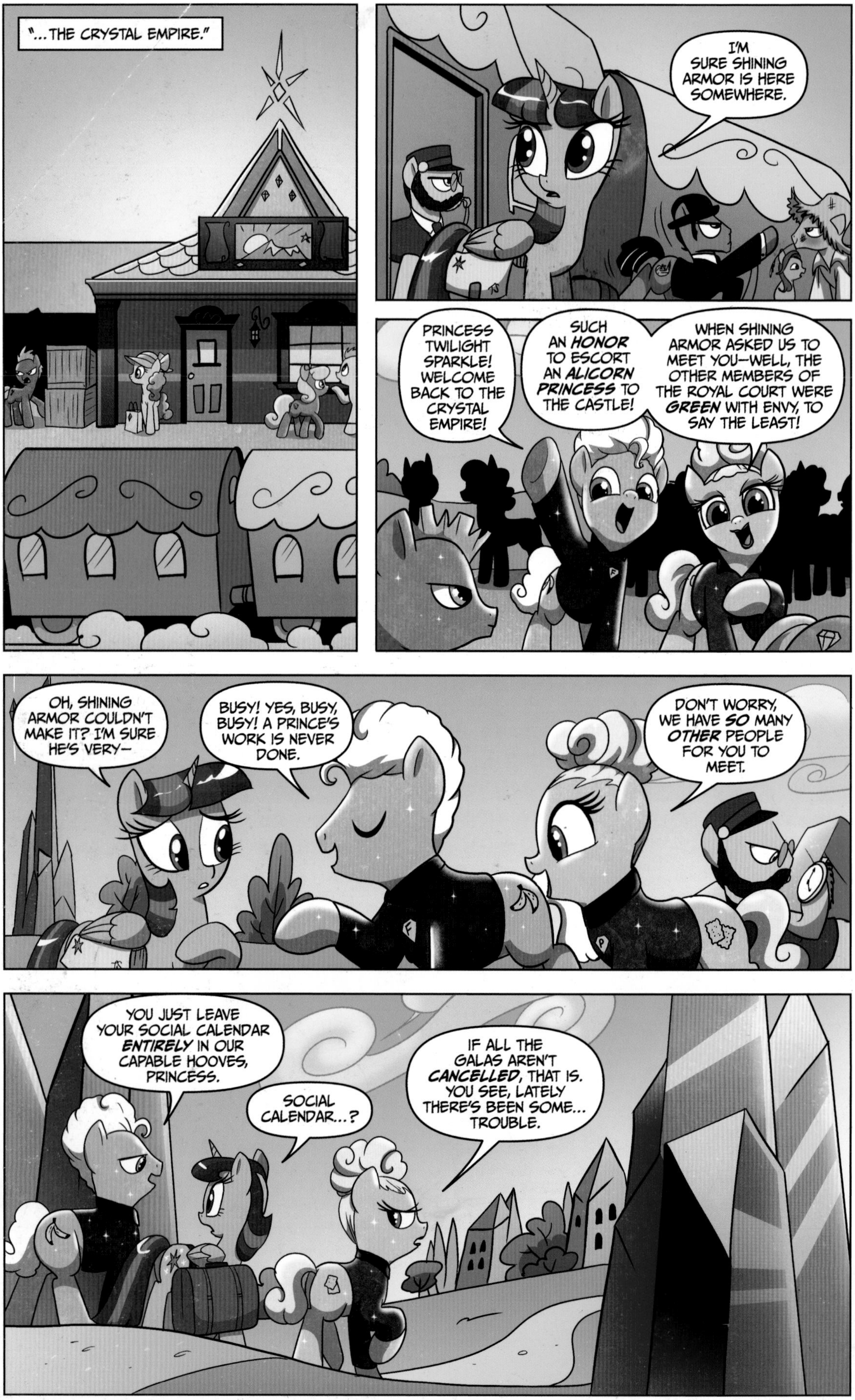
"...THE CRYSTAL EMPIRE."
I'M SURE SHINING ARMOR IS HERE SOMEWHERE.
PRINCESS TWILIGHT SPARKLE! WELCOME BACK TO THE CRYSTAL EMPIRE!
SUCH AN HONOR TO ESCORT AN ALICORN PRINCESS TO THE CASTLE!
WHEN SHINING ARMOR ASKED US TO MEET YOU—WELL, THE OTHER MEMBERS OF THE ROYAL COURT WERE GREEN WITH ENVY, TO SAY THE LEAST!
OH, SHINING ARMOR COULDN'T MAKE IT? I'M SURE HE'S VERY—
BUSY! YES, BUSY, BUSY! A PRINCE'S WORK IS NEVER DONE.
DON'T WORRY, WE HAVE SO MANY OTHER PEOPLE FOR YOU TO MEET.
YOU JUST LEAVE YOUR SOCIAL CALENDAR ENTIRELY IN OUR CAPABLE HOOVES, PRINCESS.
SOCIAL CALENDAR...?
IF ALL THE GALAS AREN'T CANCELLED, THAT IS. YOU SEE, LATELY THERE'S BEEN SOME... TROUBLE.

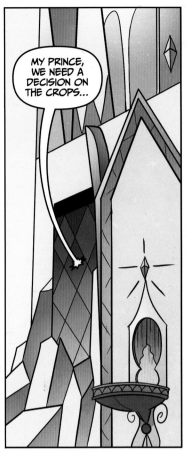

MY PRINCE, WE NEED A DECISION ON THE CROPS...

...I THINK WE SHOULD CONTINUE TO CONCENTRATE ON CRYSTAL BERRY PRODUCTION—

WHY, THAT'S JUST FOOLISH! WE SHOULD BE DIVERSIFYING INTO APPLES AS WELL. IN PONYVILLE, THEY—

YOU TWO ARE ALWAYS FOCUSED ON FRUIT! I'M HERE TO DISCUSS HOW OFF-KEY THE FLUGELHORNS WERE AT THE LAST—

TWYLIE, YOU'RE HERE!

I'M SO HAPPY TO SEE YOU! I'M SORRY I COULDN'T MAKE IT TO THE TRAIN STATION. THINGS HAVE BEEN A LITTLE CRAZY WITH CADANCE OUT OF TOWN.

I CAN SEE. BUT I BROUGHT SOME THINGS TO CHEER YOU UP—

I'M SORRY TO INTERRUPT, MY PRINCE, BUT WE REALLY MUST DISCUSS SOMETHING MORE SERIOUS THAN BERRIES AND FLUGELHORNS...

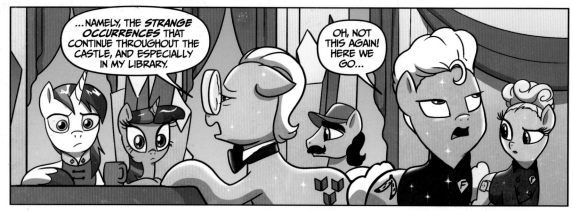

...NAMELY, THE *STRANGE OCCURRENCES* THAT CONTINUE THROUGHOUT THE CASTLE, AND ESPECIALLY IN MY LIBRARY.

OH, NOT THIS AGAIN! HERE WE GO...

LEXICON IS RIGHT! I KEEP HEARING VOICES AND MOANS IN THE HALLWAY AT NIGHT. AND THE PLUMBERS ARE HEARING THINGS, TOO.

IT'S TRUE!

WE KEEP HEARING CHAINS WHEN WE'RE WORKING IN THE LAVATORY!

AND THEN THERE'S THE MATTER OF THE *GLOWING EYES* I'VE SEEN IN THE LIBRARY, RIGHT BEFORE THEY VANISH INTO THIN AIR. AND ALL THE MISSING BOOKS!

I'M SO SORRY TO RAISE THIS DURING YOUR VISIT, PRINCESS CELESTIA.

UH... I'M NOT CELES—

LEX, YOU DID PROMISE TO GET YOUR EYES CHECKED AGAIN, RIGHT?

HOLD ON, BIG BROTHER. LOOK WHAT I BROUGHT!

DOESN'T THIS ALL SOUND FAMILIAR? MOANS IN THE DARK? GLOWING EYES. DRAGGING CHAINS. AND *STEALING BOOKS!*

IT SOUNDS JUST LIKE A *CRYSTAL GHOST*—ON *PAGE 89!*

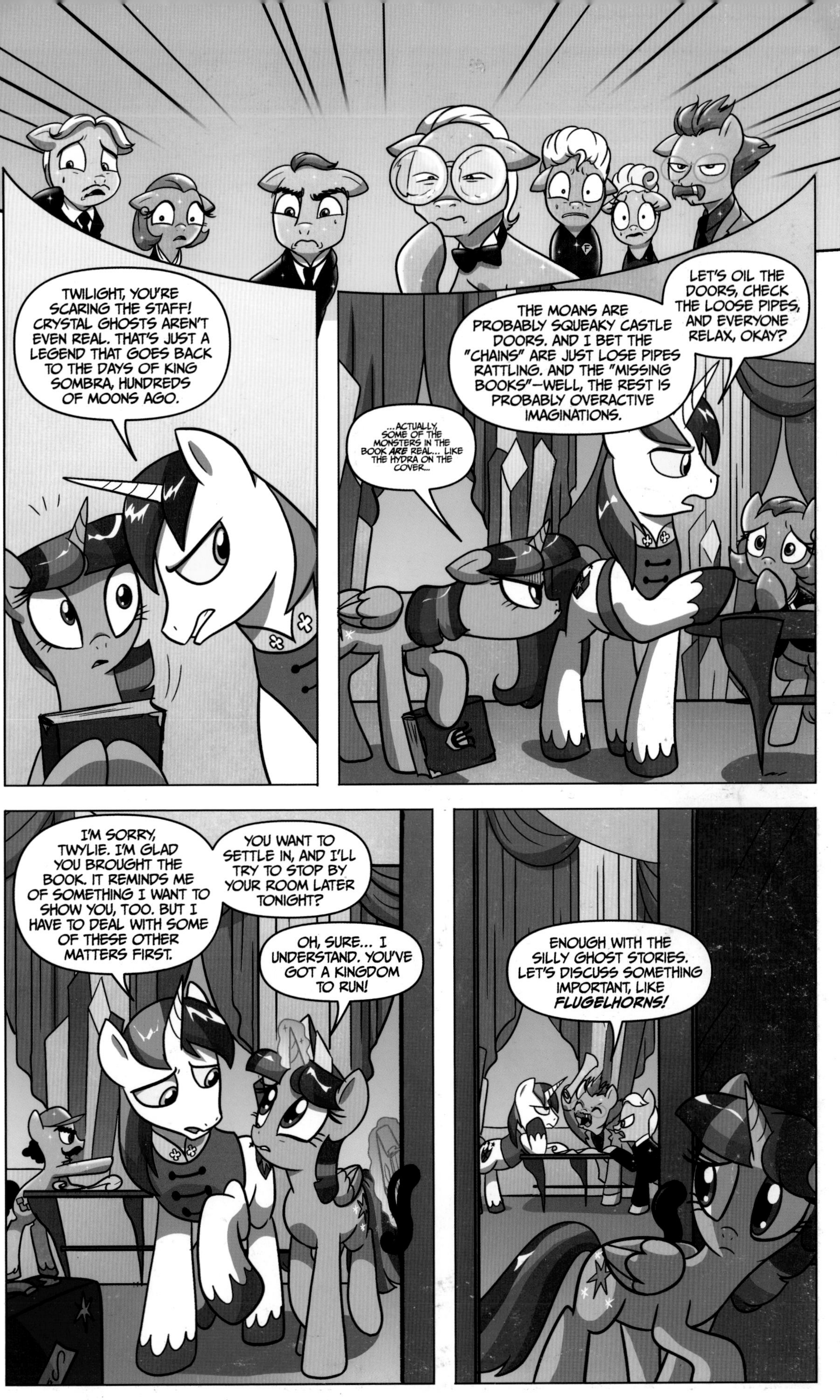
TWILIGHT, YOU'RE SCARING THE STAFF! CRYSTAL GHOSTS AREN'T EVEN REAL. THAT'S JUST A LEGEND THAT GOES BACK TO THE DAYS OF KING SOMBRA, HUNDREDS OF MOONS AGO.
THE MOANS ARE PROBABLY SQUEAKY CASTLE DOORS. AND I BET THE "CHAINS" ARE JUST LOSE PIPES RATTLING. AND THE "MISSING BOOKS"—WELL, THE REST IS PROBABLY OVERACTIVE IMAGINATIONS.
LET'S OIL THE DOORS, CHECK THE LOOSE PIPES, AND EVERYONE RELAX, OKAY?
...ACTUALLY, SOME OF THE MONSTERS IN THE BOOK *ARE* REAL... LIKE THE HYDRA ON THE COVER...
I'M SORRY, TWYLIE. I'M GLAD YOU BROUGHT THE BOOK. IT REMINDS ME OF SOMETHING I WANT TO SHOW YOU, TOO. BUT I HAVE TO DEAL WITH SOME OF THESE OTHER MATTERS FIRST.
YOU WANT TO SETTLE IN, AND I'LL TRY TO STOP BY YOUR ROOM LATER TONIGHT?
OH, SURE... I UNDERSTAND. YOU'VE GOT A KINGDOM TO RUN!
ENOUGH WITH THE SILLY GHOST STORIES. LET'S DISCUSS SOMETHING IMPORTANT, LIKE ***FLUGELHORNS!***

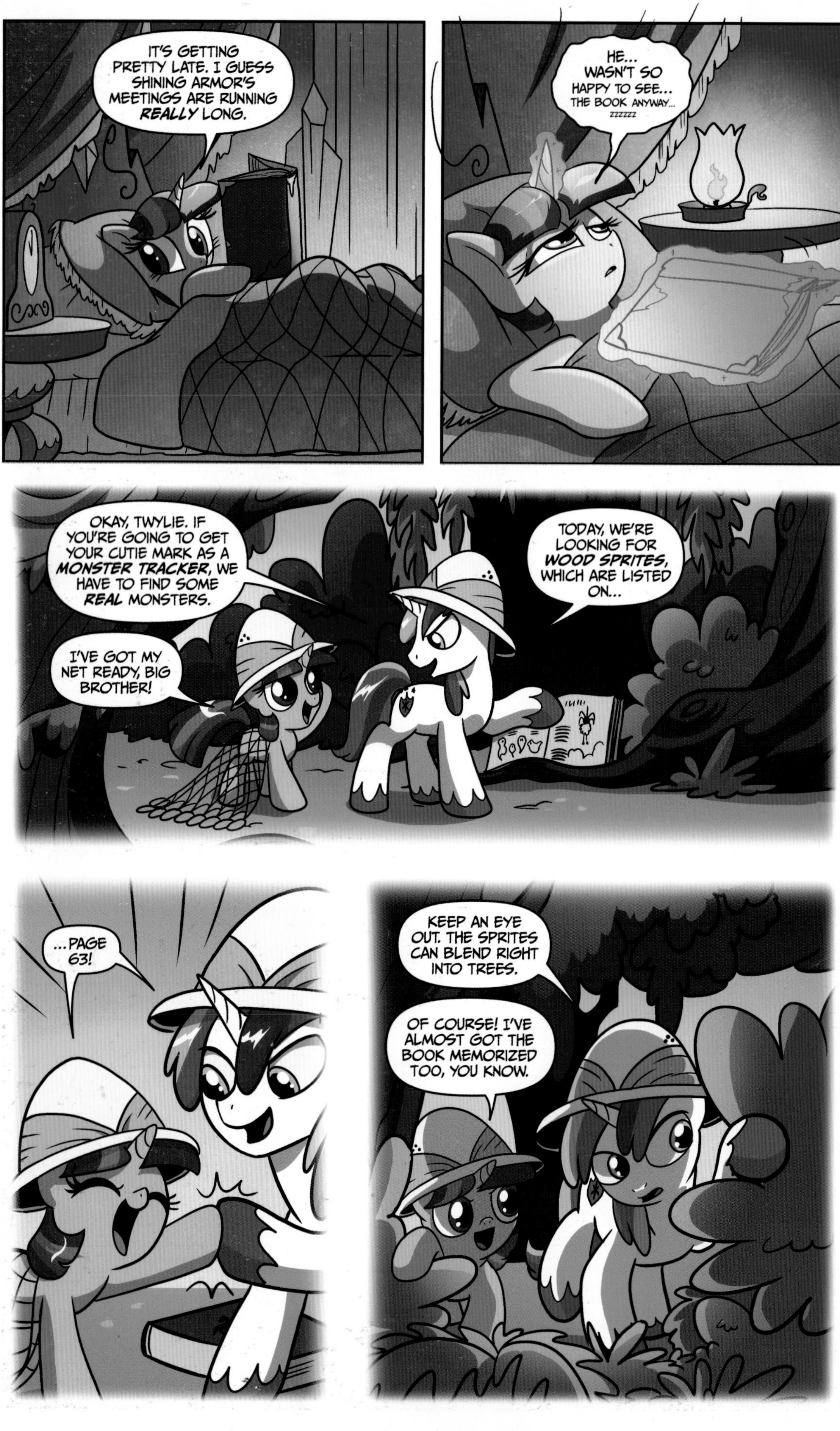
IT'S GETTING PRETTY LATE. I GUESS SHINING ARMOR'S MEETINGS ARE RUNNING REALLY LONG.
HE... WASN'T SO HAPPY TO SEE... THE BOOK ANYWAY... ZZZZZZ
OKAY, TWYLIE. IF YOU'RE GOING TO GET YOUR CUTIE MARK AS A MONSTER TRACKER, WE HAVE TO FIND SOME REAL MONSTERS.
I'VE GOT MY NET READY, BIG BROTHER!
TODAY, WE'RE LOOKING FOR WOOD SPRITES, WHICH ARE LISTED ON...
...PAGE 63!
KEEP AN EYE OUT. THE SPRITES CAN BLEND RIGHT INTO TREES.
OF COURSE! I'VE ALMOST GOT THE BOOK MEMORIZED TOO, YOU KNOW.

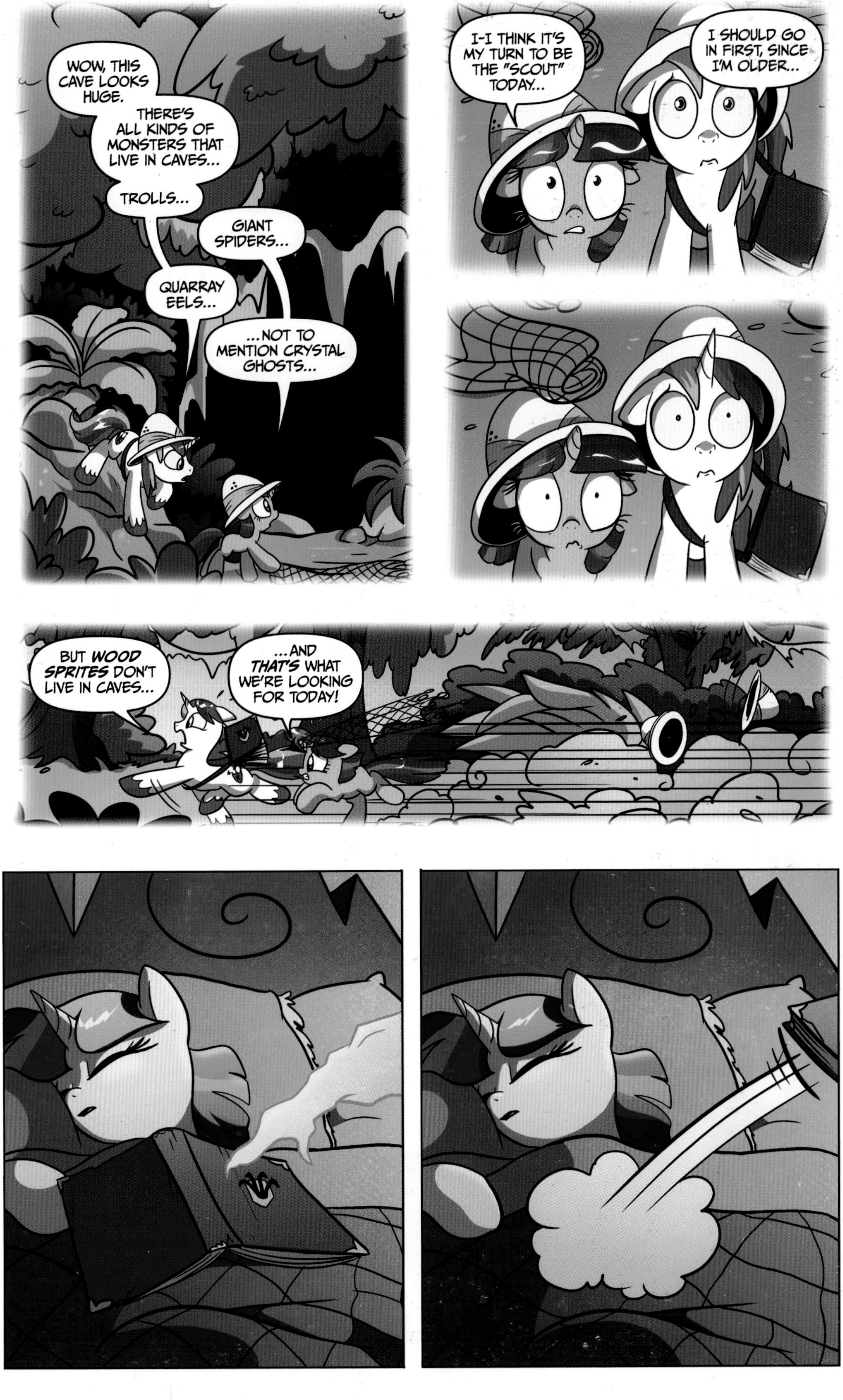
WOW, THIS CAVE LOOKS HUGE.
THERE'S ALL KINDS OF MONSTERS THAT LIVE IN CAVES...
TROLLS...
GIANT SPIDERS...
QUARRAY EELS...
...NOT TO MENTION CRYSTAL GHOSTS...
I-I THINK IT'S MY TURN TO BE THE "SCOUT" TODAY...
I SHOULD GO IN FIRST, SINCE I'M OLDER...
BUT *WOOD SPRITES* DON'T LIVE IN CAVES...
...AND *THAT'S* WHAT WE'RE LOOKING FOR TODAY!

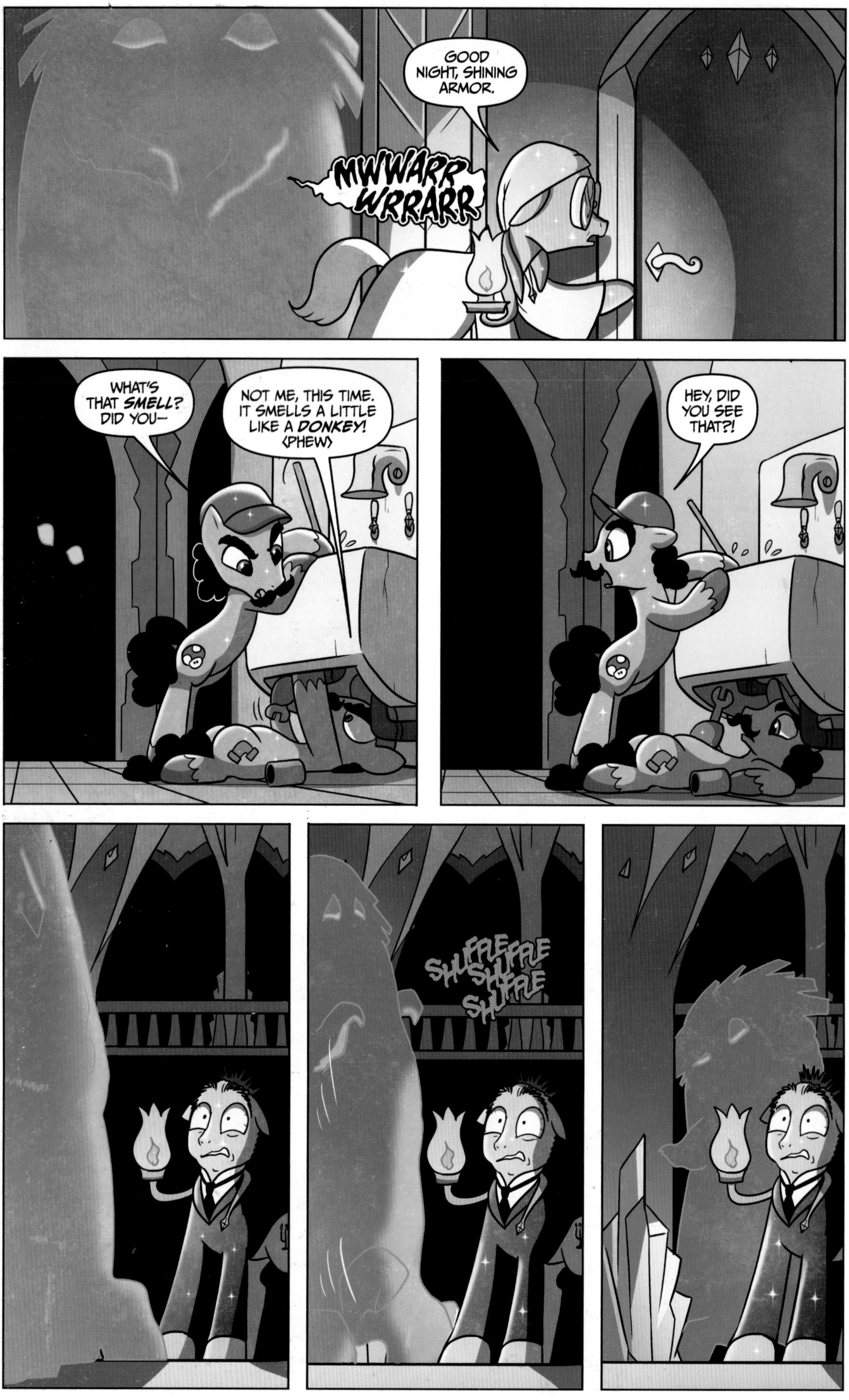
GOOD NIGHT, SHINING ARMOR.
MWWARR WRRARR
WHAT'S THAT SMELL? DID YOU--
NOT ME, THIS TIME. IT SMELLS A LITTLE LIKE A DONKEY! ⟨PHEW⟩
HEY, DID YOU SEE THAT?!
SHUFFLE SHUFFLE SHUFFLE SHUFFLE

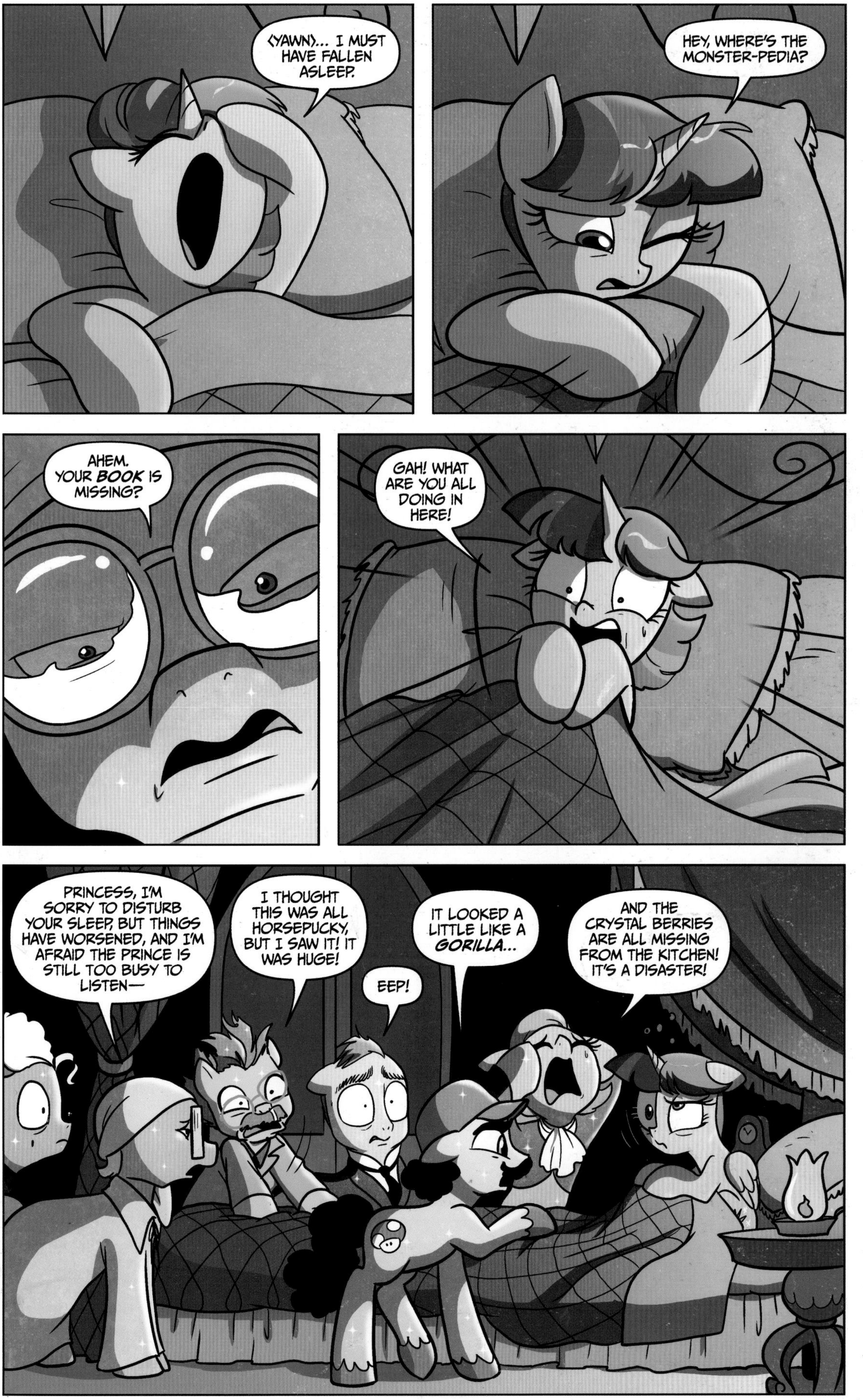

‹YAWN›... I MUST HAVE FALLEN ASLEEP.
HEY, WHERE'S THE MONSTER-PEDIA?
AHEM. YOUR BOOK IS MISSING?
GAH! WHAT ARE YOU ALL DOING IN HERE!
PRINCESS, I'M SORRY TO DISTURB YOUR SLEEP, BUT THINGS HAVE WORSENED, AND I'M AFRAID THE PRINCE IS STILL TOO BUSY TO LISTEN—
I THOUGHT THIS WAS ALL HORSEPUCKY, BUT I SAW IT! IT WAS HUGE!
EEP!
IT LOOKED A LITTLE LIKE A GORILLA...
AND THE CRYSTAL BERRIES ARE ALL MISSING FROM THE KITCHEN! IT'S A DISASTER!

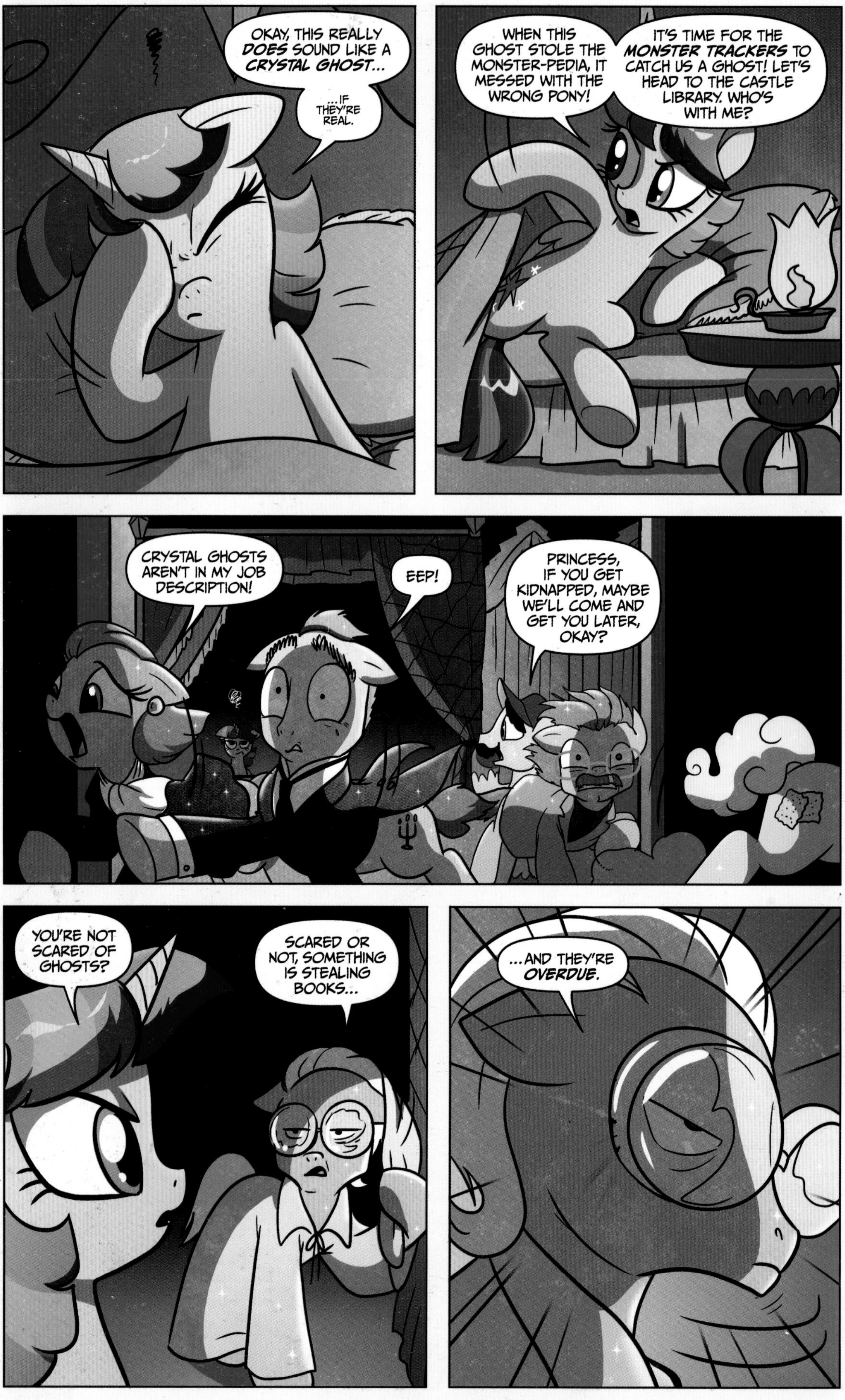
OKAY, THIS REALLY DOES SOUND LIKE A CRYSTAL GHOST...
...IF THEY'RE REAL.
WHEN THIS GHOST STOLE THE MONSTER-PEDIA, IT MESSED WITH THE WRONG PONY!
IT'S TIME FOR THE MONSTER TRACKERS TO CATCH US A GHOST! LET'S HEAD TO THE CASTLE LIBRARY. WHO'S WITH ME?
CRYSTAL GHOSTS AREN'T IN MY JOB DESCRIPTION!
EEP!
PRINCESS, IF YOU GET KIDNAPPED, MAYBE WE'LL COME AND GET YOU LATER, OKAY?
YOU'RE NOT SCARED OF GHOSTS?
SCARED OR NOT, SOMETHING IS STEALING BOOKS...
...AND THEY'RE OVERDUE.

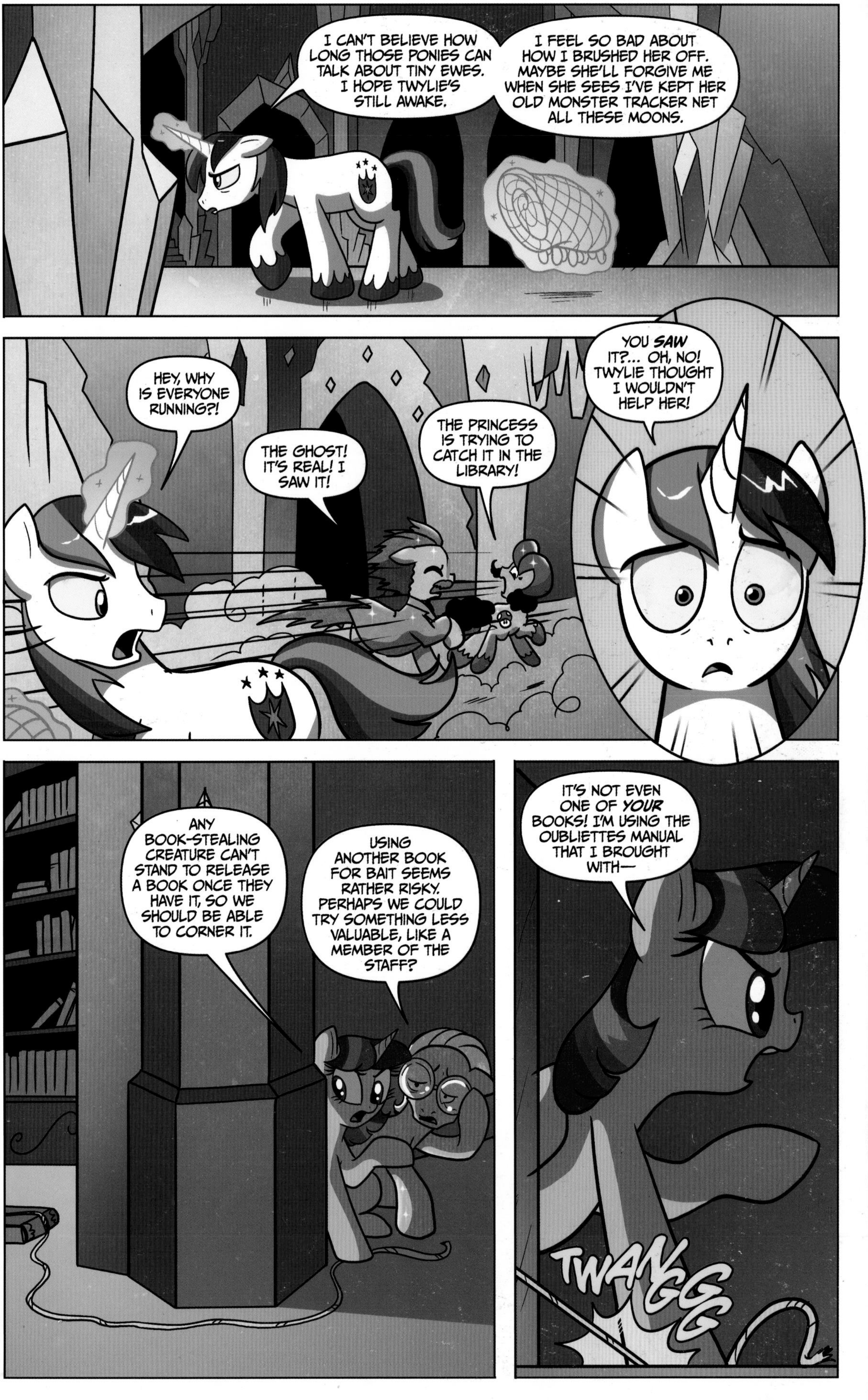
I CAN'T BELIEVE HOW LONG THOSE PONIES CAN TALK ABOUT TINY EWES. I HOPE TWYLIE'S STILL AWAKE.
I FEEL SO BAD ABOUT HOW I BRUSHED HER OFF. MAYBE SHE'LL FORGIVE ME WHEN SHE SEES I'VE KEPT HER OLD MONSTER TRACKER NET ALL THESE MOONS.
HEY, WHY IS EVERYONE RUNNING?!
THE GHOST! IT'S REAL! I SAW IT!
THE PRINCESS IS TRYING TO CATCH IT IN THE LIBRARY!
YOU SAW IT?... OH, NO! TWYLIE THOUGHT I WOULDN'T HELP HER!
ANY BOOK-STEALING CREATURE CAN'T STAND TO RELEASE A BOOK ONCE THEY HAVE IT, SO WE SHOULD BE ABLE TO CORNER IT.
USING ANOTHER BOOK FOR BAIT SEEMS RATHER RISKY. PERHAPS WE COULD TRY SOMETHING LESS VALUABLE, LIKE A MEMBER OF THE STAFF?
IT'S NOT EVEN ONE OF YOUR BOOKS! I'M USING THE OUBLIETTES MANUAL THAT I BROUGHT WITH—
TWANGG

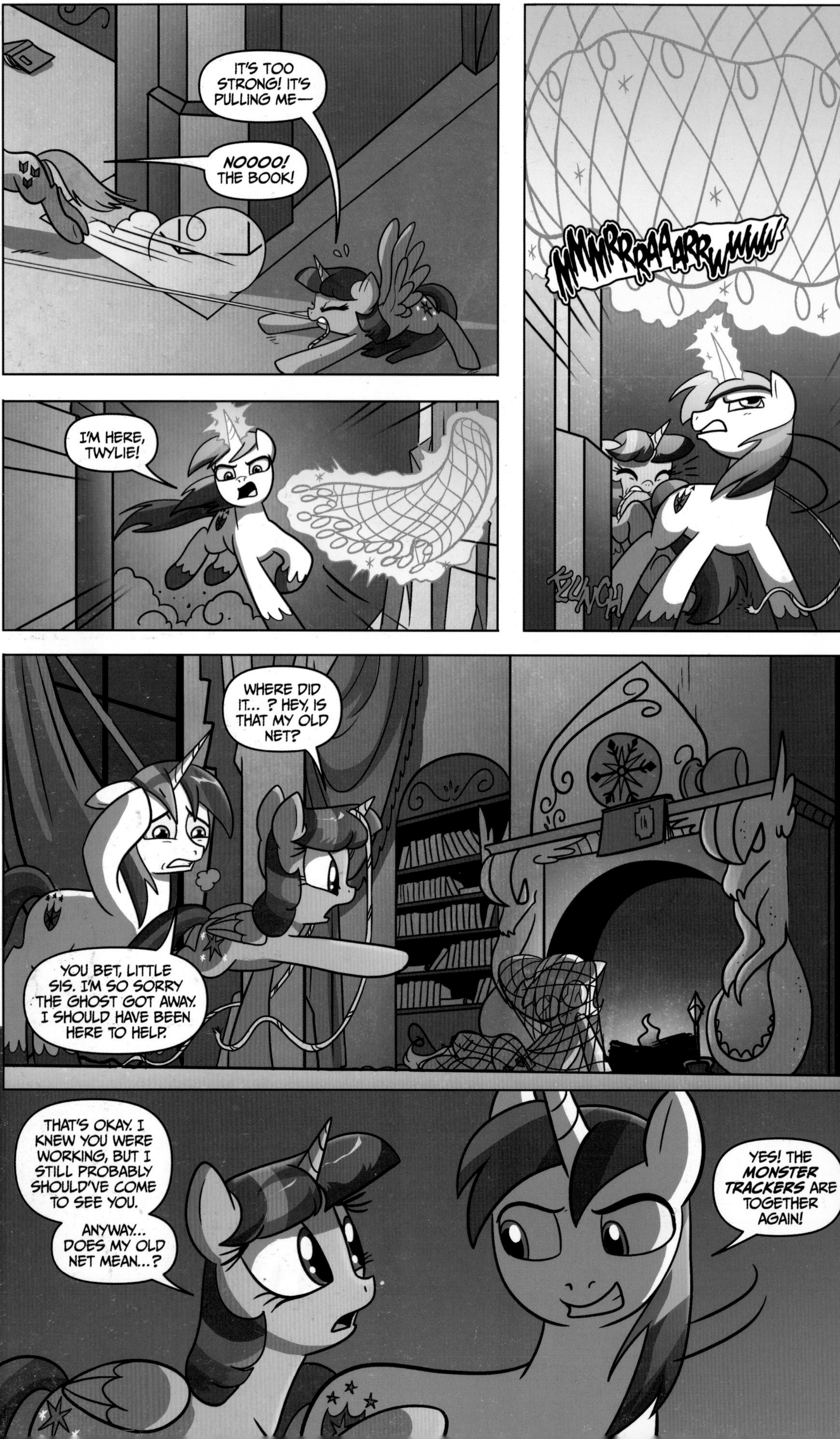

IT'S TOO STRONG! IT'S PULLING ME—
NOOOO! THE BOOK!
MMMRRRAAARRWWWW
I'M HERE, TWYLIE!
KLUNCH
WHERE DID IT... ? HEY, IS THAT MY OLD NET?
YOU BET, LITTLE SIS. I'M SO SORRY THE GHOST GOT AWAY. I SHOULD HAVE BEEN HERE TO HELP.
THAT'S OKAY. I KNEW YOU WERE WORKING, BUT I STILL PROBABLY SHOULD'VE COME TO SEE YOU.
ANYWAY... DOES MY OLD NET MEAN...?
YES! THE MONSTER TRACKERS ARE TOGETHER AGAIN!

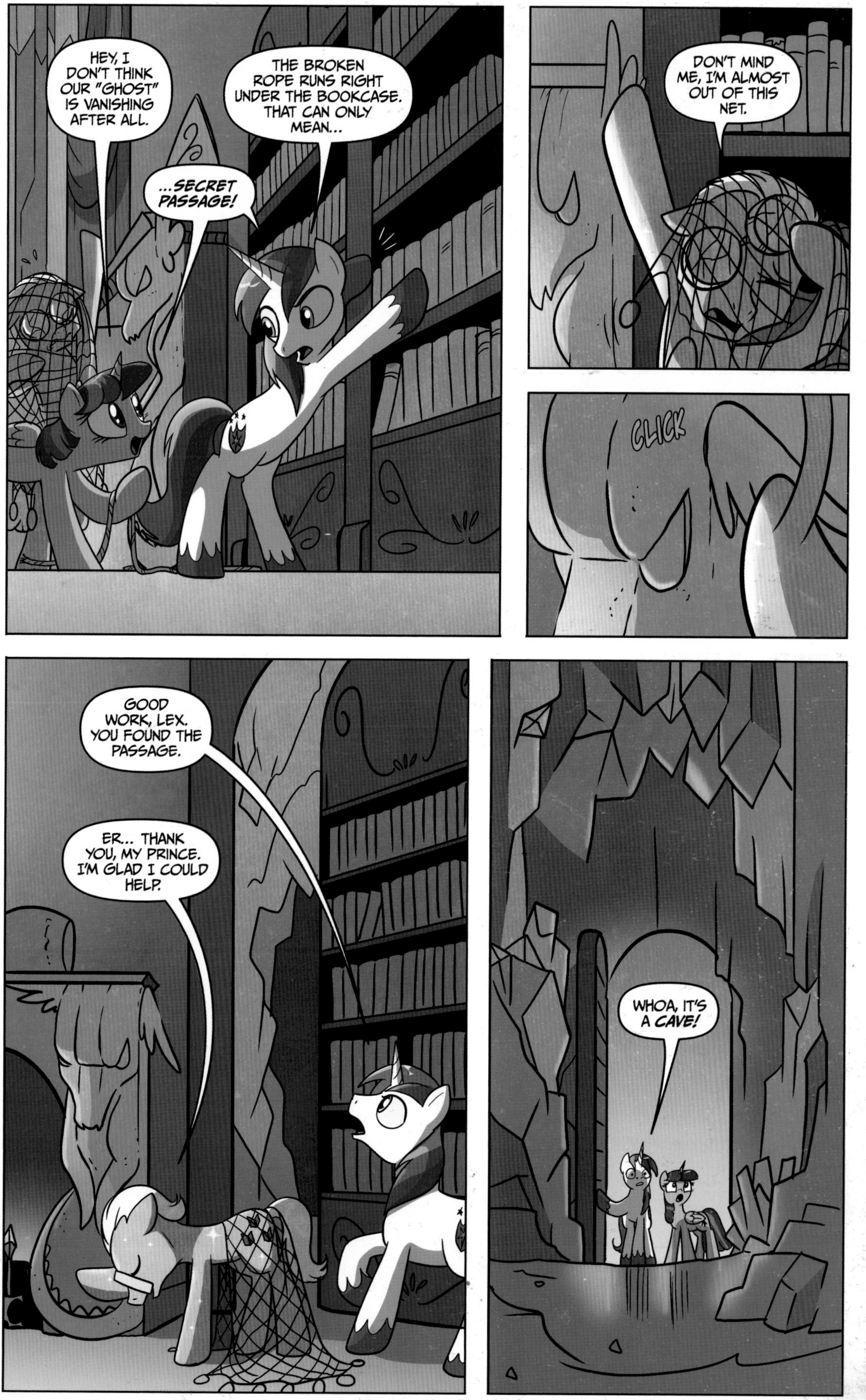
HEY, I DON'T THINK OUR "GHOST" IS VANISHING AFTER ALL.
THE BROKEN ROPE RUNS RIGHT UNDER THE BOOKCASE. THAT CAN ONLY MEAN...
...SECRET PASSAGE!
DON'T MIND ME, I'M ALMOST OUT OF THIS NET.
CLICK
GOOD WORK, LEX. YOU FOUND THE PASSAGE.
ER... THANK YOU, MY PRINCE. I'M GLAD I COULD HELP.
WHOA, IT'S A CAVE!

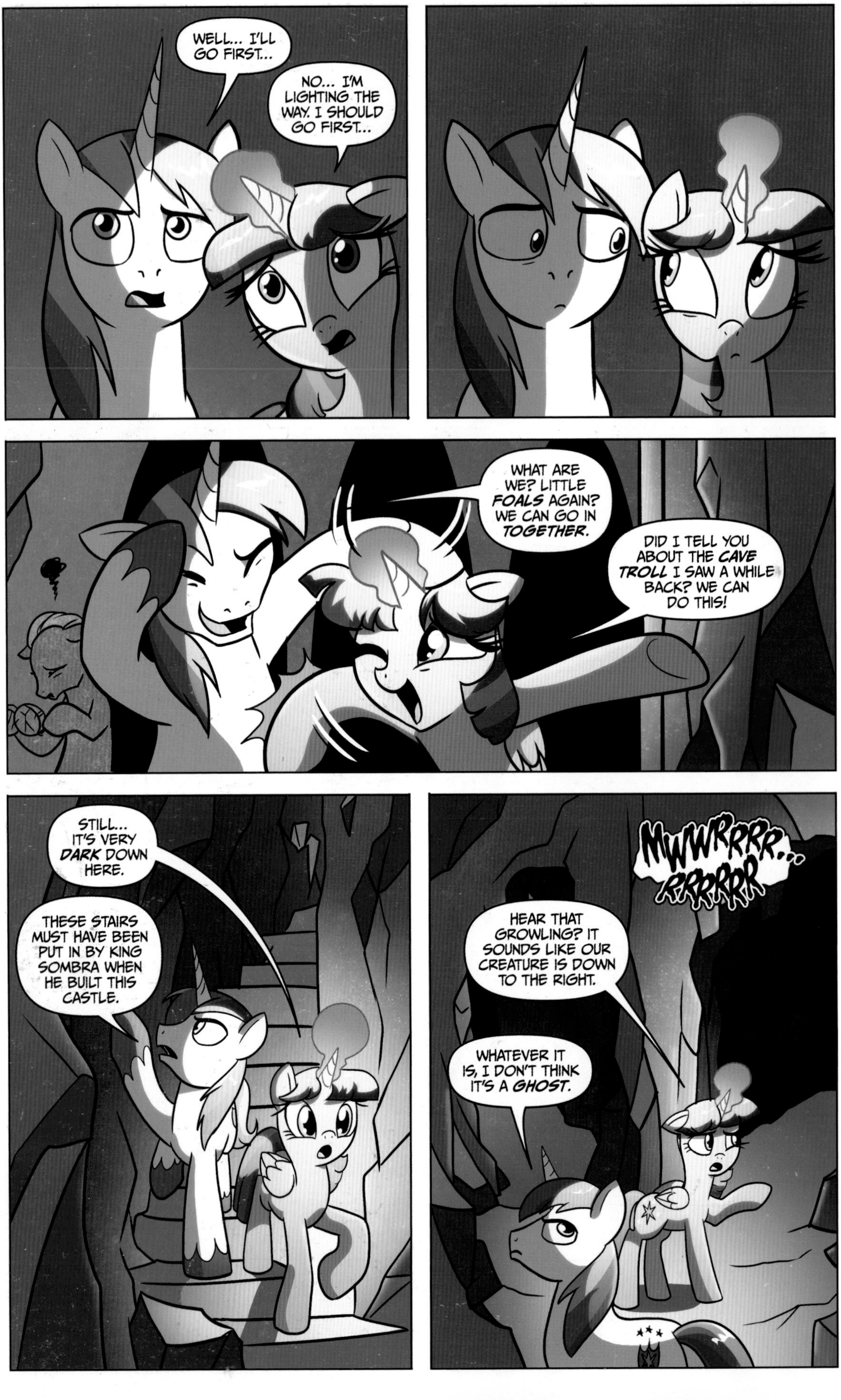
WELL... I'LL GO FIRST...
NO... I'M LIGHTING THE WAY. I SHOULD GO FIRST...
WHAT ARE WE? LITTLE *FOALS* AGAIN? WE CAN GO IN *TOGETHER*.
DID I TELL YOU ABOUT THE *CAVE TROLL* I SAW A WHILE BACK? WE CAN DO THIS!
STILL... IT'S VERY *DARK* DOWN HERE.
THESE STAIRS MUST HAVE BEEN PUT IN BY KING SOMBRA WHEN HE BUILT THIS CASTLE.
MWWRRRR... RRRRRR
HEAR THAT GROWLING? IT SOUNDS LIKE OUR CREATURE IS DOWN TO THE RIGHT.
WHATEVER IT IS, I DON'T THINK IT'S A *GHOST*.

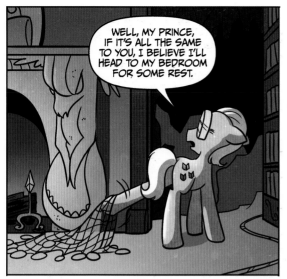

WELL, MY PRINCE, IF IT'S ALL THE SAME TO YOU, I BELIEVE I'LL HEAD TO MY BEDROOM FOR SOME REST.

HMMM... I SEEM TO HAVE GOTTEN TURNED AROUND. I MUST BE HEADED DOWN TO THE KITCHEN... WILL HAVE TO GO THE BACK WAY, I SUPPOSE.

THIS IS JUST LIKE OLD TIMES... EXCEPT, YOU KNOW, WE MIGHT ACTUALLY CATCH SOMETHING.

HEY, WE SAW A WOOD SPRITE THAT ONE TIME—

OR AN *OWL*, MORE LIKELY.

BUT, YEAH, IT'S BEEN TOO LONG SINCE WE HAD FUN TOGETHER. I WISH WE LIVED CLOSER.

ME, TOO. IT SEEMS LIKE NOWADAYS I'M ALWAYS BUSY STUDYING OR WRITING A SCROLL REPORT...

...OR WE'RE DEALING WITH SOME CRISIS—

WAIT, BIG BROTHER. DO YOU SEE WHAT I SEE?

YES! SOME OF THOSE COBBLESTONES ARE RAISED. IT—IT LOOKS LIKE A "CAGE DROP" TRAP.

RIGHT! FROM THE MONSTER-PEDIA'S TRAP APPENDIX. IT'S HANGING UP THERE.

BUT THAT'S A MONSTER TRAP. WHY WOULD A *MONSTER* SET A TRAP... FOR MONSTERS? LET'S KEEP MOVING, BUT WATCH YOUR STEP.

WOW! YOU THINK THIS STONE "ARMY" BELONGED TO KING SOMBRA?

I BET THEY DID, BACK WHEN THIS WAS HIS CASTLE. HOLD ON, THOUGH. THERE'S SOMETHING ABOUT THE WAY THEY'RE TILTING THOSE LANCES.

YEP, LOOK, THEY'RE FILLED WITH GEARS. THESE THINGS WERE MADE TO SALUTE KING SOMBRA...

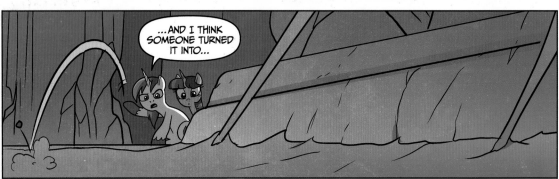

...AND I THINK SOMEONE TURNED IT INTO...

...ANOTHER MONSTER TRAP!

NICE CATCH! I THINK I SEE A BIGGER CAVERN AHEAD.

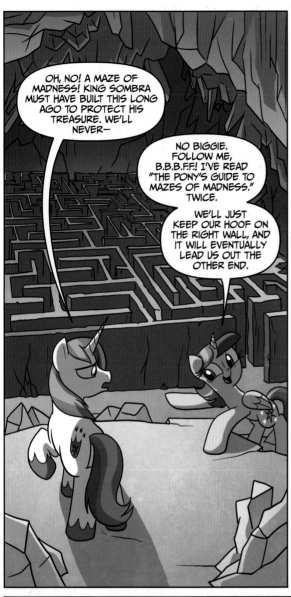

OH, NO! A MAZE OF MADNESS! KING SOMBRA MUST HAVE BUILT THIS LONG AGO TO PROTECT HIS TREASURE. WE'LL NEVER—

NO BIGGIE. FOLLOW ME, B.B.B.F.F.! I'VE READ "THE PONY'S GUIDE TO MAZES OF MADNESS." TWICE.

WE'LL JUST KEEP OUR HOOF ON THE RIGHT WALL, AND IT WILL EVENTUALLY LEAD US OUT THE OTHER END.

YOU MEMORIZED MAZES OF MADNESS, TOO? IMPRESSIVE. NO WONDER WHY I WAS ALWAYS STRUGGLING TO KEEP UP WITH YOU ON THE MONSTER-PEDIA.

NO WAY! I WAS STRUGGLING TO KEEP UP WITH YOU! I BET THAT'S WHY WE LEARNED SO FAST. WE PUSHED EACH OTHER.

I THINK ABOUT THOSE DAYS ALL THE TIME, YOU KNOW. AND WHAT A GREAT PONY YOU'VE GROWN INTO. I MEAN, YOU'RE AN ALICORN PRINCESS NOW!

NOW I'M BLUSHING. I'M JUST GLAD WE'RE TOGETHER... EVEN IF IT IS IN A MAZE OF MADNESS.

HEY, WE'RE OUT! I CAN HEAR THE CREATURE AHEAD.

I HAVE A HUNCH THIS THING IS GOING TO GUARD ITS BOOKS LIKE A DRAGON GUARDING GEMS. THIS ISN'T GOING TO BE EASY, BUT WE'RE...

MWRRRRRRRR...

SCRITCH CLATTER KLANG

...THE MONSTER TRACKERS!

ONE...

TWO...

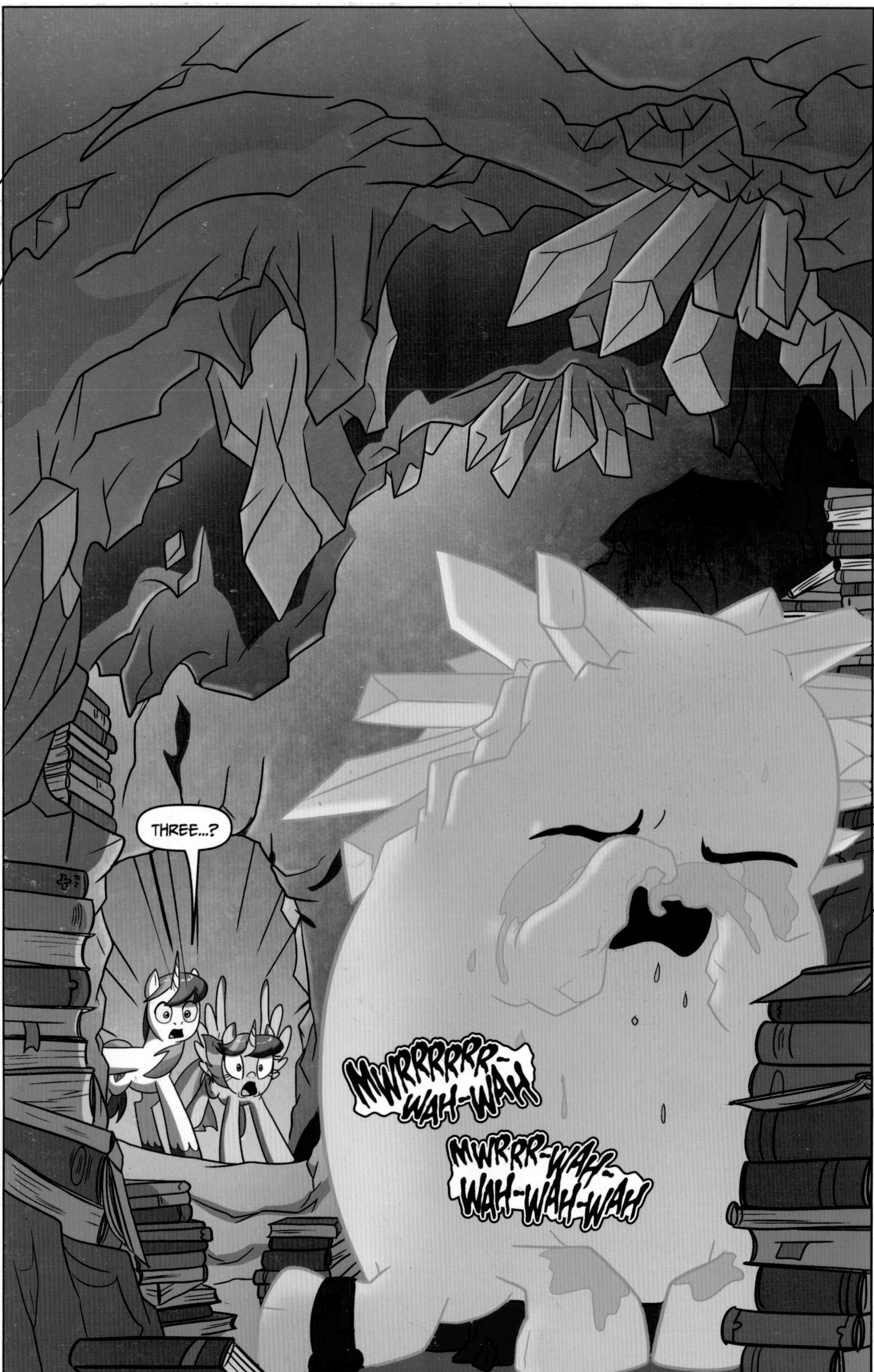
THREE...?
MWRRRRRR-WAH-WAH
MWRRR-WAH-WAH-WAH-WAH

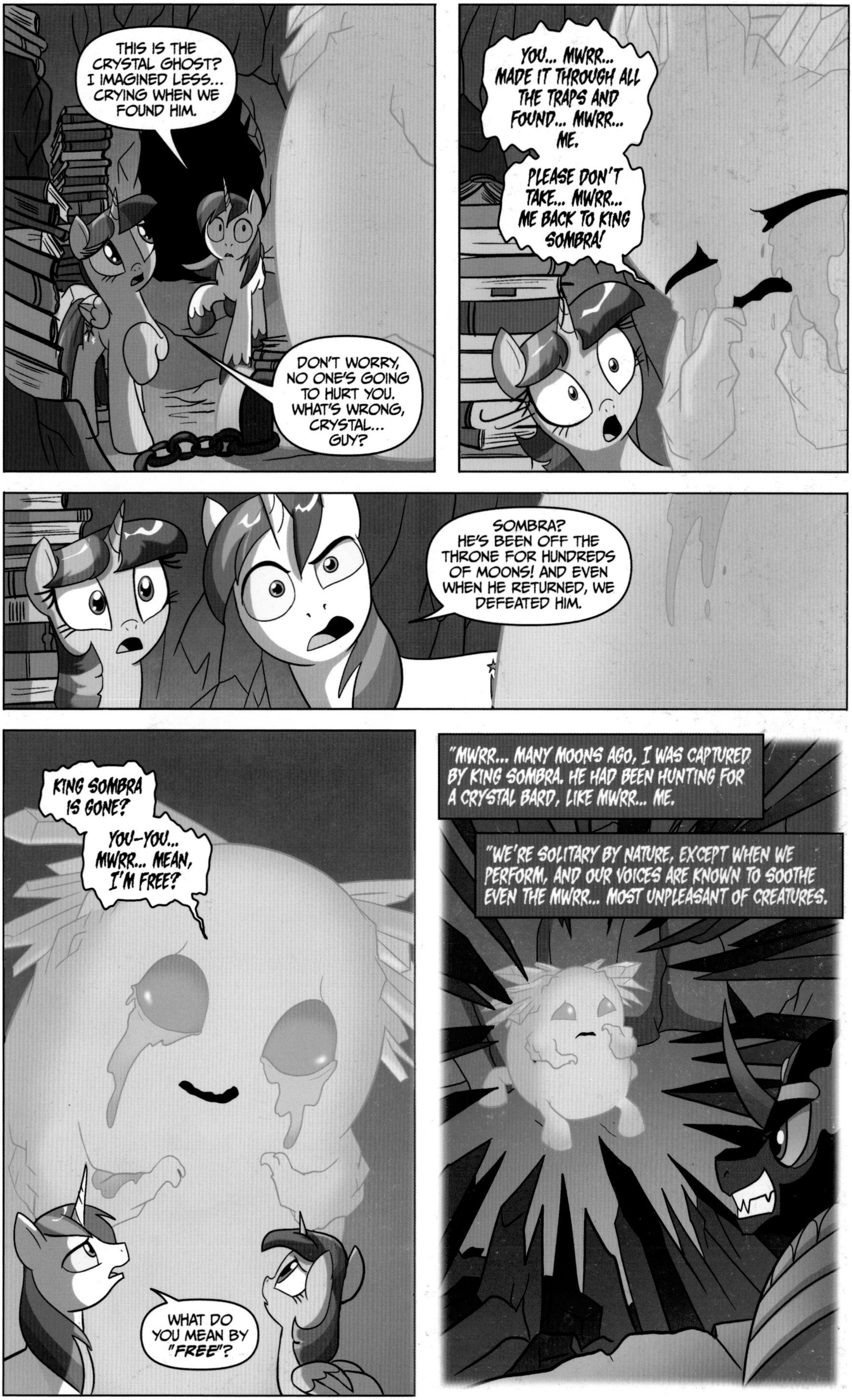
THIS IS THE CRYSTAL GHOST? I IMAGINED LESS... CRYING WHEN WE FOUND HIM.
DON'T WORRY, NO ONE'S GOING TO HURT YOU. WHAT'S WRONG, CRYSTAL... GUY?
YOU... MWRR... MADE IT THROUGH ALL THE TRAPS AND FOUND... MWRR... ME.
PLEASE DON'T TAKE... MWRR... ME BACK TO KING SOMBRA!
SOMBRA? HE'S BEEN OFF THE THRONE FOR HUNDREDS OF MOONS! AND EVEN WHEN HE RETURNED, WE DEFEATED HIM.
KING SOMBRA IS GONE?
YOU-YOU... MWRR... MEAN, I'M FREE?
WHAT DO YOU MEAN BY "FREE"?
"MWRR... MANY MOONS AGO, I WAS CAPTURED BY KING SOMBRA. HE HAD BEEN HUNTING FOR A CRYSTAL BARD, LIKE MWRR... ME.
"WE'RE SOLITARY BY NATURE, EXCEPT WHEN WE PERFORM, AND OUR VOICES ARE KNOWN TO SOOTHE EVEN THE MWRR... MOST UNPLEASANT OF CREATURES.

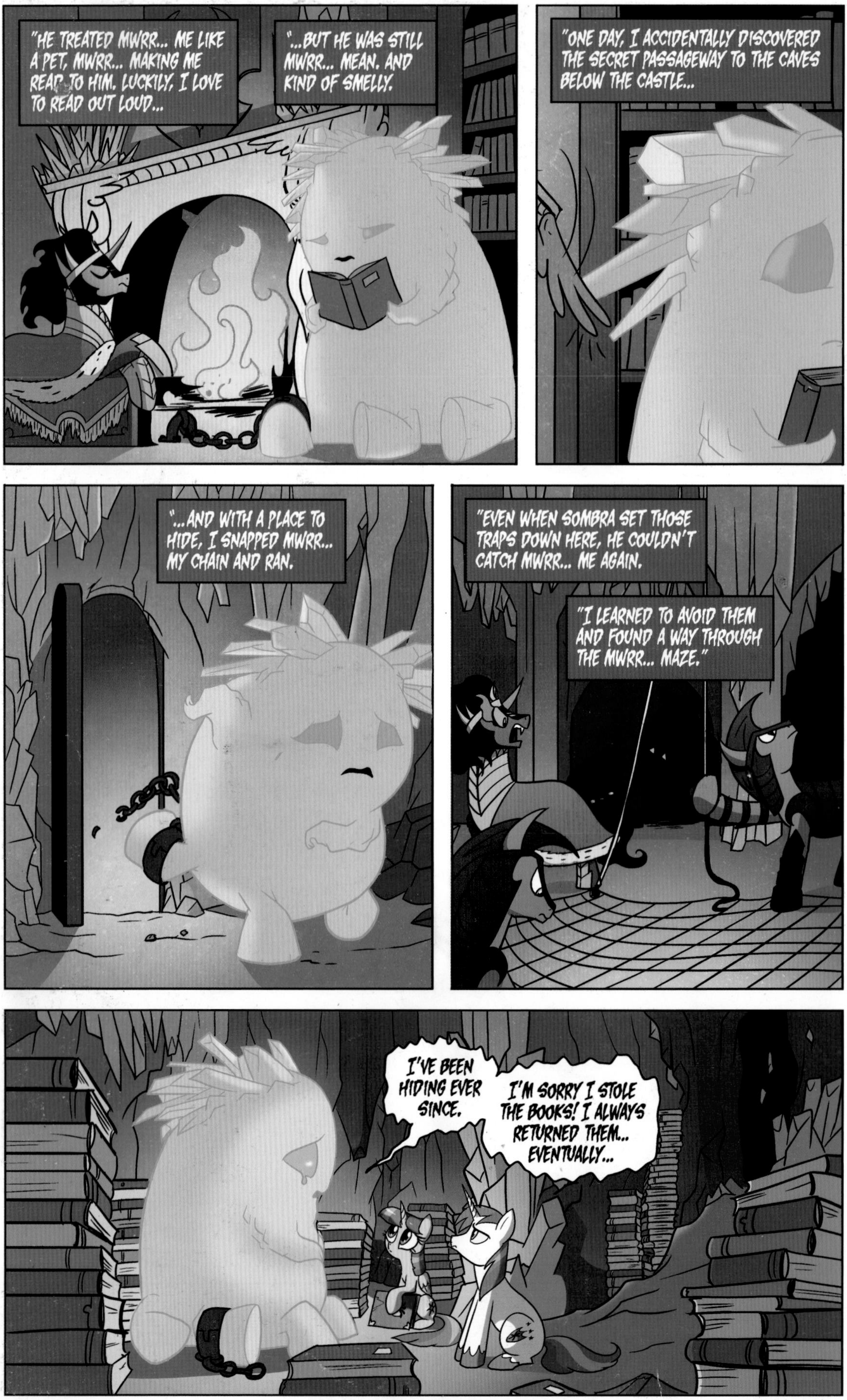
"HE TREATED MWRR... ME LIKE A PET, MWRR... MAKING ME READ TO HIM. LUCKILY, I LOVE TO READ OUT LOUD...
"...BUT HE WAS STILL MWRR... MEAN. AND KIND OF SMELLY.
"ONE DAY, I ACCIDENTALLY DISCOVERED THE SECRET PASSAGEWAY TO THE CAVES BELOW THE CASTLE...
"...AND WITH A PLACE TO HIDE, I SNAPPED MWRR... MY CHAIN AND RAN.
"EVEN WHEN SOMBRA SET THOSE TRAPS DOWN HERE, HE COULDN'T CATCH MWRR... ME AGAIN.
"I LEARNED TO AVOID THEM AND FOUND A WAY THROUGH THE MWRR... MAZE."
I'VE BEEN HIDING EVER SINCE.
I'M SORRY I STOLE THE BOOKS! I ALWAYS RETURNED THEM... EVENTUALLY...

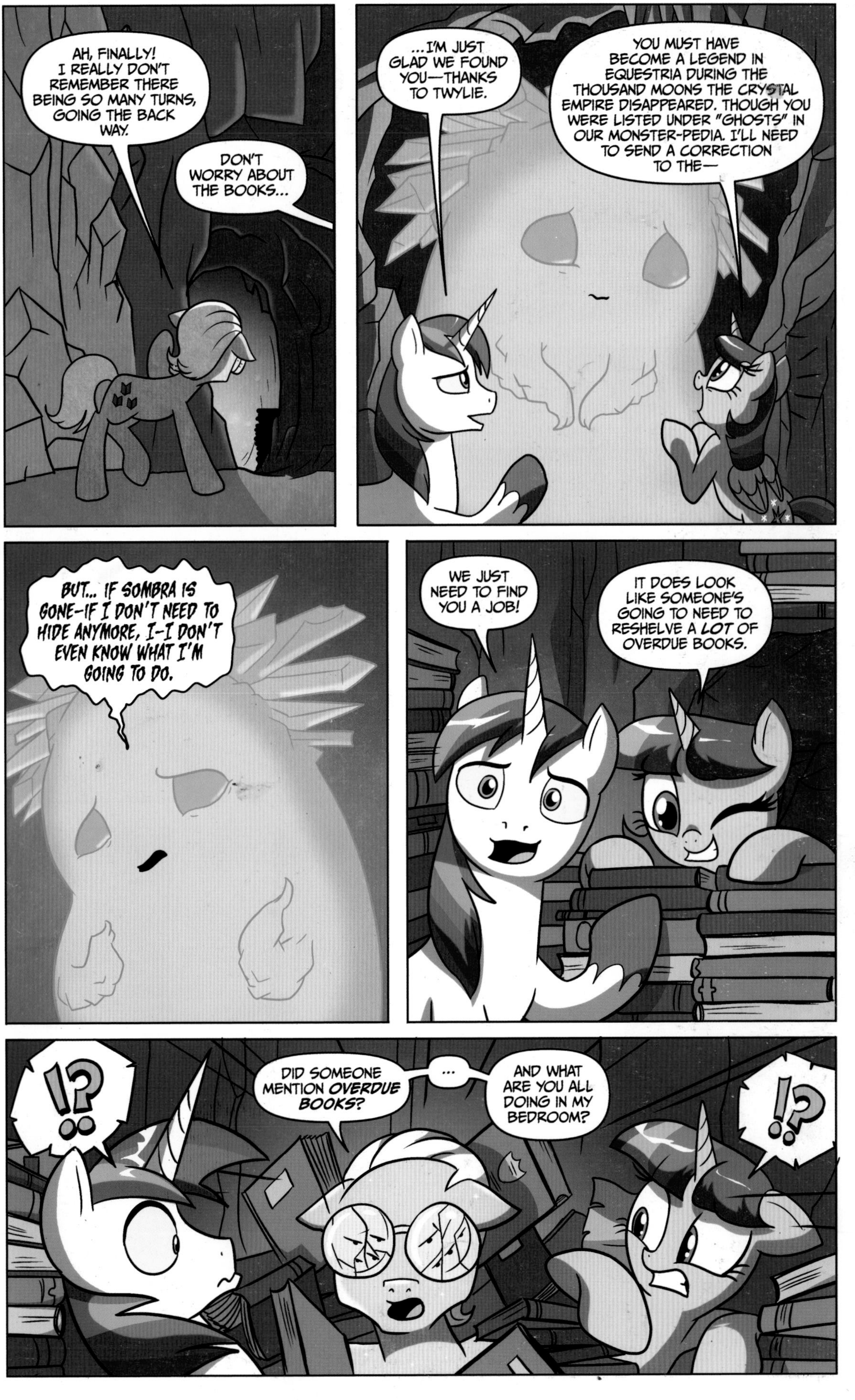
AH, FINALLY! I REALLY DON'T REMEMBER THERE BEING SO MANY TURNS, GOING THE BACK WAY.
DON'T WORRY ABOUT THE BOOKS...
...I'M JUST GLAD WE FOUND YOU—THANKS TO TWYLIE.
YOU MUST HAVE BECOME A LEGEND IN EQUESTRIA DURING THE THOUSAND MOONS THE CRYSTAL EMPIRE DISAPPEARED. THOUGH YOU WERE LISTED UNDER "GHOSTS" IN OUR MONSTER-PEDIA. I'LL NEED TO SEND A CORRECTION TO THE—
BUT... IF SOMBRA IS GONE—IF I DON'T NEED TO HIDE ANYMORE, I-I DON'T EVEN KNOW WHAT I'M GOING TO DO.
WE JUST NEED TO FIND YOU A JOB!
IT DOES LOOK LIKE SOMEONE'S GOING TO NEED TO RESHELVE A *LOT* OF OVERDUE BOOKS.
!?
DID SOMEONE MENTION *OVERDUE BOOKS*?
...
AND WHAT ARE YOU ALL DOING IN MY BEDROOM?
!?

THE NEXT DAY...

I SEE SOMEONE HAS FOUND A JOB TO DO.

HE'S A WIZARD WITH THE BOOKS; HE KNOWS EVERY ONE BY HEART. PLUS, HE'S PERFORMING AT STORY-TIME TONIGHT!

MMRRR RRRWW!

HERE'S THE NEXT BATCH READY FOR RESHELVING.

I WISH YOU COULD STAY LONGER.

ME, TOO. BUT WE BOTH HAVE THINGS TO DO. AND WE CAN VISIT AGAIN SOON. I'M NOT GOING TO LET DISTANCE OR "GROWN-UP" STUFF KEEP ME AWAY FROM MY B.B.B.F.F. FOR LONG.

I'M JUST SORRY MY "GROWN-UP" RESPONSIBILITIES ALMOST MADE ME FORGET WHAT'S REALLY IMPORTANT TO ME. LIKE TRACKING MONSTERS... WITH MY LITTLE SIS.

HEY, YOU FIND ANOTHER MONSTER, I'LL BE HERE IN A FLASH!

IT'S GETTING DARK. WATCH OUT FOR NIGHT SPRITES. YOU KNOW HOW THEY LOVE TRAINS!

YEP, THEY'RE LISTED ON...

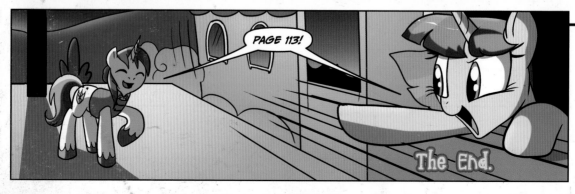

PAGE 113!

The End.

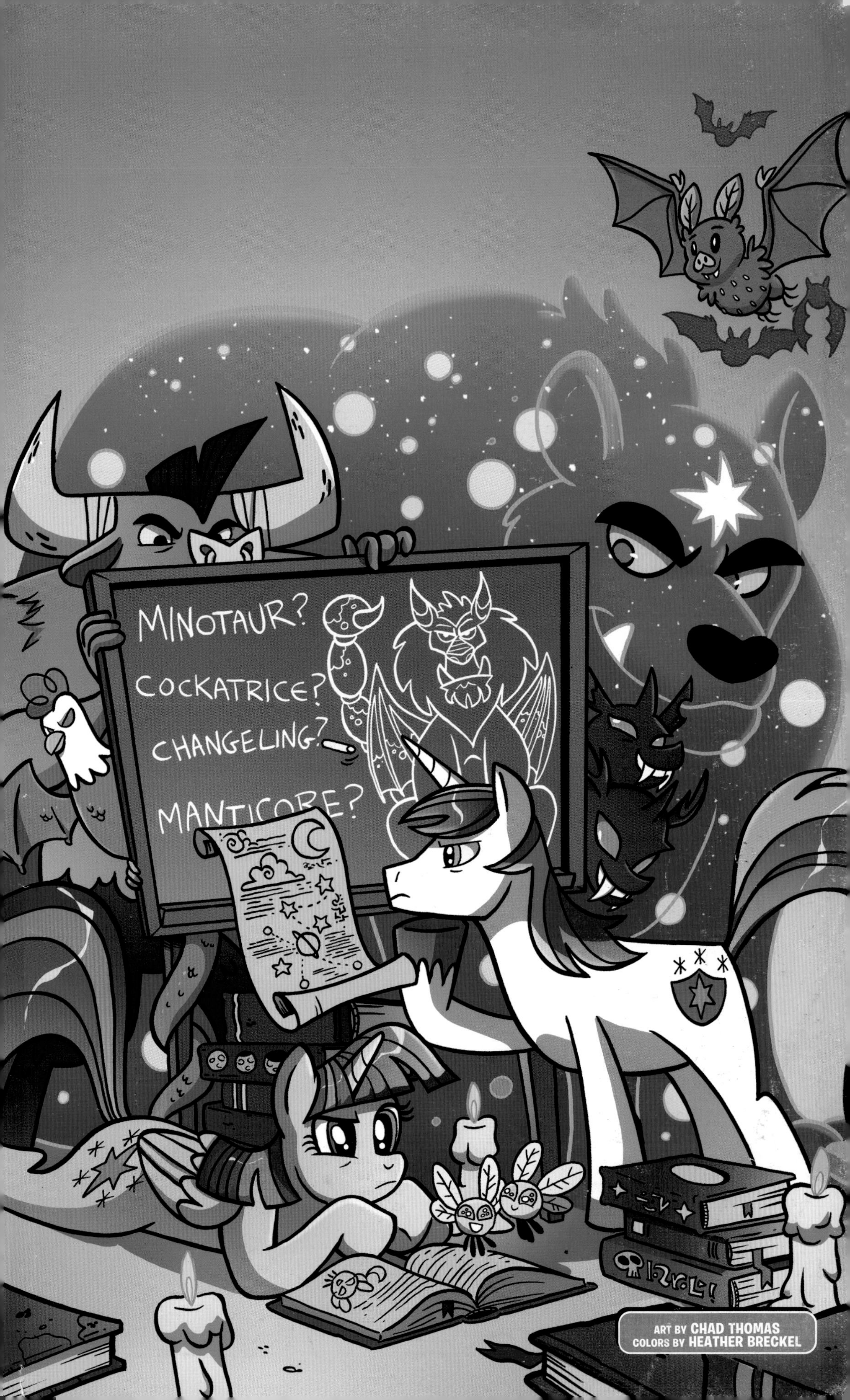
MINOTAUR?
COCKATRICE?
CHANGELING?
MANTICORE?

ART BY CHAD THOMAS
COLORS BY HEATHER BRECKEL

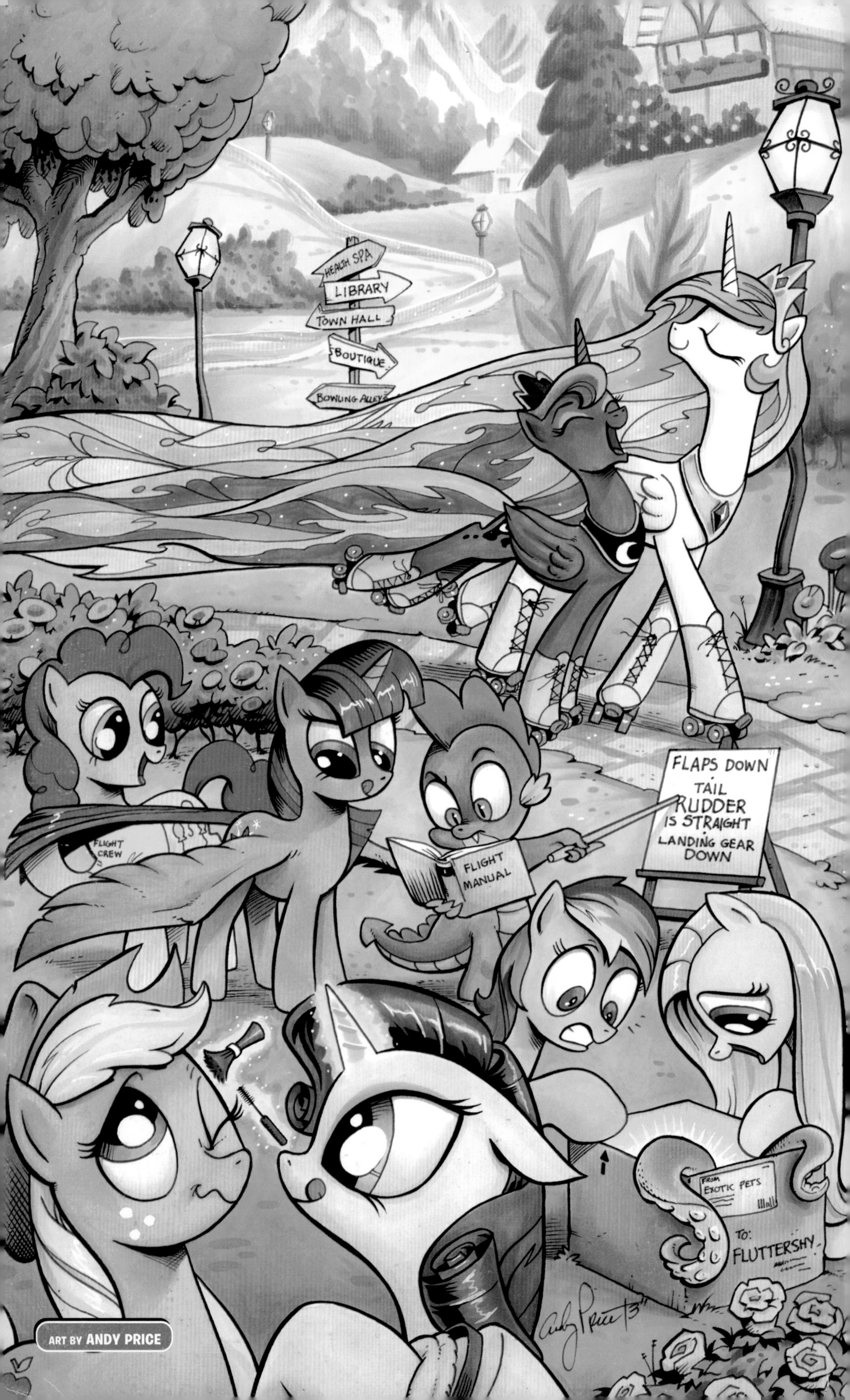
HEALTH SPA
LIBRARY
TOWN HALL
BOUTIQUE
BOWLING ALLEY
FLIGHT CREW
FLIGHT MANUAL
FLAPS DOWN
TAIL
RUDDER
IS STRAIGHT
LANDING GEAR
DOWN
FROM
EXOTIC PETS
TO:
FLUTTERSHY
Andy Price '13

ART BY ANDY PRICE

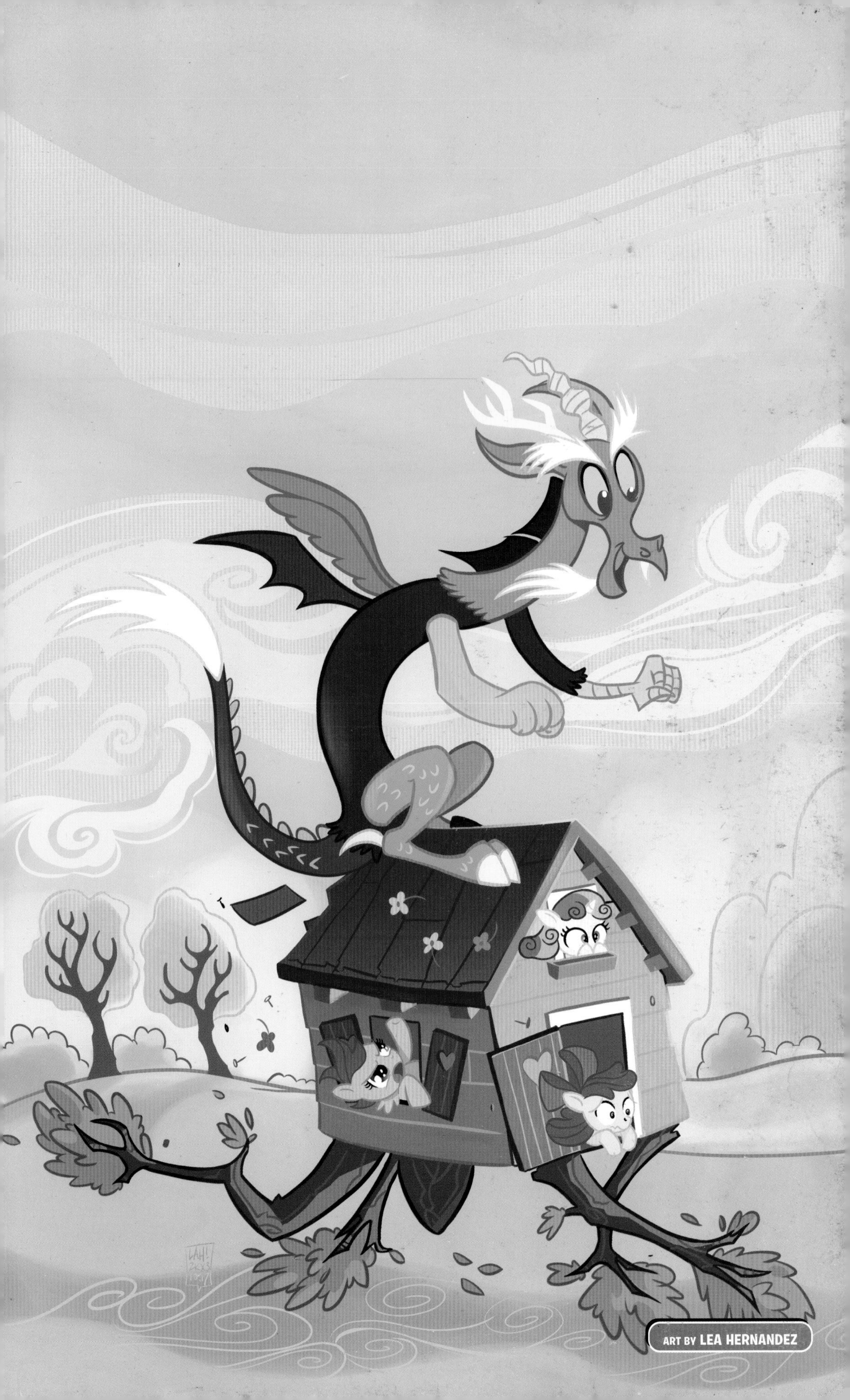

ART BY LEA HERNANDEZ

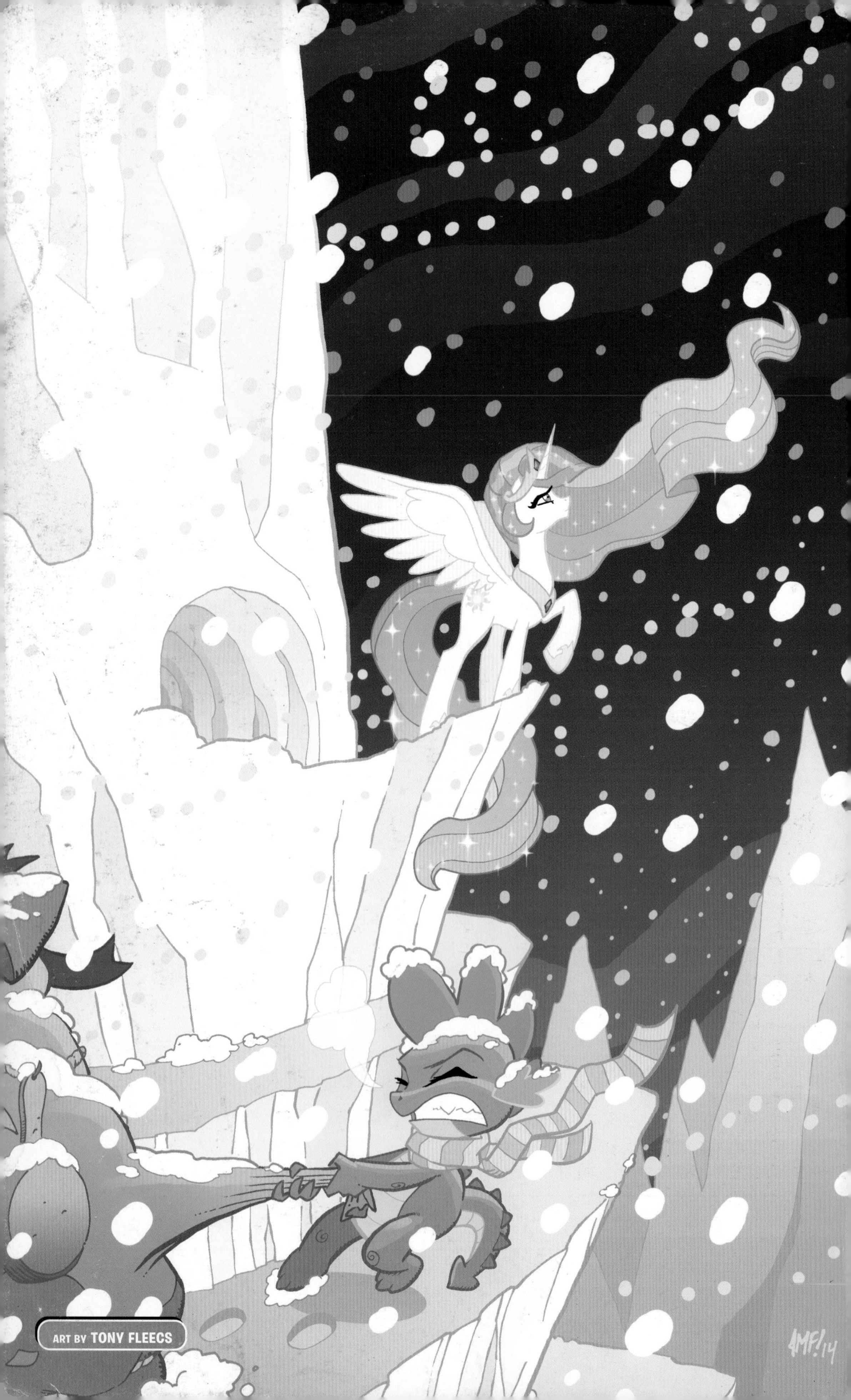
ART BY TONY FLEECS
AMF! '14

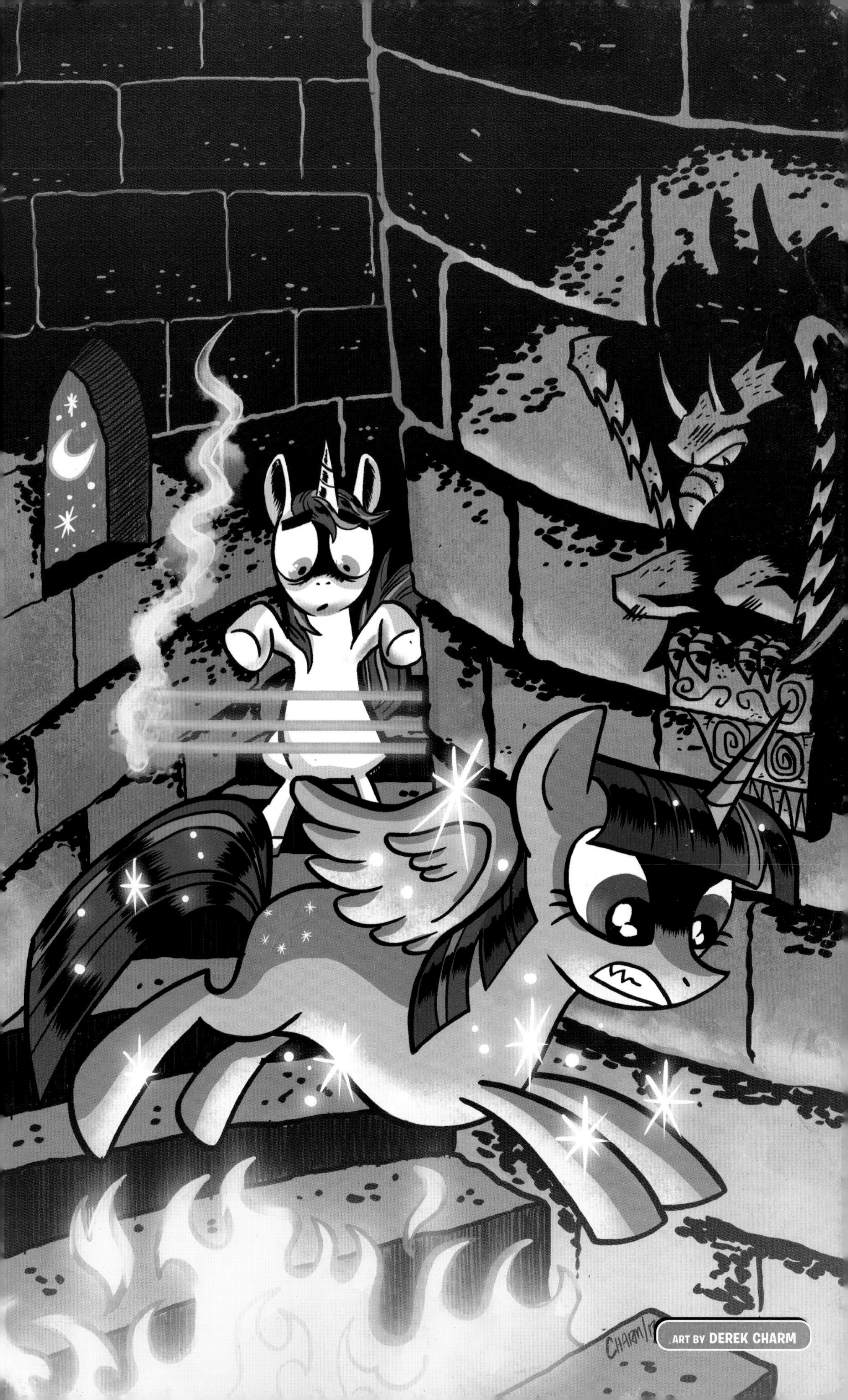
CHARM

ART BY DEREK CHARM

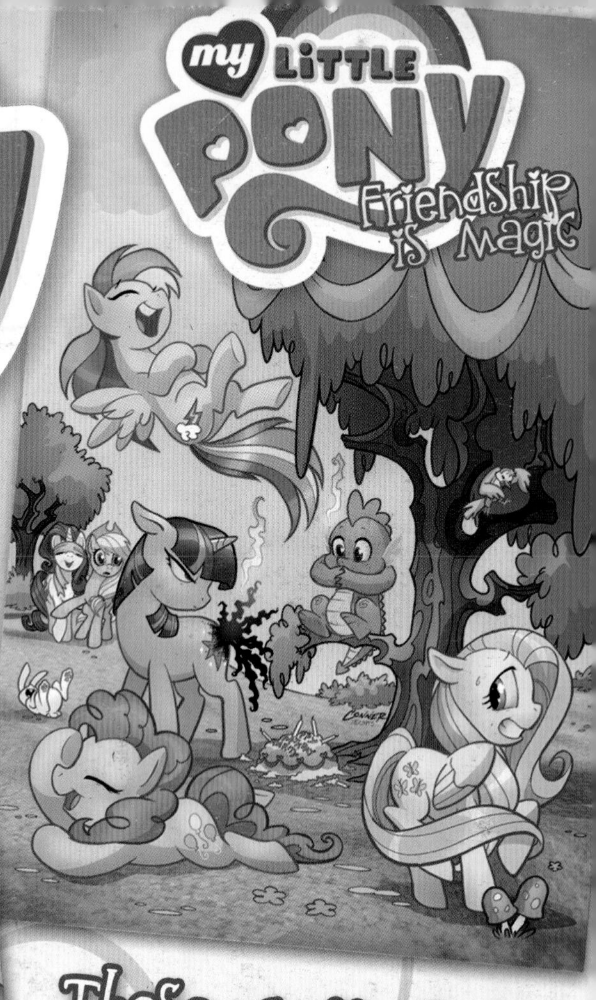
my LITTLE PONY
Friendship is Magic

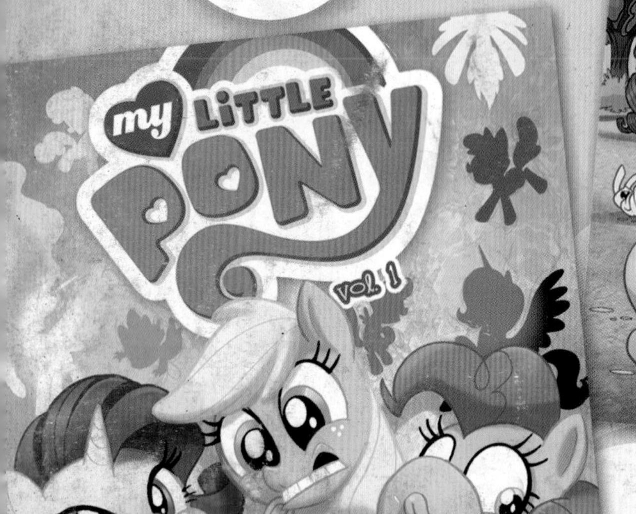
my LITTLE PONY
vol. 1
PONY TALES

These Collections on Sale now!

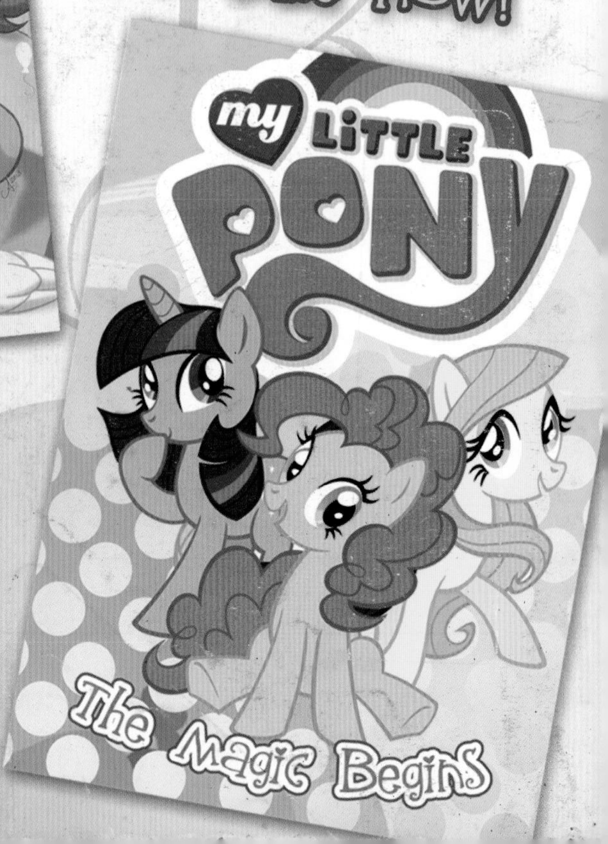
my LITTLE PONY
The Magic Begins

My Little Pony: Friendship Is Magic, Vol. 1
ISBN: 978-1-61377-605-6

My Little Pony: Pony Tales, Vol. 1
ISBN: 978-1-61377-740-4

My Little Pony: The Magic Begins
ISBN: 978-1-61377-754-1

Licensed By: Hasbro

IDW

www.idwpublishing.com